PROPERTY OF ATLAS

DJKRIMMER.COM

ATLAS

HEL'S INK

BOOK TWO

DJ KRIMMER

For Raeleen -
Without you, there would be no Atlas, therefore he belongs to you. Thank you for your ongoing love and support and for talking me out of my throwing my laptop into the street on more than one occasion. Enjoy your sexy, sweet cinnamon roll book boyfriend.

CONTENTS

Hel's Ink

CONTENT & TRIGGER WARNINGS

I do my best to present any and all content in the gentlest of lights but please, take care and make sure to check in with yourself. Only you know you well enough to decide if you should proceed.

Remember to always put your mental health first and you matter.

Possible Triggers:

Atlas Contains:

- Off Page Abuse
- Assault
- Death
- Drug Addiction (not MCs)
- Emotional Abuse From A Parent/Relative

Content:

- Type One Diabetes
- Explicit Language
- Explicit Sexual Situations

PROLOGUE

ATLAS

The pounding of my rapidly beating heart and the whooshing of boiling blood rushing through my head is all I can hear. I look at the beautiful blonde standing in front of me. Her long hair acting as a curtain around her soft, and oh so fucking breathtaking face hides her rich chocolate eyes. Her lush body trembles and I watch as her tears hit the picnic table we are standing over.

I've had enough. I can handle many things but...not this. Not her crying. Reaching my hand out, I catch her soft chin in my grasp and force her to look me in the face; the fading bruise on her cheek fills me with a dark murderous rage I've spent most of my adult life suppressing. But not anymore, the light, fun version of Atlas that I've spent so long creating, he's nowhere to be found right now and the monster that has laid dormant inside me has taken the reins.

Through teeth gritted so tightly I don't know how they haven't cracked, I growl in a voice I barely recognize as my own. "Where did the bruise come from?" I enunciate each word as my hand holds her trembling chin firmly, making her look me in the eye.

"Atlas..." My name is a weak and desperate plea falling from her full lips. I watch fresh tears slip from her red eyes and splatter against my hand. Later, I will relive her tears, the look of terror in her eyes, the wobbling of her lips, and it will tear my heart apart. But right here, right now, all I can feel is this fire coursing through my body. "Please, you don't have to do this."

Don't have to? What other choice is there? Looking once more at her abused cheek, I run the back of my fingers across it, ever so gently. I see the wince on her face and I take that slight expression as the green light I need to end this. To end him. So yes, I do have to do this. I have to protect her.

"Get out of here, Princess." I say as I move away from her to head back inside the bar. I had come here earlier this evening just for a beer and to meet a tinder match. Then Ren showed up with *him.* I chose to ignore them and try to be the mature adult that no one thinks I'm capable of being. It was going as well as it could until Ren saw me and our eyes locked. Being the polite people pleaser she is, Ren came over to say hi and that is when I saw the layers of makeup she had applied to her face to cover what appeared to be a bruise over her cheek. In that moment I realized two things. One, Ren absolutely sucks at cover-up makeup and would've done well to have her best friend, Janie, teach her the art. And two, I was, without a doubt, going to get arrested tonight.

I've been waiting for the moment I could beat her dick-less, mother fucking loser ass boyfriend's face in for far too long and I am about to enjoy every fucking second of it. She deserves better than him, better than his wandering eyes, better than the way he looks down at her, how he doesn't spoil her. She deserves everything that he is unable and unwilling to give her. And now? Now that I know he is hurting her? Well, now is when I can no longer stand back and "stay out of it".

"Atlas, please!!" Ren cries as she grabs my wrist to stop my movements. "Please, I'm sorry! But please, if you do something, it could ruin us both."

I run my fingertips along the side of her face as I tuck some of her hair behind her pretty ears. I love her ears. She has those constellation piercings that go all the way up in this unique design and I love looking to see what cute little pieces of jewelry she adds in to reflect her mood. Right now they are plain silver colored balls, and it doesn't sit well with me. Ren is anything but plain with her pretty dresses, bright blonde hair and knee-weakening smile. It angers me to my very core that the bright goddess I knew has turned into this dimmer, quieter version of herself, and it's all *his* fault.

"Princess," I let out a breath, trying everything in my power to not allow her to see the level of fucking rage I have inside. I don't want her to be scared of me. "I need you to trust me on this, okay? I would never let anything happen to you. And *he* will never hurt you again. You hear me?" My heart skips when she grips the chest of my shirt in her hands and buries her face into me.

"Atlas," she sobs as her body crumples against mine. "I don't want you in trouble over me. I'm not worth it. Please."

Not worth it? I'm going to kill this fucker and anyone else responsible for making her believe such an asinine thought.

Wrapping my arms around her soft body, I give her a squeeze and silently mourn over the fact our first real embrace is like this. It's not fair. The woman I've been pining over in secret for more than a year, waiting for the right moment, the perfect romantic setting for our first hug, and it's been stolen from us. Leaving her and I in a desperate embrace in the back patio of a local bar by the employees' break table and the trash bins. I'm going to punch him extra for this moment.

"Listen to me," I say as I pull her back, my heart breaking all over again. There is a part of me screaming to forget all of this and to leave with her. I could force her into my car and I would take her back to my place, where I could protect her. But that isn't enough. He deserves to pay for what he has done. He needs to realize that he can *never* touch her again. And I need her to realize that she is worth protecting and fighting for. "I want you to get an Uber and go to Janie's, alright?" I watch as she opens her mouth to fight me, but I stop her by pressing my index finger to her swollen, wet lips. "I wasn't asking Lauren. Go."

I don't give her the opportunity to argue again, because I know she will. I turn my back to her and head into the bar, only one thing on my mind now.

Walking up to the bar, I see him, *Andrew*. He is flirting with my tinder girl, Rachel. Rachel is twenty-three with raven hair, grey eyes and a gymnast's body. Her hobbies include celebrity-hunting and spending her days looking for ways to "live her best life" and "find the vibe" or something. Also, her favorite color is *Purple Pizzazz*. I looked it up. It's a real color, it's also known as hot pink, but that debate is neither here nor there.

I smile at the two as I pat Andrew on the back, just a *friendly* slap that makes him cough out a cry upon impact. It makes me wonder, did Ren cry out when he hit her across the face?

I give Rachel my best flirtatious smile and it works like a charm. She swoons and her cheeks go pink as she giggles.

"Sorry Rach," I say, my voice low and husky, even though the heat and anger rushing through my body is making it next to impossible to stay in my "sexy Atlas" persona. "I'm going to have to get a raincheck. Andrew and I actually have some important business to take care of." I don't wait for her response as I grip the man by his boney shoulder and shove him towards the front door.

"What the fuck, man!" Andrew shoves me off of him once we are outside. I look down at him, yes down. I have at least six inches on this fucker, and I'm loving every bit of it. I am not one that believes in criticizing others based on looks, especially something they have no control over, like height. But nothing fills me with joy quite like looking down at this guy and knowing that I'm taller, stronger and bigger than he will ever be. Andrew is forty-two, balding with strawberry blond hair, a goatee, zero muscle mass, and this one eye that looks slightly outward. When I first met him in person, I knew exactly how he landed the absolute knockout that is Lauren Locklear. Ren works for the shit stain and he made her go out with him. I never could prove my theory though, and my best friend Fox told me not to make those assumptions if I ever wanted the tension between Ren and I to go away. I should've never kept my mouth shut. She's been in an abusive relationship for months now, and I could've stopped it sooner. That is a guilt and shame I will live with for the rest of my life.

"Fuck you asshole!" Andrew growls as he tries to push past me, but he fails to move me even the slightest. I almost feel embarrassed for him...almost. "I'm going back in, get out of my way, Hart. I need to get back to my girlfriend." I am not sure why that sets me off. In all honesty, that phrase is the most respectful way he could've addressed Ren. Maybe it was the "*my*" he had added? I don't know, I'm sure my therapist would be able to unravel and explain the reasons behind the emotions. But we aren't there and I am completely fine with not understanding the emotion. Andrew tries to move away, and in an instant, I grab him by his polo shirt and shove him up against the brick wall of the bar.

"You hit her." I snarl as my grip tightens. The absolute fear in his eyes is not as thrilling as I had been hoping for. All I keep thinking is–*did Ren look this scared when he attacked her?*

"Atlas," Andrew whimpers as he shakes in my grip. "I-I didn't hit her!"

My fist collides with his face, and I nearly groan at the satisfying *crunch* of his cheek and nose I feel upon impact. He lets out a cry that I feel is way too dramatic for the blow I delivered.

"Shut up," I groan as I look around to see if anyone is noticing our commotion. "You know people are trying to have a nice night out, and you screaming like a bitch is going to really put a damper on their evening."

Andrew snots all over my hand, which...fucking gross. He looks up at me, blood covering his face. "You hit me!" He yells and I jerk my head back as blood and saliva land on my face.

"Say it, don't spray it, man." I groan as I wipe my face on the sleeve of my black henley. "Alright, so here are your options. You can tell me the truth about beating Lauren, or you can lie to me. Keep in mind the outcome of your ass kicking will vary drastically depending upon which way you decide to go."

There is a pause before the sniveling idiot looks at me

with watery eyes. I mean seriously, grow a pair and take the beating like a man. Of course, I suppose referring to him as a man is incorrect. Real men don't put their fucking hands on women in violence.

"Okay," He lets out this nasally whistle breath through his nose that causes me to cringe. It's actually a super annoying sound.

"You may want to get that looked at tomorrow," I state as I tap my own nose. "That noise will become distracting as fuck."

Andrew looks at me as if annoyed. I shrug and wait for him to continue, most people can't deal with my brain and energy, and I don't really care if I am "too much" for him. In fact, I want nothing more than to be too much.

"Yes," Andrew says slowly. "I... hit her."

"For how long?" I snarl through my tense jaw, the white hot rage coursing its way through my body making me shake. I want him dead, I ***need*** him dead. But first, I must make him *wish* he were dead.

"Just the one–" I punch him in his soft abdomen with such force I swear I can almost feel where his spine would be, if he had one. Instead of continuing to prop him up, this time I allow his body to fall to the ground before kicking him in his side. Grabbing him, I heave him back to the standing position and push him back against the building. His head won't stop nodding and lulling.

"Try again." I bark as I grip his hair to hold his head straight. "And think real fucking hard about whether you should lie to me." I would give him this, he is able to take a beating a lot better than I initially thought, though his pleading is becoming a little too annoying.

"It's not how it looks! And she forgave me and we worked it out! We always do! I love her." Those words snap something inside me and time no longer exists. Nothing exists. No, *he* does not get to say those words. This worthless fuck does not get to love her. You don't steal someone's light if you love them. Everything is red, I can't see him or any of my surroundings. My hearing is muffled, just faint cries and yells from what seems like miles away. The sirens are what pull me out of my blackout, followed by the screams and shouts, guns drawn, handcuffs and me being forced onto the hard concrete ground.

Letting out a breath, I stare out the window of the cop cruiser–allowing the blur that's been the last few minutes finally to come together in my head. I shift, the handcuffs are a little tighter than necessary in my opinion and my shoulders are too big to be squeezed like this behind my back. Watching, I see the paramedics load the stretcher into the back of an ambulance with Andrew's bloodied, beaten, and motionless body strapped to it. I'm momentarily pleased with myself, but that moment is gone fast once the realization of what I've done hits me like a ton of bricks.

Andrew Cambridge, son of one of the biggest defense attorneys in this city, is laying–possibly dead-on that stretcher. And I'm the one that put him there.

Fuck.

CHAPTER 1
ATLAS

"I really appreciate this, Fox." I pat my friend on his back as we walk from the courthouse to his truck. "You know, you really ought to look into a greener vehicle besides this gas guzzler." I smirk as I watch the dark blonde brow on Fox's face twitch slightly.

"It's diesel." He mutters in his deep *'I'm a grumpy badass'* way.

Gasping, I clutch my chest. "You heathen. Do you not care for your mother earth? You are in Southern California, you cannot drive a diesel truck."

"Listen fucker, first off, you drive a fucking Tahoe, so shut the flapper."

"It's a hybrid." I counter and he scoffs.

"It's still shit on gas. And second, anybody that has a problem with my truck can gladly say it to my face. And you shouldn't be talking shit since you are expecting a fucking ride." Today was sentencing for my assault charges. Thankfully, *I guess*, Andrew didn't die or end up in a coma after the beat down I gave him four months ago. And with the help of our tattoo shop's shark of a lawyer, Frank, I didn't serve any more jail time than when the cops picked me up at the bar after I hit... okay, beat the ever-loving fuck out of Andrew. I do, however, have six hundred and seventy-five hours of community service to atone for my sins.

It's fucking bullshit if you ask me. He beat his girlfriend and *I* am the one being punished. And I mean that in every possible way, except for the sexy ones. During the last four months, I've lost clients at the tattoo shop I work at, I've missed conventions I was supposed to attend, and had to move out of my apartment that I rented with my friend and co-worker, Ash. But the absolute worst thing I've had to deal with is the fact that Ren hasn't spoken to me since that night. No texts, no calls, no visits. Nothing. While I'm not happy about my punishment, I would take it over and over again for her, gladly. Hell, I was ready to face prison time. So to not hear from her even once in four months, yeah, it stings.

"Have you talked to Ren?" I ask Fox once we are on the road. He rolls his eyes and glares at me before turning his attention back to the road.

"You know I have. She is Torch's best friend." *Torch* being Janie Pierce, Fox's girlfriend. Janie is the daughter of mine and Fox's now deceased boss and mentor, Tony. About a year and a half ago, Janie came in to co-run her father's tattoo shop, *Hel's Ink* with Fox. After more drama and angst than a soap opera, those two idiots realized they were disgustingly in love with each other and even though Fox is like seventy-four and Janie is barely legal, they've seemed to have made it work...

Okay, she's like twenty-seven and he's forty-five or something, same difference. Anyway, Janie, Torch or as I call her, *Red*, or *Mama J*–yes, she is a woman of many personalities and it's best to have a name for them all. She is the queen bee of our hive and she is as close to Ren as one can get, which is awesome, unless you are on Ren's shit list and want to contact her. Which is where I currently am and have been for the last four months. Then the short red head becomes this tiny freckled impenetrable wall between you and Ren.

Groaning, I look out the window at, well, nothing in particular, it's the city, it's roads and cars and billboards, there is nothing to look at, ever. "I just want to know if she's okay." I state softly, keeping my eyes fixed on the nothingness outside the window. Fox gets uncomfortable with feelings that don't involve general irritation. Unless it's with Janie, then he turns into this gross marshmallow fluff oversized man with a magnificent beard. But, because of his selective aversion to feelings, I try not to talk about mine too much.

Sighing dramatically, I roll my head back on the headrest and look towards him. "I mean, I was just trying to save her life, and what if you were trying to save Janie and she iced you out, didn't even show up for your sentencing and you didn't know how she was?"

Fox parks the truck outside the hotel I've been living in for the last couple of months. He stares out the windshield, a scowl firmly planted on his face before sighing, "Ren is sick," his grave tone grabs my attention and I sit upright as he continues.

"That's why she wasn't there today. She actually did plan on being there, despite everyone telling her it would be a bad idea considering Andrew would be there and you are trying to keep her name out of this, but she got sick and is in the hospital right now. So I need to drop you off and then go get Bruno and pray that this doesn't give Janie furbaby fever again. Every time we pet sit, I have to hear about

Winston being an only child for weeks and it's becoming a problem."

"Wait..." I shake my head, trying to pull the important information out of that mess and pack away the questionable relationship Fox and Janie have with their rescue cat. "Ren is sick? Sick enough to be in the hospital?"

Fox nods and shrugs. "She's stable, from what Janie said this morning. But yeah, she was sick with some nasty cold or something and then her sugars were acting up or something. I don't know man, I'm sure it has something to do with her diabetes."

I frown as I look forward while trying to wrap my brain around his words. "She never told me she's diabetic."

Fox lets out a dry laugh. "Well, it's not like you two have ever been super close."

"I'm as close to her as you are!" I snap in defense, feeling annoyed at his insinuation. Of course Ren and I are close. I've known her for years! She's one of my best friends.

"At, man, I love you. But you know that not everyone thinks like you do, right? A lot of us need more than casual conversations to consider someone a friend. So that's probably why Ren hasn't ever felt comfortable enough with you to talk about her condition. I mean, Janie didn't like talking about her tremors until she had to. Ren is definitely more open about it, but I also saw her pump when I did her last tattoo." I nod, though still not really satisfied with this information. I say my goodbyes to Fox before getting out of the truck, but not before he made me promise I wouldn't be late for community service tomorrow.

Once I see his truck disappear, I run over to my motorcycle and start her up. There are multiple hospitals in the city, but, while I may not know everything about Lauren Locklear, I do know that her mother, Dr. Melonie Locklear, is a big wig doctor at the university hospital downtown. So, my guess is she would put her daughter in the hospital she has the most pull in.

With the destination decided, I back my motorcycle out of its space and take off downtown.

"SIR, I AM SORRY, BUT IF YOU ARE NOT IN THE IMMEDIATE FAMILY, I cannot take you to see her." The nurse gives me a sympathetic look as I run my hands over my scruffy face. Ren is in a room on this floor. I've flirted, smoldered, and bribed my way to *this* area where the private rooms are. But this woman is a fucking immovable mountain. She reminds me of the black knight in *Monty Python.* "None shall pass" blah blah blah.

"Ma'am..." I've tried flirting with her and she laughed in my face. So, let's go with soft, respectful Atlas. "Please, I just need thirty seconds...ten seconds. Hell, walk me by her room and let her see me and I'm telling you–"

The nurse sighs, okay so respect won't work, but I know that type of sigh. That's the sigh of a mother with an overly excited child who is being worn down. Luckily, I am an expert in this art. The nurse must realize that she's shown the chink in her armor because defeat washes over her.

"Alright! Come here." She hisses and pulls me by my jacket away from the nurses' station, muttering about being on a sixteen hour shift. *Note to self: go get her something as a thank you after I leave.* She walks me up to a glass window and I see the long blonde hair fanning over the bed. I go to run in, but the nurse blocks me. "Not so fast." She states. "Miss Locklear cannot have visitors."

"But–" The nurse holds her hand up.

"She is very ill, and being exposed to other germs in her weakened state could cause her serious harm. She is isolated right now for her own protection. If she wants to talk to you, you must do so through the phone here, or... you know, a cell phone." I give her a sheepish smirk at her last remark.

"She's kind of, umm, avoiding me?" I rub the back of my neck.

The nurse rolls her eyes. "Can't imagine why. You have five minutes and then I am calling security." I press my hands together in the prayer position and bow.

"You truly are a saint." When she leaves, I turn to the phone on the wall. Picking it up, I press the button and watch as Ren grabs her bedside remote.

"Hello?" Her voice is so weak and tired, and instantly my entire body feels so heavy.

I need to stay cheery. *Brave mask, Brave mask.* "So what?" I force my overly confident, cocky demeanor to come out. "You decide to hide here, pretending to be sick, instead of coming to my hearing? I'm heartbroken, completely wounded." I watch through the window as Ren slowly sits up. I can see from here her body is shaking as she tries to pull herself to the edge of the bed. "Stop Princess." My voice goes serious and I watch her freeze.

"Atlas," she breathes out, her breathing ragged. What is going on with her? "Why are you here? How did you know?"

I smirk and give her a half shrug. "I am here because today was an important day, and you weren't there. Very rude, by the way." I check to make sure she knows I'm joking. I think she does, but her pale, nearly grey skin and dark circles are making it hard for me to know for sure. "Fox said you were in the hospital, and I just spent the last hour flirting and paying my way back here to get five minutes....now three and a half minutes with you."

Her face scrunches in confusion, "Why?" *Why? Is she serious?*

"Because," I say slowly. "You're my friend. Something is wrong, and I was worried about you?" I watch her shift away slightly. Fearing that I've somehow said the wrong thing, I go back to playfulness. "Not to mention I know you're dying to hear how I'm doing. Did you know that you're not allowed to flirt with the bailiff?" Did she just roll her eyes?

I watch as she lies back down in her bed as she gives me a small wave. "Goodbye. Atlas."

"Rennnn..." I groan as I tap on the glass. "Come onnnn. Talk to me, please! I just got sentenced to a year of community service, not to mention the fines and retributions, and I'm standing here about to get a trespassing arrest because I need to talk to you."

She doesn't respond verbally. But I hear the click as she turns off the speaker on the remote, silencing me. Looking at the useless phone as if it betrayed me, I drop it onto the receiver before placing my palm on the glass, wishing like hell I could get her to just look at me, but she doesn't. Her body turns to face out the window. I glance around the empty room and frown. The room is white, like most hospital rooms. There is a television attached to the wall that she has turned off and her window outside gives her the view of the other part of the hospital. Her room is so bare, there is nothing in there for her to look at.

"Alright Romeo," the nurse sighs as she comes back to me. "Am I calling security or are you leaving?"

I blink slowly before looking down at her. "I'll leave," my voice is quiet as I remove my hand from the glass and follow her to the elevators. "Is she going to be there a while?"

"Can't disclose patient information...but yes." I wince as I watch her stab the button to call the elevator.

"Can she have gifts? Like from the gift shop?" Maybe she's not allowed to have anything in there and that's why her room is empty?

The nurse nods. "Yes, no food items though, she's on a monitored diet. And that's the last question you get to ask." She warns when I open my mouth again. The nurse points to the opening elevator doors. "Now go."

I give the nurse a small bow before stepping into the elevator and heading down to the main floor. I will leave like she asked, but first I need to make a pit stop. Now that I know Ren is allowed to have things in her room, I'm going to make sure she can't turn without seeing something pretty.

CHAPTER 2
LAUREN

It's been an irritating week or so. Hell, this last year can kiss my fucking ass really, but this last week has been the rotten cherry on the top of this shit sundae I really didn't need.

I'm sick.

Well, that's kind of a vague statement. I am a Type One Diabetic, so technically, I am *always sick*. But what I mean is, I have the flu, a severe case of it. So bad that my body shut down, and I had to be admitted to the hospital. The hospital itself isn't so bad. My mom is the chief of surgery here, so I get the royal treatment, which is nice, for the most part. Though I get checked four or five times more than necessary, and being as I prefer to be on my own, it's grating on my nerves.

But besides being sick, the hospital stay, the constant invasion of privacy and the fact that my job, where everyone already has been brainwashed into hating me, is trying to tell me I'm out of sick days; my irritation is not because of any of those things. It's due to the fact that I woke up from my nap to a gift shop explosion in my room. I stopped counting the vases of flowers after seventeen. There are at least twelve balloons, including a pink one that says "it's a girl", and at the foot of my bed sits a cow. Not just any cow, it's a brown highland cow stuffed animal. Those really soft, round marshmallow stuffed animals.

I'm irritated because it's a highland cow. Cows are my favorite animal. The highland cow is my all-time favorite animal. I don't care if people find it weird; they are entitled to their wrong opinion. Atlas has something, or everything, to do with the gift shop relocating to my room, but this cow...how did he know that is my favorite animal?

Or did he?

I think back to the limited conversations he and I have had over the past couple of years, but after about a minute, I give up. My head hurts too much. I'm tired and really just want to go home. Grabbing my phone off the bedside tray, I go to my text messages and open up a group chat I am in with my best friends – Janie, Sunday, and Stevie. I snap a pic of the cow and send it to them.

Janie: Holy cow... he's so fucking cute

Stevie: SO FLUFFY

Sunday: Your obsession with cows is becoming creepy. How did you even get him?

Me: I think Atlas Hart got him for me. Along with this

I take a panoramic photo of the massive collection of balloons and flowers and send it to them.

Stevie: How have you not married that man?

Sunday: At least fucked him. It's obvious he is into you.

Janie: Ohhhhh....makes sense now lol

Me: What makes sense??

Janie: At sent me a text earlier asking what your favorite flower and color is. I was... busy so I ignored the message *angel face emoji*

Stevie: JANIE!? You have been at WORK all day! Stop being a slut at the tattoo shop!

Janie: *crying emoji* I CAN'T HELP IT! So you know how we are working on expanding the building? Well, Fox was in there and lifting these bags of concrete-shirtless-I am not ashamed to say he dominated EVERY part of me.

Me: As someone with NO sex life... I hate you.

Sunday: Sammme

Stevie: Okay but Ren, seriously, did you talk to Atlas about the stuff?

Me: No. I just woke up and it was all here. I know he's been trying to get a hold of me and I've been ignoring him since he was arrested.

Janie: You really should text him. He is going through something mentally and it's killing him that you two aren't cool

Me: It's not like we've ever been close...

Stevie: But we all know you COMPLETELY avoid him now. You two used to goof with each other and now there is nothing from your side. He's not an idiot, he can feel it. At least he's trying to make an effort.

I sigh as I look up from the screen, eyes falling on the cow again. Why won't he leave me alone? Can't I just live in my humiliation without having to look at him again?

No one besides the guys at Hel's Ink and my girls know why Atlas nearly killed my ex-boyfriend at the bar. When asked, I would shrug and say I didn't know. Atlas never said why, not even when there was a bargain offered. I'm not sure why he hadn't, it would've definitely helped his case. Though a colleague at the court emailed me to say Frank had gotten his sentence reduced to a slap on the wrist.

I think back to the night at the bar. That night, my ex, Andrew and I were going out, not something that I was too excited about. Mainly because I was still sporting a bruise and when we went out to drink, Andrew usually ended up getting angry. That night, Atlas had seen me and I was terrified that he would say something smart to Andrew, as was customary every time they crossed paths. Atlas did not like Andrew and was very vocal about it. That day, Andrew had had a bad day in court and I knew if Atlas started teasing him like normal, I would get in trouble for it later. So I went over to say hi to him and tried hard to ignore the jealousy churning in my stomach as I saw his pretty date. When I walked up to Atlas, his eyes zeroed in on my face. The bruise was several days old and I have no idea how in the dimly lit bar he had seen it as quickly as he did, but when he looked from my cheek to my eyes, I was terrified by what I saw.

Atlas is the happy, easy-going guy of the group of men

that make up *Hel's Ink.* I am a frequent customer, legal advice giver and... let's be honest, I *had* a major-**major-** crush on Atlas for like, two years. Not that he ever looked my way, even once by accident. But Atlas is goofy, excitable, a showoff, the jokester of the shop. Everyone is his best friend, and he always has a smile on his perfectly angled, scruffy face. So when he looked into my eyes and I saw a darkness in his that I didn't know existed, I was taken aback. And when he stood up and walked into my space, I realized for the first time just how massive he is.

I'm a bigger girl. At five foot eight, and purchasing my clothes from the plus size section, I am used to not feeling small, but at that moment, Atlas' six foot three, heavily sculpted body made me feel so small and frail. And when he growled for me to go to the outdoor patio of the bar, in such a low, almost primal tone, I couldn't do anything besides nod and numbly follow him out there.

Growing up the way I did, the eldest sibling, plus size, type one diabetic, law school, I've learned to *suck it up,* shove my emotions down and push through whatever I was feeling. But when Atlas looked at me, when his strong hand caressed my face. I felt every wall I've spent twenty-nine years building begin to crumble.

"Hello Lauren," I jump as my mother's clipped, no-nonsense voice startles me out of my thoughts. I stare at the fair woman standing in front of the glass door, phone to her ear. My mother, Dr. Melonie Locklear, is known in the hospital as the ice queen. Tall and slim with pale blonde hair, high cheekbones, steel-grey eyes and zero smile lines.

"Hey mom," I give her a small smile that she doesn't return as she looks over her tablet, business as usual.

"Your sugars are finally stabilizing again. I know you like your monitor, but I want you to do finger pricks for at least a few days after you leave, so you know for sure that it is accurately reading your levels." I stop myself from rolling my eyes. My mother isn't the biggest fan of new medical technology, and she doesn't trust most of it. For a long time, I found it odd that she was so against the newest developments in modern medicine, especially with her being the head of a teaching hospital, but my dad made a good point. While she does see the benefits, she also sees what happens when it all goes horribly wrong. So, for her sake, I try my best to smile and nod like always. Needing to be the good girl and the dutiful daughter.

"You haven't had a fever in the last twenty-four hours," she tells me, as if I didn't know. "And your urine output looks satisfactory." *Swell. Can you have the nurse rip the catheter out now?* "Stay here again tonight and as long as your levels continue improving and stabilizing, I'll talk with your endocrinologist and I'm sure he will discharge you in the morning." *Of course he will. She trained him, she is his boss. I am only in this glass viewing room instead of a regular hospital room because she ordered it.*

"Can I start peeing on my own now? Eating some real food maybe?" I mutter the last part as I didn't want to get into the diet portion of our typical conversations. My mother is, for the most part, relatively calm about my size and has come to my defense on multiple occasions due to the fat phobia in medical settings. No matter my ailment, a doctor's advice has been to *lose weight.* That included my type one diabetes, which has ***zero*** to do with my weight. But, I am plus size and if you are plus size, regardless of your symptoms, losing fifty pounds wouldn't hurt.

That being said, my mother is still a woman that feels a size six is the only acceptable size and you never finish your plate, no desserts and when out, it is a salad and water.

"I'll talk with your doctor about allowing a few options for you to eat." She says sharply while tapping on her tablet. "I'll also send a nurse in to remove your catheter. I have to go scrub in for surgery, so I may not be back until later tonight." For the first time since this conversation started, my mother looks up and stares into the room. "What is all of this?" She asks, gesturing to the floral shop in my room.

Shit. If I tell her it's a guy, she will demand a complete rundown, and I can't handle that. I smile lightly and shrug. "The girls thought they were being funny. I'm just going to have the nurses take them to another floor once I'm discharged." Mother nods and looks back down at her tablet before turning and walking away.

Guess that was the end of our chat.

CHEWING ON MY BOTTOM LIP, I STARE AT ATLAS' LAST TEXT. I must have gotten eighty from him that I've never responded to. I always wanted to, and... I still do. The problem at first was, he wouldn't tell anyone the truth about what happened that night, and I didn't want anything I said to get back and screw up the case for him, it's very common to want to see text message records and I thought if I kept quiet, it could only help his case. Then it morphed into embarrassment. Embarrassment that he saw me cry, that he felt the need to do what he did, that he went to jail for me and kept my name out of it. But the real reason I became so embarrassed was, he knew that I was being abused and allowed it to continue. No one knew at that time. Not my girlfriends, not my parents, no one. I didn't mean for it to happen. I am not someone that ever took shit from anyone, but Andrew had me over a barrel. He was...is... my boss. When I got my promotion, I thought it was because of my job performance, but I was wrong. It was because he wanted me. And when he got me promoted, he made it very clear that the moment I decided not to date him anymore, my career would be over.

I didn't believe him at first. I can recall the first time he said it, I laughed because I truly believed he was joking. But something nagged at me and after a week or so, I looked into him and noticed the rather long list of female lawyers that had held my current position, and the fact that they all tended to end up fired at his firm. I should've said fuck it and left then, but I didn't because he had been nothing but nice to me. Then one night, after a cocktail party with his colleagues, he insisted that someone had been flirting with me. I laughed and brushed it off because there was no way that was true, the man in question had only said "good evening" to me. Andrew flew into a fit of rage that ended in bruises, *him* sobbing, and then his sliding on top and inside of me.

I shake my head, needing to think about *anything* else besides what I allowed that man to do to me.

Letting out a breath, I tap on the icon to call Atlas, but cuss when I realize I hit the FaceTime button instead. Before I can hangup, Atlas answers. I see his massive smile appear and his green eyes sparkle as they crinkle at the edges.

"Oh my god," I groan when I see myself on the screen. I put my phone on the table so that it faces the ceiling. "I meant to call you, but I hit the wrong button."

"Ohhhhh no no no..." I hear him moving, but I don't

dare look at the screen. "You get that beautiful face back here!"

I try not to allow his words to affect me, but they do, like always. Atlas is a charismatic man, and... well, a shameless flirt. I think he gets off on it, so one has to learn fast to not take him seriously because in two minutes he'll be talking the same way to your grandma. The problem is, I know all of this, but my body still likes to react as if it thinks he means it. Case in point, my face is on fire right now.

I slowly bring the phone back to my face and I stare at him through my lashes while keeping my head somewhat down. I notice him looking at me and...I feel naked all of a sudden. His eyes change and his goofy, flirty grin is replaced with a small, soft smile.

"There's my beautiful Princess." *Princess.* He's called me that only a couple of times and every time I hear it, well, it's probably my absolute favorite nickname ever, not that I'll tell him that. "Man," Atlas breathes out, shaking his head and his goofy grin is back. "I might need to come join you at the hospital. Your face has my heart pounding every which way."

"Stop..." I groan as I roll my head back. "I didn't call you so you could practice your cheesy pickup lines on me."

He smacks his hand over his chest and scoffs. "Ren....you wound me! To think I would use you as practice?" He gives me a smirk and a wink. "Like I need practice, anyway. You know I am the panty dropper in this city."

"You're a pig." I can't help but laugh though, as I cross my arms. "Does calling the girls Princess actually work?"

He raises a dark brow and I hear a can crack open right before he takes a sip of his energy drink. *Really? It's nine pm.* Though the shop is open until eleven and it looks like he's in the break room. "What do you mean?" He asks.

"Do the girls eat it up, fall in love with you, and rip their clothes off when you call them Princess?" I can't help the smile that pulls at me as he laughs loudly.

"Well," He turns his intense stare towards me. "I don't know, you're my only Princess. So tell me Ren, are you falling in love with me?"

I open and close my mouth several times before huffing. "Not a chance in hell, bud."

Holding his index finger up, he smirks and arches one brow. "Not a chance in hell, *yet.* I can be pretty persistent and when that doesn't work, I'm a master at wearing people down."

Rolling my eyes, I drop my head in my hand. "ANYWAY. Did you really buy out the main lobby gift shop?"

"No." I blink at his completely straight and short answer.

"No?" I repeat, looking around the room. "So all the flowers and balloons aren't from you?"

"Oh no, they are, but I bought out the gift shop on the maternity floor. The stuff there was nicer, they have a Starbucks on that floor too." Well, that explains the 'It's a girl' balloon.

"Okay, but why? Why did you buy all of this?" I watch as he shrugs and takes another sip of his drink.

"You needed something pretty to look at. I got upset when I saw that your window only had a view of the other part of the hospital."

I will not cry. But goddamn it, that was the sweetest fucking thing. No, stop it Lauren. "Okay, and the cow?" I ask, while clearing my throat.

"It's a highland cow," he states with a grin. "Those are your favorite type of cow."

"Yes, I am aware of my favorite animal. My question is,

how do you know?" I watch as he is quiet for a very short second, but in that flash, his eyes darken and his jaw ticks.

"You were coming in for your first tattoo at Hel's and the douchebag that used to work there, Les, was up for the next walk in, but he passed on you and Fox took his spot because he said he didn't work on..."

"Cows." I finish and watch him wince as if it hurts *him*.

"Yeah, and once back there, you told Fox and Tony that you love cows so you were choosing to take his comment as a compliment. And then you showed them your keychain with the highland cow on it."

Speechless. I am speechless. Thinking back to that day, I remember that dick making the comment, but I wasn't going to allow him to ruin my day because it was my first tattoo and I had graduated law school. I was getting a tattoo at the famous *Hel's Ink*. Fox and Tony had apologized over and over again, and Tony said he would be handling that guy. The comment was slightly embarrassing, but nothing I hadn't heard before, so it was easy to hide.

"I don't even remember you being there.... like at all. I'm surprised you remember that." I say as I absentmindedly stroke the stuffed cow.

"Yeah, I heard him. Then I beat his ass, and came inside and said I fell trying to do a handstand." He speaks as if it's no big deal. I feel my lower lip tremble and I go to cover it. "Stop it Princess." I look up at him, his green eyes almost glowing. "Pretty girl, don't–"

"Don't what?" I whisper softly. I am feeling way too much right now. It's all too confusing. Atlas has to stop looking at me this way.

"Don't cry when someone can't be there to wipe your tears away. Please...it will kill me." I hear Derek, another tattoo artist, yelling to Atlas that his client is here. "Tell him

I'll be out in a few!" He calls back before looking right back at me, all his attention directly on me.

I give him a smile, "You better go do that tattoo, you're going to need the money." I joke and he hangs his head and lets out a breathy laugh.

"Ah, I'll be okay. It'll all get taken care of." He gives me a smile, not a grin, but a soft beautiful smile which makes my heart flutter in a way that I hope doesn't alert my monitors.

"You should've let me say–" I stop speaking when I notice his eyes have the same dark look in them from the night at the bar and I feel my stomach knot. "Atlas?"

"It was worth it," his voice is low and I feel a current run through me. "It would've been worth years in prison if that had been my fate. But my fees, my community service, it's all worth it because he got what he deserved for daring to raise a hand to you. And that's all that will be said on this subject because..." He exhales harshly, and his jaw ticks as he grits his teeth. "Because that fear in your eyes already haunts me in my sleep. If I see it while I'm awake ever again, I will lose it Ren. I will lose it and I will kill him."

We stare at each other in silence for several seconds before I finally give him a weary smile. "You need to go to your client, Atlas."

"I don't give two shits about that client," He scoffs as his stare continues to burn through me. "I'm not leaving if you aren't okay."

Damn it, that stinging in my eyes is back. I look at the ceiling and blink back the tears before turning my gaze back to him. "I am okay, go on, and do your thing." He opens his mouth to protest, but I stop him. "I get out of here in the morning, as long as there are no hiccups tonight. How about I text you after I'm out? Will that get you going?" I smirk playfully at him as he bows his head and sighs.

"Fine," He states, his voice holding a hint of annoyance that I find far more adorable than I have any right to. "But just know, if you ghost me again, I'm going to steal your dog." My mouth falls open and I stare in shock. Atlas shrugs, "Yeah that's right, I met Bruno at Fox's. He likes me so I'll just take him and then you'll be forced to talk to me."

"Fine. Now, **GO**, do your job." I grumble as he gives me a half salute.

"Good night Princess, try not to have ***too*** many dirty dreams about me." He winks and ends the call before I'm able to react. I stare at the dark screen in shock as I feel my face heating up. That is the most Atlas and I have ever talked to each other. It felt so natural and easy. God, the way his eyes never left me. Atlas has a very difficult time focusing on one thing for long, but that conversation, he never strayed, not even when his client showed up. I've never felt so... seen. So important.

Resting my head on my pillow, I stare out the window at the dark sky and groan. My crush might not be as over as I had previously thought.

"Is this everything?" Sunday, my silver maned friend asks as she loads the back of Stevie's car. From my wheelchair, I see Stevie's turquoise hair through the car window.

"Yeah," I smile weakly as Sunday comes over to help me into the back seat. I'm more than a little impressed at the strength she has when she all but supports all of my weight to help me. Then again, I shouldn't be that shocked. Sunday is a lead pole instructor, before that was a very sought after ballerina, and before that still she grew up in Alabama working as a bar loader under the table. Her body is long, tanned, and toned. "I'm so exhausted," I groan as I close the door once I'm inside. "I hate that I have to go to work tomorrow."

Stevie scoffs. "You aren't even better yet." Her northern Louisiana accent mixing in harmony with Sunday's southern Alabama drawl is such a rare, sweet melody. Here in California, everyone tries their best to sound void of any accent. It makes it easier to brand you here if you're a blank slate. But these girls never tried to get rid of their roots when they moved here and I love it.

My phone buzzes and I fear it's Atlas. While I do plan to text him, I really don't want to have a conversation with him in front of the girls. Looking down, my heart sinks and my palms go sweaty. Not Atlas, no, it's Andrew.

Slowly, I accept the call and place it to my ear. "H-hello?"

"Miss Locklear!" Andrew's voice comes over the phone loud and too eager. "I'm so happy to find you are able to answer your phone calls now." I see Stevie's blue eyes look at me from the rearview mirror and I instantly avert my gaze, feeling like I am doing something wrong.

"I was just discharged," I say softly while trying to get a handle on my nerves. "I-I will be to work tom–"

"Oh, no no no..." His chuckle is cold and full of malice. "You see, I received a photo this morning of Atlas Hart hanging around your hospital floor. Now, need I remind you of the heinous acts of violence I endured because of that man? The acts that *you* are responsible for, even if that was never brought up in court."

Oh, fuck no. I feel the blood rushing from my face and my stomach begins to churn. "Andrew," My mouth is bone dry as I try to speak. "What are you–"

"You're fired, Miss Locklear. For not only fraternizing with a convicted criminal that nearly killed your superior and could still be a threat in the future, but due to your lack of availability."

"Lack of–I've been in the hospital! You cannot fire me for being diabetic!" I yell into the phone, causing both women to look back at me.

"Well, then blame your idiot in shitty armor. I really don't care. Either way, you can come get your shit, it will be at the front desk. Have a great day." The call ends and I don't know if I want to scream or cry.

"Ren?" Sunday says softly. I look up and see that we are in a parking lot and both women are turned to face me.

Holding back my tears, I give them the fakest smile I can as I shrug. "Guess I'm unemployed."

CHAPTER 3
ATLAS

"Bro, you're going to hurt yourself." I barely hear Ash's hesitant voice over the loud metal music blaring through the gym, but I ignore him as I continue my weighted leg curls while hanging from the chin-up bar. I hope I do hurt myself. I pray that when I crawl into that uncomfortable fucking hotel bed tonight, I am so exhausted I cannot stay awake and overthink one more damn thing. I want the ripping pain to lull me into a heavy, dreamless sleep. It's why I am constantly here. Breaking my body down is the only thing that shuts my mind up. Unfortunately, here lately, I'm needing longer and harder sessions to achieve the same temporary peace.

"AT!" Ash grabs me and rips the weights off my legs. I stare down at him. Ash is about my age, dark hair, piercing black eyes and swimmer's build. He actually hates weight lifting, believing that endurance training is the best way to go. I know he is only here because Fox is playing the role of "dad" again and is "concerned" about my mental state or some bullshit. "You have to stop." He growls, forcing me to give him my attention. Blinking, I pull myself out of the trance and I can no longer hold myself on the bar. I let go and expect to land on my feet, but my legs give out and I collapse.

"Fuck..." I huff out a laugh from the floor as Ash helps me sit up.

"What the fuck dude," he smacks my sore arm and I whine. "I stopped counting at fifty. You are going to rip your muscles apart."

I smirk as I reach over for my water bottle. My entire body screams. Oh yeah, this is going to hurt tonight. "Fuck man, I hope so."

Ash gives me the same look I've been getting from everyone lately. The *"Are you okay? You're spiraling."* look. I'm fine, great even. Top of my career, in excellent shape, can have any woman I want in my bed.

Well, *almost* any woman.

"Any news on Ren that you know of?" I ask, trying to appear casual. In actuality, I'm a ball of stress. Ren said she would text me when she got out of the hospital today, but she hasn't. At first, I thought that something had happened that made her have to stay in the hospital longer, but while at the shop, Janie had to leave early, saying she was taking Bruno back to Ren. When I asked Janie about Ren, she just shrugged and said, *"Ren who?"* Those women and their fucking code of silence are driving me fucking insane.

Ash rolls his eyes before taking a pull from his water bottle. "Yeah, because you know I get all the hot gossip. I know nothing man, the only woman I talk to for more than five minutes besides Janie is Indy." A smirk forms on his face. "Usually, I prefer conversations with ladies to revolve around grunts and moaning."

It's my turn to roll my eyes, which I know wounds my friend. Ash and I were notorious for one-night stands. No repeats, no dates, out every night finding the next lay. The only problem is I've stopped. I've tried, God knows I've tried to pick a woman up, the closest being Rachel from tinder the night I got arrested.

I've spent the last...holy shit. Has it been a year since I got laid?

I stare up at Ash in horror. "Dude," I breathe out. "When did I have sex last?"

Ash's face falls, "At, please don't tell me the last time you fucked a girl was one of our nights out. Man, that was... holy shit you didn't even fuck a girl in Vegas last year, that was Derek. It's been like thirteen months. Are you ill?"

I stare at my gym shorts covered junk in disbelief. *Thirteen months?*

"Oh my god." I whisper. "Is... am I broken?" I'm thirty-five years old. I am smack dab in the middle of peak sexual prime. But I don't even think I've rubbed one out in a month.

Ash pats my shoulder. "I think you've just been stressed, man. Have you given any thought to moving back in with me? You know Indy stays locked away." Indy is Ash's baby sister who needed somewhere to stay, so I offered up my half of the apartment that I used to split with him.

Shaking my head, I begin to stand while biting back a cry. Fuck, this hurts. "Nah man, I'll probably find my own place now that I know I'm not headed to prison." I laugh lightly, but Ash doesn't seem to see the humor.

"You don't deserve the sentence you got." I give my dark-eyed friend a shrug.

"It could've been worse." Ash huffs as he shakes his head.

"At, it could've been better! You were defending R–"

Clasping my hand over my friend's face, I shush him. "That's enough." I hiss out.

Ash smacks my hand away and wipes his mouth. "Gross, your sweat went into my mouth, dick-hole."

"I'm just worried about you, At."

"Yeah, seems to be a common theme nowadays. Really, I'm fine and I'm completely fine with the sentencing. It's fair for what happened. Now, can we drop it?" Ash wants to say more but doesn't and I am so very grateful that my friends know when I need them to stop pressing.

Giving Ash's shoulder a pat, I make my way to the locker room, silently cursing myself for taking the motorcycle instead of my Tahoe.

I WINCE AS I URGE MY TIRED, SCREAMING LEGS TO MOVE FORWARD, stepping off the elevator and into the modern hallway of *The Tides* - the tower of an apartment building that Ren lives in. The original plan, though no one would believe me, was to leave the gym, go back to the hotel, take an ice shower and pass the fuck out. I pinky promise, that was one hundred percent what I was going to do. But, as I got closer and closer to that fucking hotel with its uncomfortable bed, weird cleaner smell and the guy that is going through a divorce and living next door to me weeping all night, I just couldn't handle it. Then, I thought about Ren not messaging me, and I will admit, I got pissed off. I have a thing, a pet peeve if you will, I don't like when people do not follow through on what they say they will do. Big or small, if you tell someone something, you do it. A therapist could look at that and say it stems from my dysfunctional childhood and my constant lack of stability, but who cares? The point is, you say it, you do it. Ren said she would message me and didn't. And now I will not be able to relax until I've seen her face and find out that she's okay. So, here I am, in front of her door. I knock on it twice and I hear a small "woof" from Bruno. Followed by the unlocking of the door.

Ren's polite smile falls when she sees it's me, because, of course it does. Why wouldn't it? Forcing the feeling of rejection that is trying to suffocate me aside, I give her my biggest flirtatious smile before leaning my arm on her door frame.

"W-what are you doing here?" She asks and I notice even she flinches at how harsh her tone sounds. "Sorry," she whispers, sounding embarrassed. "I didn't mean to sound that rude."

"You said you would text me when you got out of the hospital," I shrug, while trying to act like me showing up here is no big deal. "You didn't, and then you didn't respond to any of my calls or texts."

Ren leans against the door and it's at this point I really get a good look at her. She looks like, well, shit, she looks like shit. Pretty shit, breathtaking shit, but shit nonetheless. She has that sick, clammy hue to her skin. Her hair looks like a rat's nest on top of her head and her bloodshot eyes contrast terribly against her dark rings.

"Okay," she rolls her head to look up at me and lets out an exhausted breath, as if just that movement took all the energy she had left. "You're right, I'm a dick. What were you texting me for?"

"Well, I've been trying to get a hold of you to tell you, you're beautiful," I smirk and give her a wink. "That's all, just needed to give you your daily reminder that you are a goddess among us."

Ren stares at me in stunned silence and I wait for her to tell me that I'm a dumbass or a liar, but it never comes. No, something much, much worse happens. I watch as her chocolate eyes become glossy and a big tear falls down her shocked face, another following its path.

No. No. No. No.

"Ren," My voice cracks on her name. Fuck! I made her cry. "No, Princess, please." Her face crumples and an actual sob escapes her throat. Instantly, I step into her apartment and wrap my arms around her. She feels...frail. I don't know what I was expecting. Ren has never been in my arms before except the night at the bar, but the energy she puts out in the world, her presence, I didn't expect her to feel this weak, and now all I want to do is keep her as close to me as possible. I need to protect her.

My heart skips a literal beat when I feel her push herself deeper against me. Her soft body curling into my hard one and, oh, you have *got* to be kidding me. I feel ***him***, he's really going to betray me like this? She is CRYING you sick fuck!

As I continue to mentally scold and battle with my traitorous cock, Ren sniffles and pulls away from me. "I'm sorry," she sobs and falls against me again. "I'm so sorry, Atlas." Her body shakes with each ragged breath.

"Come on," I whisper as soothingly as I can, "Let me carry you to your bed."

Ren half sobs half laughs at my comment which, why? I am trying to be a caring person here. "That's sweet, but I'm not a small girl, Atlas." She pats my chest and laughs again before slowly making her way to her end table to grab a tissue.

I cross my arms over my chest. “So? What does that have to do with anything?”

Ren rolls her eyes and has the nerve to look annoyed with me. Even though I am the one that got laughed at. “Atlas, you will blow out both your knees and a testicle if you try to lift me.”

Is she serious? Yeah, Ren is a larger girl. She’s got large breasts and an ass that... nope not thinking about that. Point is, she is curvy, plus size, whatever they call it. But I can still lift her. She has no idea what I do in my free time. I want to prove her wrong. I want to throw her over my shoulder and toss her on her bed like a fucking cave man. But as I watch her pulling out a small pouch and pricking her finger, I am thrown back into the real world.

Ren is sick.

I watch her put a little stick into a small handheld machine, after a second, it beeps at her and then she begins to clean up.

“Did,” is she going to yell if I ask? “Are you alright?”

“Yeah,” she says from her small kitchen before coming back to the couch. “I’m diabetic, so I have to check my blood sugar. Usually I have a monitor that is checking it constantly, but after being in the hospital, my mom wants me to check the old-fashioned way for a little bit.”

I take a seat on her couch and smile when Bruno whines and lies his head on my lap, begging for attention. “You never told me you were diabetic.”

“I didn’t realize it was something I needed to advertise to everyone.” She mutters, and I can feel that I am approaching a sensitive topic.

Deciding to back off, I scratch Bruno’s ears as I change the subject. “Why are you sorry? And why are you crying?”

Evidently not much of a subject change. She shifts in her seat and I see her lip wobble.

"I-I was fired today." Her voice was barely audible.

"What?" I roar, jerking forward and startling Bruno. "How? When? Why?"

I watch her head fall into her hands as fresh tears fall. "He called me when Stevie and Sunday picked me up from the hospital." She grabs another tissue and wipes her eyes. "He said I'm not reliable enough for them to keep on." She shakes her head and starts crying harder. "I'm going to lose everything. My apartment, my savings, my health insurance. Oh god! How am I going to pay for my medication?!"

I stand up and walk in front of her before kneeling down. "Hey," I grip one of her hands and while trying to ignore the heat rushing through me at the contact, I give her a reassuring smile. "Breathe, it will be okay."

She scoffs and rolls her eyes. "Easy for you to say. Do you have any idea how much my medicine is *with* insurance?"

"Okay, so you get new insurance. I'm sure it can't be that hard, there are insurance compan–"

"Just stop Atlas. I know you are trying to help, but you have no idea what you are talking about. Without my job, I cannot pay for my insurance. And getting new insurance is not like going and getting a new pair of pants, especially when you have an illness like mine." I watch her deflate and I hate it. I want to fix it for her.

Wait, I can fix this for her. I have insurance...good insurance.

"What if you use my insurance?" I ask, while running my thumb over the top of her hand. God, her skin is so fucking soft.

She chuckles softly, "We aren't married, aren't in the

same household, there is zero way for me to be under your insurance, and even if I could, I'd still have a monthly payment that I cannot afford on the income I'm about to be on until I can get this all squared away. I've royally pissed off a large law firm. I'm going to be seen as tainted now."

"Marry me." I firmly blurt out, causing Ren to start choking. On what I don't know, she wasn't drinking anything.

After a long coughing fit, Ren stares at me, eyes wide and wild. "What?" She breathes.

"I said, marry me." I repeat, and her eyes somehow get bigger.

"Atlas, what are you talking about?" She looks around the room in confusion before her eyes land back on me. "Is this a joke?"

"What? No! I'm serious. This could actually work out good for the both of us! I need a place to stay, you need health insurance. Let's get married, and then we both have what we need."

"Okay," she says slowly as she stands up and begins pacing. "And how do you suppose that will work? Obviously, our friends could know. But my parents, they would have to be told a lie. And what about your parents? And what does that mean for us? And what about potential future partners? How long would this go on for? Why are you smiling?"

I breathe out a laugh. "Princess, calm your pretty ass down. We don't need to have all the answers right this minute."

"The fuck we don't! If I'm marrying you, I need a color coded list of rules, expectations, hard limits, preferably at least a basic timeline, and of course what our lie is." She stops mid pace and arches a brow in annoyance. "Why are you grinning now?"

I am grinning, like a fucking idiot because her need to know absolutely everything before starting on anything is adorable. I mean seriously, a color coded list?

"How about we just play it by ear?" I have to bite back the laugh threatening to come out from the look of utter horror and disgust plaguing her face. You would've thought I recommended sacrificing puppies to appease the gods or something.

"Princess," I reach out and grab her soft hand again, missing the way it felt in mine. I wonder briefly if she feels the same pull between us that I'm feeling. "If you want a color coded list, I will go to the store and buy an assortment of different color pens, maybe some different writing pads, annotation tabs and we will get to work."

Her face falls, and her bottom lip begins to wobble. I'm about to ask her what I said wrong when her shaking voice rings out. "You know what annotation tabs are?"

I let out a breathy chuckle. "Yes, I am well aware of all the office supplies. So, what do you say?"

She blows out a breath before tucking a fallen blonde strand behind her ear. "I mean, in theory, as long as we don't get caught, it makes sense, but what you are proposing, I'm not seeing the benefits for you."

You are my benefit.

Nope, can't say that. I roll my neck and give her hand a squeeze. "I need a place to stay, I need someone to help make sure I don't fuck up this community service shit, and I could use some good karma."

She seems hesitant, but I watch as she glances over to a black storage cabinet and her shoulders hunch inwards. She looks back at me and nods.

"Okay. Atlas, I will go to the office supply store with you."

My face falls. "W-what?" I laugh at the unexpected words.

"You said if I wanted lists, we would get pens, note cards and tabs, so I'm agreeing." She shuffles to the end table and grabs her keys. "Come on."

"Ren," I rub my hand over my unshaved face. "You are too sick to go out. You look like death." I see the disappointment in her eyes and an idea hits me. "How about I order the goods to be delivered, and I get us dinner?"

She stares at me skeptically for a moment before nodding. "One condition," she says while holding her pointer finger up. "We shower while the stuff is on its way."

Did I just die? Surely having all of the blood coursing through one's body suddenly change direction and dive straight to one's cock with such swiftness and veracity as mine just did would kill you.

I watch as Ren's eyes go wide and she clasps a hand over her mouth. "Oh my god." She muffles through her palm.

Trying with everything I have to "turn it on", I give her my playful grin and step closer to her. "I mean," I whisper huskily as I waggle my eyebrows suggestively. "My job, no, my duty, no, it would be my honor to please you, my Princess." I drop to one knee and reach out to grasp her palm. I bring it to my lips and press a kiss to it. Funny. I've seen this done on TV and in the theatre countless times. Hell, I've even done it. But it's never felt this intimate.

I hear her breath catch but when I go to look up, Ren has moved back and regained her composure. "I meant," she huffs, her cheeks still pink. "That I feel gross from being in the hospital, and you look..." Her slender nose scrunches slightly. "Sweaty." I stand and run a hand through my hair.

"Well, I was at the gym. I gotta keep myself looking like a snack for your viewing pleasure." Her cheeks get redder and her mouth forms an "O".

"I don't 'view' you." She snorts as she avoids my gaze. I playfully bite my lower lip as I take a step towards her.

"Oh Princess, you think I haven't seen the way your eyes linger over my body?" I whisper as I take another step.

It's then Ren apparently regains her composure because her lips purse together, and her eyes narrow. "Sorry to burst your bubble, but you must be thinking about one of your other girls." She turns to walk away and I am about to applaud her comeback when I realize she left an open.

"So you admit you're one of my girls!" She freezes, and her shoulders cringe upwards. I wait for her to admit defeat but instead, Ren turns her head and stares at me, her eyes hot and laser focused.

"Let's get one thing crystal clear," she says cooly as she turns to completely face me again. "As long as you have ***girls*** in your life, I will never be one. I do not share." And with that, she turns and heads down the hall, leaving me standing in silence with Bruno licking my hand.

"No, I don't like that." Ren's comment makes me want to smack my face into her wall.

"And why this time, Princess?" I say through gritted teeth. Usually I am the one to wear people down, but those people have obviously never been in debate with Lauren Locklear about proper color coding.

"Red and green are Christmas colors - you never alternate those two side by side in a list." We are two hours in and we have yet to write anything down because *"organization and proper color coding are key parts to any and all lists"*. If she says no to one more suggestion, I'm going to draw a red and green penis on her face.

"Okay, what would *you* suggest?" She stares thoughtfully at the markers for a moment while scratching Bruno's head.

"The blue and the green. They are both positive colors and are similar yet different enough that we can easily differentiate between them." I blink once and then again.

"Ren... I said blue and green an hour ago."

"Yeah, but we hadn't gone through all the possible options to make sure *this* blue," She holds up the marker. "And *this* green would be the match."

"I cannot even respond to your lunacy." I say, shaking my head. "Fine, go on and write your rules down."

"You write them. Your handwriting is prettier." Her words send prickles over my skin as I stare at the markers nervously.

"I uhh. I would rather you do it if you don't care." I rub my neck nervously as she gives me a skeptical look. "Sorry, it's just, I'm dyslexic. It's not going to look as pretty as you think it will."

"Wait... what?" Ren shifts up from her slouched position on the couch. "You're a tattoo artist, your script work is well, it's amazing."

I smile at her compliment before shrugging. "Spell checks and triple checking with the client and everyone around me. There are definitely people out there with far worse dyslexia than mine. I can still read, sort of. It just takes me a little longer." I chuckle nervously, feeling a little exposed and maybe embarrassed? My dyslexia isn't something I talk much about. When I was a kid I was picked on, terribly, by classmates, my siblings, and even my mother. So I kept quiet about it. Now the only people that know are the guys at Hel's and Ren.

"So anyway," letting out a breath, I slap on my goofy grin. "Seeing how particular you are with color coding, the last thing I want to do is mess your list up by writing it."

Ren shoots me a pained look. Is that a look of pity? Oh god it is! My muscles tense as the dark feeling of inadequacy fills me.

She probably thinks I'm an idiot now. This will be the number one reason she says no to this–

My thoughts are interrupted by her taking the marker and beginning the list. "Okay, I'll write and you tell me anything you want to add. I'll be blue and your color will be green."

"You aren't going to tell me you feel sorry for me?" I asked cautiously as I watch her write the letters and do some kind of god awful scrollwork in an effort to make it look fancy, I assume.

She scoffs, "Of course not. Why would I feel sorry for you? We all have obstacles to overcome. You seem to be overcoming yours just fine."

"But you're really smart, and you read a lot." I state as I gesture to the large bookcase taking up one side of her living room. Hundreds, there are hundreds of books, all displayed in a very pleasing and organized way. I have no idea what constitutes a library but I swear, she has one in her apartment.

Ren shrugs as she rips the page and starts over,

unhappy with her floral work around the writing. "Yeah, I read, you don't have to. Nor do I expect you to read to me. Your pancreas works and mine doesn't, we all have shit."

I let out an uncomfortable laugh as I sit on the floor next to her on the couch. "I think your diabetes is a little different than my dyslexia."

"They are, goddamn it!" She growls as she rips off another page, her brows furrowing in either concentration or irritation or maybe both? "But they are the same in the sense that neither of us can help it. It's nothing we did and we have to just find a way to keep moving forward. So no, I'm not going to feel sorry for you. I may feel bad about the situations you've dealt with because I can empathize. But pity is something that I get often and I hate it. I wouldn't do it to someone else. Ugh! Why!" She yells, and I snicker while placing my hand over top of hers.

"I'll tell you what," I smile while trying to ignore what just the touch of her hand is doing to me. "You write the words and I'll draw the little pictures you want, okay?"

CHAPTER 4
LAUREN

When I was growing up, certain expectations were placed on me. Being the first born child of a well-renowned surgeon and judge, my life was mapped out from day one. I had always been okay with that though. I like lists, plans, and I like having all my ducks in a row. So, at nine, when my school project was to write about what I wanted to be when I grew up, the five-page essay I turned in detailing every single plan I had up to the age of thirty-five was apparently alarming to my teacher. I remember her calling my parents in, who didn't come – they sent Abigail, my nanny. My parents were too busy to be leaving work to go to school meetings. Plus, how would that look if Judge and Dr. Locklear had been spotted at their daughter's elementary school for a meeting? *The scandals.* There would be rumors that we were losing money, that I was troubled. It would completely ruin their image. And my parents are all about image.

Which is why I went to law school instead of pursuing my crazy dreams. It is why I was to marry another lawyer by thirty, have at least one but no more than two children by thirty-five and be ready to jump off a cliff when I catch my husband banging the secretary and or nanny before forty. See? All planned perfectly from start to finish. No surprises.

At sixteen, I went through this rebellious phase. It's kind of silly to call it rebellious, though. Most teens were sneaking out to drink or party, have sex or whatever. But not me. No, my big middle finger to my parents was my plan to run away, go live in the mountains and do voice over work. God, that was my dream, to be able to escape the real world and become the characters I read in books. I would listen to all the big books on CDs and dream of getting to be just like them. So, I planned to run, but unfortunately my mom found out my plan– because I was a teenager and used Dad's credit card to get a bus ticket. They were so furious with me. I was irresponsible, ridiculous, and ungrateful. I wasn't taking my life or my health seriously. How was I going to pay for my medication? My insulin? All of my inevitable stays in the hospital?

So, like the good daughter I was... and still strive to be, I threw my no longer hidden dreams of a cabin and a job I loved into the trash. I pushed all of those words they shouted at me into a box so that it wouldn't affect my relationship with them, but I would still be able to hear them if I ever thought to try to step out of line again.

I still continued to read stories to my younger siblings, Henry and his twin sister, Adeline. They are about to turn twenty-one, but due to our age difference and the lack of attentive parents, I was seen as their mother figure. As kids, they always would want me to read them stories because I "did the voices" whereas Abigail would just read what was written. Reading out loud to Henry and Adeline was the only part of my dream

I allowed to stay alive. I became the best daughter I could. Graduated top of my class in high school, college and finally, law school. I worked harder than anyone else to make my parents proud, not that they showed it ever or said it. And I dated one abusive man after the other because they were the "proper fit" for me. Successful, wealthy, high class. Right, maybe in public. Behind closed doors, I was degraded, yelled at and lied to. But never hit–until Andrew.

Andrew was the first that got physical with me. I allowed it, stupidly. I allowed it because I'm "the good daughter". Andrew was the one that would check off all their boxes on the husband list. He is the one that when my parents saw, they smiled. Smiled like I did something right. It didn't matter how much I didn't want to be there. Or even that he was hitting me–not that I told them, though Mother did see a bruise on my wrist once. I thought for sure she would put two and two together. But she just looked away and drank her wine. Two weeks later, he hit me for the last time. Atlas made sure of that.

"Your total will be five hundred seventy-two dollars and thirty-one cents." The older woman behind the glass divider says to Atlas and I.

I watch as Atlas doesn't bat an eye, he just smiles politely and slips his credit card, along with our IDs, to the woman. Glancing over at the dark-haired man, I can't help but stare for a second. He's so tall and built. My eyes travel over the black button-down shirt he has on that fits his tapered waist perfectly. It's funny how, minus the hand tattoo, he could actually pass for someone my parents would approve of. As long as they didn't know his name, educational background, or profession. Or that he rides a motorcycle, yeah they would hate that... or his criminal record. Yep, as long as he stood there, not moving or speaking, he would definitely get my parents' approval.

"So I owe about three hundred." I whisper to myself as I pull out my phone to put the amount in my note app. Atlas' hand lands over my screen and I'm now staring at his black and grey realism skull tattoo on the top of his right hand.

"I know my soon-to-be wife did not just offer to go dutch on our wedding service and try to make me look like a cheap asshole in front of this lovely clerk."

Shit. How fucking stupid am I? We are supposed to be playing this like we are in love. I give him what I hope is an apologetic smile, though by the growing look of concern spreading over his features, my guess is it's not working.

"Okay, I'm here!" Janie's bright voice echos as she struts in wearing a tight emerald green halter dress that ends above her knees and glittery gold strappy heels. Her curly red hair is done and wild and wow, she looks like she's really going to her best friend's wedding. My eyes land on the reluctant giant of a man walking behind her, her boyfriend Fox. His eyes scan the area in that protective, possessive way he does with Janie. Fox has had to learn the hard way that Janie is a social butterfly about eighty-five percent of the time. Mix that with her obvious good looks and her warm energy that just draws you in, it's safe to say she gets checked out, often. Fox being the large, massive *"lumbersnack caveman hybrid"* that he is–Janie's words–gets to spend his time glaring and growling at everyone that turns to look in my best friend's direction.

"Where is your wedding dress?" Janie asks after hugging me. "These places usually rent them out."

"How would you know that?" Fox asks skeptically.

Janie flashed him a cheesy grin. "I've gone to many of these chapels for influencer weddings."

I feel my cheeks getting hot and I shake my head. "I'm happy wearing this." I say, gesturing to my jeans and my old law school t-shirt.

Janie stares from my clothes back to my face and I watch her upper lip curl. "You're kidding. Look at how I'm dressed, and the guys! Come on, let's at least look, I know it's not a bridal boutique, but you know I can turn a sack into a gown easily." She goes to pull my arm and I want to cry when Atlas speaks.

"I thought you already looked back there while I was getting dressed." He says in a questioning tone.

I look at Janie, giving her the "help me" look that *every* woman can pick up on. Thankfully, it doesn't take long for her skeptical look to melt away. She stares at me for a long second and I see the realization hit her. Yep, that's right, the dress sizes don't go high enough. I'm too big for the chapel's dresses, but didn't want to make it a big deal, so much for that.

She rolls her lips inward as she realizes that now the guys are looking at us expectantly. Sighing, I roll my shoulders back and stare directly at Atlas. "Well, you wanted to marry me, so I guess we aren't hiding things. The dresses in the back only go to a size fourteen. I'm too big for them, sorry. If I had known–"

"Excuse me, Ma'am?" Atlas turns his attention away from me and to the clerk. What the fuck? It was taking a lot for me to vocalize this to him and he just... dismisses me? I am about to yell at him for interrupting when he gives the woman a smile and starts to speak again. "Do we have time to run down the street to go dress shopping? I would like my wife to have the dress she wants."

I have no idea what else he says to the lady because my brain is too busy shorting out. He turns to look at me and cocks his head to one side. "Ready?" He asks and I continue to stare at him dumbly.

Evidently, my brain starts functioning again about the time we get to his Tahoe parked outside. I stop walking once we reach his car and look up into his green eyes. "Atlas, what are we doing?"

"Going to get you a dress." He says simply while opening the passenger door for me.

"What? Why? It's not like this is a real wedding. I don't need a dress." Something flashes in his eyes, but before I can pinpoint what emotion it is, it's gone and his neutral smile is in place. Some people, *i.e. me*, have *RBF* or "resting bitch face". Well, Atlas has a "resting happy face", it is equal parts adorable and irritating.

"It is a real marriage." He says as he moves close enough to me that I can smell his masculine scent, woodsy and clean. Not what most would expect this giant tattooed goofball to smell like, but it has always drawn me in. Like a crisp autumn morning in the woods.

"We are going to say our vows, sign a license. This is real, pretty girl."

Rolling my eyes, I back up closer to the inside of his vehicle. His scent is causing feelings to surface that need to stay buried deep down. "There is no love," I mutter as I avoid his eyes. "This is a marriage of charity. Nothing more, so you don't have to take me to get a damn dress."

I go to move away from him and head back inside. So what? My pictures will look shitty, my parents are already going to hate that I had a quickie marriage, my attire won't matter. A firm hand grabs the back of my shirt and yanks me back. I gasp and instinctively put my hands up over my face before I realize I've done it. When I move them, my heart aches.

Atlas looks wounded, like I stabbed him. I watch as the look disappears and morphs into the dark expression I've become all too familiar with. "Lauren," His low tone and the fact that he says my full name sends a shiver through me. "Did you think I was going to hurt you?"

I look from him, back to the chapel, and then back to him. "Atlas," I plead as I reach out and grab his arm. "Please, just take me to get a dress and forget this." I try, but the man isn't falling for it. He backs me against his vehicle and I shiver when his hand cups my face. I look from his arm back to his eyes and notice the darkness is gone. His green eyes stare at me with so much warmth and protectiveness, it's almost overwhelming.

"Pretty girl," He breathes as his thumb strokes my cheek. "I know you can't help it. And I'm sorry if what I did scared you. But I promise you, Princess, I will never hurt you. I will never lay a hand on you in anger. And I promise you, no one else will either, understood?"

I open my mouth to speak, but nothing comes out. I look away and then look back at him. "Understood." I manage weakly.

He gives me a short nod and helps me into the vehicle before he rounds the front and slides into the driver's side before driving to the nearest dress shop.

"REN?" JANIE'S ELBOW DIGGING INTO MY SIDE CAUSES ME TO flinch, breaking me out of my trance. I look up to Atlas, his brows are pulled together in concern. Fuck, I'm not feeling good, is it showing?

"I-I'm sorry, what?" I look from Atlas to the woman performing our ceremony. She has a look of annoyance on her overly tightened face because I dared ask her to repeat herself.

"You may kiss the bride." She states again, and I watch in horror as Atlas steps forward. I forgot about the kissing! We didn't practice this! This wasn't on the list for today! So do I open my mouth? Tongue? Partial open?

Atlas interrupts my thoughts when his soft lips land on mine. I let out an unfortunately audible squeak, causing him to laugh against my mouth as he places the sweetest chaste kiss on my lips. It's so gentle, but it awakens something in me. And I know what that something is. It's the something I've been trying to hide, the something I'm trying like fuck to deny, to keep in the fucking box, but this sweet kiss, his soft lips, it's too much to contain.

As we walk down the makeshift aisle, the four of us make our way to a side room to have our ten photos taken that were included in our package deal. Those cheesy "by the minute" chapels in Vegas have nothing on this place. I can't help but laugh at the balloons that are half deflated, the obviously fake flowers that look thrown together to hide broken parts and chipping paint on the trellis and my personal favorite, the deep green carpet with blue dots.

I turn to look at Atlas, who looks just as amused as me and can't help laughing despite how exhausted I'm feeling. What we are all doing, it's so reckless and ridiculous. It's something that I would never think in my wildest dreams I would do. Me? Lauren Locklear, marrying Atlas fucking Hart? And for health insurance?? But here we are, his arms around me as the woman snaps the last photo. Thank God for that because I need some cold water on my neck. I'm starting to feel weak and really warm.

I excuse myself to go into the bathroom and change. Once in the restroom, I catch sight of myself in the long mirror, and for a moment I think about how this isn't the dress that was planned for me. It wasn't the wedding I had envisioned or planned for in great detail, in a scrapbook that is in a box under my bed. I do feel pretty, though. The cream-colored dress is floor length, off the shoulder flounce with a pretty eyelash lace. When I put it on and showed Atlas, his mouth dropped open, which was definitely a confidence boost.

Sighing, I slip out of the dress, but pause as I feel the familiar dizziness wash over me. Fuck, I left my bag at the apartment and I haven't placed a new glucose monitor on me since getting out of the hospital. *Real fucking smart Lauren.*

I take a slow, steadying breath as I feel myself sliding to the floor, my rapidly increasing heart rate is all I can hear and I hope like hell that I am actually calling out for help, but I don't know if I'm loud enough or not. I weakly slip off my heel and slam it with all my might over and over against the stall.

Of course this would happen. I enter into a fake marriage for health insurance and then I die.

Fucking perfect.

CHAPTER 5
ATLAS

"I cannot believe you are married." Fox chuckles as he shakes his head.

Shrugging, I lean against the wall in the hallway while the three of us wait for Ren to come out. Janie had mentioned going in there as well, but turns out the bathroom of the wedding chapel is oddly not big enough to hold more than one woman in a dress.

"She needed help. I am in a position to help her. Why wouldn't I?" Seriously, I don't get why this is so weird. I care about Ren, I have no one that I'm interested in pursuing as a wife plus, this means I get to share an apartment with the goddess of my dreams, finally win her over and get her to see that I am willing to worship her the way she deserves every single day. Something I'm starting to think has never happened. A disgusting thought, honestly. That woman deserves the best, but she offered to pay half of our wedding bill, and was embarrassed to tell me that the dresses were too small. Seeing her face in the parking lot on the way to buy her dress when I attempted to grab her shirt but missed and got her collar instead, it took everything I had to not break. The fear in her eyes when she cowered in front of me. The hurt and betrayal. Like she thought I was about to beat her. Like someone had beaten her. Had *he* grabbed her like that before hitting her? The thought made my stomach churn. I wanted to ask, but the pleading look in her embarrassed features let me know I needed to let the subject go, for now.

"Man she is taking a–" Fox stops mid-sentence when we all hear it. The incoherent yell and the banging noise. I launch myself off the wall and run full speed into the bathroom. My heart drops as I see Ren on the bathroom floor, her dress half off. She's still trying to bang her shoe against the stall.

"What the fuck?" I say, looking around for what could've attacked her.

Janie pushes in and curses. "Fox, go find some juice. Atlas call 911 and tell them there is a diabetic going low and possibly into unconsciousness."

I don't hesitate as I dial the number. I put the phone on speaker as I go to my knees and pull Ren to me, she doesn't need to pass out on a public bathroom floor. I hear her moaning something as she presses her head into my neck.

"Shhh..." I whisper into her hair, feeling completely useless as Fox rushes in with a bottle of juice.

"Ren, do you have your kit?" Janie asks while opening the bottle. Ren moans in response, giving us no indication. "Smell her breath." Janie tells me. "Is it fruity smelling?" I try to mask my confusion as I grip Ren's jaw and open her mouth as I inhale through my nose.

Shaking my head, I look back at Janie. "It's not fruity."

"She can't talk. I'm not waiting for her to fall unconscious and the EMTs to finally show up." Janie growls as she crawls over to me to help Ren drink. Janie curses as her hands shake too much to hold the bottle steady. Janie has Essential Tremors, a disorder that causes her body to involuntarily shake, and when she is anxious, the tremors become worse, like at this moment.

I grab the bottle and bring it to Ren's lips who moans and moves her head. "Ren, stop it," Janie says calmly as Ren moves again. "She's getting confused, it's not her fault."

I growl in frustration as I sit her up against me so that her back is against my chest. "You're going to drink this, either from the bottle or my mouth, so open up." I bark out. Ren lets out a small groan, but I am able to get her to drink some. I stop when she coughs and sputters. I'm about to try again when I hear commotion outside and thank the universe when an EMT knocks on the bathroom door.

HER BLOOD SUGAR WAS LOW. VERY LOW. TOO LOW FOR THE JUICE to help. Thankfully, the EMTs were fast and able to get her sugars back up.

I stare intently at the woman who is sitting on the chair in the chapel's lobby as the EMTs check her out. She had forgotten her kit at home. We were planning to get food after this, but the dress shopping took a little longer and things got pushed back. She hadn't had any drinks or food: she had no monitor.

I'm so pissed off at her that I want to scream. But I'm also pissed off at myself because I know nothing about diabetes. If I had known, I could've stopped this from happening. I take blame for that part, and I will make damn sure it doesn't happen again.

"Are you her husband?" I furrow my brows at the petite woman walking up to me. *Husband? Oh, wait, shit, that's right.*

"Uh yeah," I laughed awkwardly. "As of an hour ago, I guess I am."

"She's refusing to go to the hospital to get checked out, but her levels are increasing and she is awake and coherent now, so we cannot force her to go." I walk past the woman towards the curvy blonde still sitting in her pretty wedding dress.

"You have to go to the hospital." I state firmly as the other EMT grabs his bag and walks away from us.

Ren gives me a tired, uncomfortable laugh. "No, actually I don't. I was low, I bottomed out. I'm fine now. I'll feel crappy this weekend and be fine by Monday. When I get home, I'll hook myself back up to my monitor and I'll be good to go."

"Ren, you were fading in and out of consciousness on the bathroom floor!" Is she insane? How can she not go and get checked out?

"Look," she says calmly, as if she is trying to talk me off the edge. "I am sure that it looked scary but–"

"Yeah. It fucking did." I snap while clenching my fist. "You have no idea how scared I was, holding your limp body while your eyes kept rolling back in your head, knowing I couldn't help you."

Ren's eyes soften, and she stands up in front of me. I'm not happy that she's standing, if it were up to me, her pretty ass would be laying in the back of that ambulance on a stretcher. She takes two steps and then leans into me, curling her arms around me and gives my torso a squeeze. "I'm sorry I scared you."

I feel a lump in my throat and I make a noise as I try to

talk around it. "It's fine," I somehow manage to huff out. "I would just feel better if I could at least take you to the apartment now." Thankfully, Ren agrees to this and after we say our goodbyes to Janie and Fox, we make our short trip back to the apartment.

ONCE WE STEP OUT OF THE ELEVATOR, REN UNLOCKS THE DOOR and goes to step in when I stop her. "I'm supposed to carry you in, right?"

Ren lets out a loud, unexpected laugh, despite how worn out she looks. "Atlas! You can't carry me in!" I frown, annoyed at her comment hitting me harder than it probably should. Without a second thought, I grab her arm and pull her to me before grabbing her legs and holding her against me. Her body goes tense and I can feel her nearly trying to levitate so I cannot feel her weight.

"Guess what," I whisper in her ear and I watch the goosebumps run down her arms. Now that is fucking hot to watch. I wonder where else those goosebumps are. "You can't fly, so I still feel you, even if you wiggle your ass out of my arms."

"Atlas," she breathes, and I hear the panic in her voice as her arms hold tight around my neck. "T-this isn't funny. I could hurt you, or you could drop me." I roll my eyes as I walk into her apartment, kicking the door shut with my foot.

"I know everyone thinks I'm an idiot," I grumble as I set her down, easily. "But I'm not that dumb, I know how much I can hold and I know you aren't close to it. Just because the other men in your life have been too weak to carry you, doesn't mean I am. Maybe your problem has been you're dating boys but you're built for a man."

Ren opens and closes her mouth several times, and I smile in satisfaction as I spin on my heel and prance my ass into my room to change.

"You know," Ren says as she tapes her monitor on the back of her arm and looks in the mirror to make sure it's secure. "I don't think you're an idiot."

I frown as I look up from my tablet. I've been sitting on the couch "sketching" for a client for the last two hours, which is a lie. I have downloaded multiple audio books about type one diabetes. I am determined to know what symptoms to look for, things to have at the ready and I'm making a list of things to get after community service tomorrow. I pull out an earbud and look at her. "What?" I ask.

"You said that everyone thinks you're an idiot," she says, checking some touchscreen device. There is so much I have to learn, I'm terrified I'm not going to remember it all. "I don't think you're an idiot. I actually think you're really smart."

Blinking at her, I wait for the punchline, but it never comes. She sets the device down and looks over at me. I avoid eye contact and stare down at my tablet. I don't know how to respond to that. No one has ever said I was smart without a "if only" or a "but" attached to it. I'm about to respond when Ren changes the subject.

"Oh, I need your ring size so I can go get us a couple cheap bands." She says as she cleans up the wrappers and syringes that she had on her table.

"Why? Also, I'll try not to be insulted by 'cheap rings'. I mean, I just bought you that beautiful wedding. Where else in this state can you go and walk down the aisle with that color carpet? Did you notice it was green and blue?" I smirk and raise my brows.

Ren lets out a laugh that could rival an angel singing. It is otherworldly and so musical. "Oh my god! It was green and blue! It was a sign!" She sits on the other end of the couch and Bruno instantly gets up from his place next to me to go lay beside her. "But seriously," she says after her laughing fit subsides. "We need rings because my parents will expect to see them."

Right, her parents. I guess as a married couple, I will have to go with her to family events. I've never met a woman's parents before. And I get the feeling that the upper class Dr. and Judge Locklear will not welcome me with open arms when they find out about Ren eloping with me.

"And then I'll have to meet your family, I'm sure." I snap my head back up from my tablet as I turn to look at her. "Do you have siblings?" She asks.

"No." I say sharply and wince. "I mean yes, I don't know. I'm not close with anyone in my family. You don't have to worry about meeting them."

Ren's eyebrows knit together and her warm eyes narrow in suspicion. I can't blame her, everything I said sounds shady as fuck.

"I just," I sit my tablet on the end table and turn to look at her. "I don't get along with them very much and I've tried to keep my distance the last few years. I don't really have much contact with any of them, besides my mom on a rare occasion." And those rare occasions I will protect Ren from at all costs. The emotional vampire that is my mother is something I never want Ren to have to be around.

"But what about the holidays?" Ren asks softly. "What do you do for Thanksgiving or Christmas?" I shrug, feeling a little uncomfortable like I'm sitting here naked, but not in a fun way. More so like my soul and feelings are bare, and it's not a pleasant feeling.

"Uhh well, usually I'll eat with Ash or Fox on Thanksgiving and I don't really do anything on Christmas. Maybe watch a corny movie or something. Pig out on cookies from the store."

Her eyes watch me for a beat before she looks away and shakes her head. "Well, you will be expected to come to my family's holiday parties. They are torture, but afterwards I'll find a way to make it up to you."

A smirk pulls at my lip, and I watch her eyes roll as she stands. "Not that way, you pervert! I meant I might bake you cookies!" She can "pervert" me all she wants, but I see the blush she is trying to hide as she storms off.

Yeah, I definitely made the right choice in marrying her.

CHAPTER 6
LAUREN

Sunday stretches on the floor of her pole dance studio while I sit on the bench watching her, envious of the ease in which she performs each move. I shouldn't be, it's no one's fault that my body is currently going through what it is. I'm still recovering from the hospital and the illness. Add to it the high amount of stress and lack of sleep, and it's no wonder I have no energy or strength.

"So how's married life treating you?" Her sweet voice instantly puts a smile on my face. Sunday Sutton has been my friend for a few years now, though our friendship is unlike mine and Janie's or even Stevie's. Sunday is a very private person and will tell you immediately to mind your own business if she doesn't want to talk about something. It's probably why she and I are as close as we are because I am very much the same. Janie and Stevie are the "share your feelings" types, and I love them for it. But Sunday and I are just different, we don't talk about problems, we just try to fix them on our own.

I shrug as I lean back on the bench, stretching my legs

out in front of me. "Okay. I need to go ring shopping in the next day or two. Dad's birthday party is this weekend and my parents are expecting us."

"How did it go telling your parents about Atlas?" I wince, unwilling to meet her gaze. Sunday laughs lightly. "So why take him if you haven't talked to them?"

I blow out a breath, feeling a little overwhelmed all of a sudden. "Sunday, how about we discuss why I haven't seen where you live?"

Sunday's face goes stoney as she nods. "Point taken. So you wanna go get the girls and day drink?"

Whining, I roll my head back. "I wish I could, but I have to go get an outfit for the party and the damn rings." After letting out a breath, I stand, deciding it's time to face the music and head out to go shopping.

THINGS TO KNOW ABOUT ME: I WOULD BE CLASSIFIED AS A GIRLY girl. I like dresses, skirts, florals, funky jewelry and hats. My favorite color is blue, but I never wear that color because I was once told it made me look even fatter than I am and regardless of me trying my best to love myself, some things just stick with you. And finally, my dream is to one day go into one of those fancy clothing boutiques where they have a private room and I get to have clothes brought to me.

But that dream is not today. Today, I am in the very busy department store in the very busy mall, looking between a green dress with a high neck and a black one with sequins and shoulder pads. I hate both and my eyes keep glancing over to the pretty fall print maxi dresses. Finding formal wear in my size in this area is not easy, unless you are willing to pay for a higher end designer, which, considering my current employment status, isn't going to be happening anytime soon.

I feel the anxiety twisting in my stomach. The dresses suck. I feel bloated and I'm not feeling like being in this crowded store. My thoughts keep drifting to my mom, and how she has been blowing my phone up for a week now since one of the EMTs from the chapel said something to somebody at the hospital and it made its way to Mom that I bottomed out at my wedding. Which I mean, I know there is doctor patient confidentiality, does that not carry on to EMT and the dumb girl that forgot her diabetes pouch?

Mom lost her ever-loving shit. Frantic calls and texts that were nearly impossible to ignore. Key word being *nearly*. I have managed to avoid–thus far–every attempt to contact me, including my Dad when he found out I was no longer working at the law firm. Funny, as much as the two of them have tried to get a hold of me, neither has come to the apartment. Typical though, always having to go to them instead of the other way around.

The ringing of my phone rips me from my thoughts, I look and see the name on the screen and I hate the smile that I feel forming as I put my earbud in and answer his call.

"What do you want?" I ask with fake annoyance in my voice.

"Oh my god..." Atlas' voice is a deep growl that sends shivers through my body. "Princess, you have a voice made for porn."

I let out a laugh and shake my head even though he can't see me.

"What are you doing, beautiful?" This man thinks he is as smooth as they come. And what's worse, I'm starting to think it too.

"I'm trying to decide between two very crappy dress choices for Dad's birth..." My voice trails off and I knit my brows together as I try to decipher what I am hearing on the other end of the call.

"Atlas...are you...peeing?"

There is a light chuckle and then Atlas quickly adds a "No."

"You are disgusting," I roll my eyes. "Fucking mute your phone, or better yet– don't call me."

"Well, that's a dumb idea. How would you hear me pee? We are married now Princess, we are one unit, nooo secrets." I hear the toilet flush and the distinct sound of a zipper. I wait a moment and when I don't hear anything, I groan.

"Really? Wash your hands!"

Atlas busts out laughing, and I hear the faucet turn on. "Just seeing if you were paying attention. Now what's wrong with the dresses?"

"Nothing," I whine as I look back at the ugly choices. They remind me of something a grandma from the nineties would've worn. "I just hate everything about them, and I still have to pick one and then go get our rings. Oh, do you have a suit?"

"Yep! I haven't worn it since Tony's funeral, but I could take it downstairs and toss it into the washer." I smack my phone against my head.

"Why are you such a pain in my ass?" As soon as I say it, I want to take it back. But there is no un-ringing this particular bell.

"Oh?" Fuck. When his voice does that low rumble, I

have to stop a moan from escaping. Talk about a voice for porn. "Princess, if you want me to be a pain in that perfect ass of yours–"

"Okay!" I interrupt, thanking god this jerk can't see my face. Not that it matters, his snickering tells me he already knows he got to me.

"Pretty girl, why don't I come pick you up and I'll take you dress shopping and then we can go get the rings together?" I hear him shuffling around and I wonder what he's doing.

"You offered that last week, remember? And then you blew me off." I decide I'm not going to waste my money on either dress and start heading towards the mall entrance. "Where are you, anyway?" I ask, trying to listen to the background noise. It sounds loud wherever he is, I thought he was doing community service.

"I didn't blow you off," He sighs in what sounds like annoyance. "I didn't realize the anger management class was that evening." I chuckle, still unable to believe that anyone could look at sweet Atlas and think, *"Oh yeah, that's an angry man."* Then again...I saw the photos of what he did to Andrew. And I've witnessed the darkness in his eyes.

Too busy in my thoughts and on the phone with Atlas, I'm not paying attention to where I'm going as I accidentally run right into someone. "Ow!" I hiss when the person shoves me away from him, causing my leg to hit a corner of the stone planter next to us.

"Watch where you are going, you dumb bitch!" The man yells as he steps up to me. He's about my height in my heels, which is a little more intimidating than if he were taller because now we are face to face.

"I-I'm so sorry." I rush out quickly. "It was completely my fault."

"Stop apologizing." Atlas' dark voice says in my ear, but I try to ignore him as the bald man with steely eyes and a deep set scowl on his weathered face glares at me. I watch his eyes travel up and down my body and his lip curls.

"I don't usually pork pigs, but you have a decent face and ass if you want to go out to my truck and make it up to me." I'm speechless as he licks his lips and reaches out to grab me. As he tries to make contact, a tall figure comes between us and I feel all the air whoosh from my body as I watch a tattooed fist clench and unclench. Atlas, he's here? How?

"Three fucking seconds." Atlas all but snarls out. I stare down and watch his hand go in front of my body and pull me behind him.

The man, either fearless or dumb, doesn't heed Atlas' warning. "Listen muscles, this was a private conversation. Now blondie over there was–"

"Her name is Lauren," Atlas says through gritting teeth. "Not Blondie, pig, or bitch. And she is *my* wife." My mouth falls open and I stare over to the man who no longer looks as fearless as he once did. I know that I am Atlas' wife, but hearing him say it, especially in that protective, possessive way, it is definitely stirring that buried feeling inside me up again.

"Listen man," The guy laughs uncomfortably. "I really didn't mean anything, I was just joking."

"So," Atlas works his jaw and my god, his entire body looks tense as hell under his form hugging blue t-shirt.

Oh, it's blue, he really pulls off blue.

"You thought it would be funny to yell and insult my absolute goddess of a wife?" *Oh god.* I cringe inwardly as I hide my face against his back. *Did he have to add the goddess part?*

The man takes a step back. “Look man, I apologize.” He stammers.

“What the fuck? Apologize to her!” Atlas moves me to his side, and the man gives me a nervous look, same dude, same.

“I am s-so sorry,'' the man offers weakly. I nod, wanting this whole thing to be over with before Atlas takes this man out.

As the man literally runs off, I turn around to face Atlas. His eyes are slits, brows together, nostrils flaring and the scowl on his face–it doesn’t belong there. Without thinking, I reach my hand up and cup his cheek, rubbing my thumb over the corner of his scowl. The action seems to snap him out of his murderous trance. In almost an instant, Atlas is nuzzling into my hand, his body melting against my touch. He turns his face and presses his lips softly against where my palm meets my wrist and I inhale sharply.

“Are you alright, Princess?” His voice is back to his soft, kind tone and his face begins to relax back into his content smile. I give him a tight smile and nod before taking my hand back, unable to hold the connection any longer. Though, the second I break it, I wish it was back. In the past, I would’ve given anything to have this moment, and now here I am, having it and it’s too much.

“What are you doing here?” I ask as we start walking.

Atlas sticks his hands into the pockets of his jeans, and follows me. “I got out of community service and drove here. I figured you would be irritated by the clothes and having to find us a ring set, so I came here to make it more fun. I called you when I was in the restroom by the food court to ask you where you were but then that fucker started some shit.”

I sigh as I look towards the sign for the jewelry store,

trying to ignore the warm feeling coursing through me at him coming here for me. “They are going to hose me on these rings, but these are desperate times.”

“So we can go somewhere else.” Atlas shrugs. “I don’t really care. I’ll tattoo lines on our fingers, whatever you want.”

I halt my walking to look at him. “Atlas,” I say, my voice filled with confusion. “You can’t–tattoos are kind of permanent.”

Atlas looks down at me in shock. “Really? You don’t say! I had NO idea.”

Rolling my eyes, I shake my head. “You know what I mean.”

“Yeah, I know they are permanent. What’s your point?”

Laughing, I look around. “My point? My point is, you and I aren’t in love! One day you will find a girl that you are in love with. You’ll want to marry her and she’s going to see that tattoo on your ring finger, and how will that make her feel? No, I couldn't do that to your real wife.”

“*You* are my real wife.” He states firmly. “You are it. I’ll never marry another woman.” When had we gotten this close to one another? Our chests were nearly touching and I know if it wasn’t for the mall crowd, he would be able to hear my rapid heartbeat.

“Why not?” I am not even sure if it’s an audible question until Atlas tucks a stray lock of hair behind my ear and smiles softly.

“Because Princess, I don’t want to give that to anyone else. No matter what happens down the road, even if you no longer need me for my insurance, I won’t marry again because it won't be special. It won’t be special because it wouldn’t be with you.”

Fucking hell. I’m in it, and I’m in it deep.

I watch the cocky grin stretch across his scruffy face. “Oh yeah,” He laughs as he starts strutting away. “I am as smooth as melted milk chocolate.”

CHAPTER 7
ATLAS

"That's gin and game!" Howard, the old man sitting across the table from me, cheers as he slams his playing cards down and reaches out to pull the pot towards him.

"Howard," Betty, the older nurse, gives him a warning tone, a disapproving frown forming over her dark painted lips. "You know you can't have all that junk food. And you," she snaps her fingers before pointing at me. "Why can't you bet quarters like all the others do?"

I shrug and give her an innocent face. "Howard doesn't like quarters."

Howard grunts his response as he loads the side bag of his wheelchair with his winnings, which consists of the entire vending machine downstairs that he is not allowed to purchase food from. "Betty, you ride my ass harder than my wife ever did. At least she made me dinner once in a while."

"Watch your mouth, Howard, or I'll put Charles on your sponge bath duty." Howard lets out a shudder before waving Betty off.

"Leave this boy alone, he brings in the goods because I'm tired of small change, these..." He holds out a snack bag of chips. "These are high stakes."

Betty rolls her dark eyes before looking back at me, exasperated. "Every time you come in here, you get him all riled up, and then I have to deal with it all day."

I give her a sheepish grin as I rub the back of my head. "I'm sorry, Ms. Betty." She hits me on the chest before walking away.

"That 'ah shucks' boyish charm won't work forever." She calls over her shoulder.

I turn back to Howard and give him a grin. "Alright man, looks like our time is up until Monday."

"Did you get a picture of that pretty new wife of yours yet?" He asks as I wheel him out of the community area of the nursing home. This is one of the community services I am required to do. Three times a week I come here and hang out with some of the residents. The first couple of times I was either being looked at like a criminal or groped. And let me tell you, those ladies may not be able to open their pill containers, but they have an iron grip on my ass.

The second or third time I came, Howard – the appointed asshole of the nursing home, told me to get my money and play cards with him. And now that is what we do. Howard is ninety-two, wheelchair bound, and is ready to go see his wife again. He has seven children, fourteen grandchildren, seven great-grandchildren and has had zero visitors since he was forced to move here after his wife died, five years ago.

"Nah," I smile as we stand outside. "I'll take some this weekend while we are at her dad's birthday party and I'll show you next time."

Howard nods and seems to look past me. "Want a word of advice?"

"Depends," I smirk as I lean against one of the pillars. "Are you the one giving it to me?"

Howard cracks a smirk, a rarity for him I'm told. "Smart ass," He shakes his head before running his hand over his stubble. I notice how splotchy his shave is and make a note to help him get a clean shave on the next visit. "Take all the pictures. Doesn't matter if she's all dolled up or she's just waking up. One day..." There is a tremble in his voice and he lets out a small cough before continuing. "Erm... You never want to look back and wish you could have that photo of her staring at you from across your bed as the sunlight illuminates her. Your generation is blessed to have the ability to capture memories so much easier than we could. Don't take that for granted."

Me: Hey Beautiful

Princess: Atlas... are you ever going to stop doing that?

Me: Absolutely! The moment you stop being my beautiful Princess goddess.

Princess: ... beautiful Princess goddess? Can someone be all three at once?

Me: Before meeting you, I would've said it was impossible, but here you are, rocking the shit out of it. A regular triple threat.

Princess: Oh you are laying it on thick thick. What do you want? Forget about a date you already had scheduled for the weekend and you need to cancel on me?

My smile falls from my face when I read her text. That stung more than I want to admit. But of course, I will never tell her that.

Me: Never! These eyes only see you, my beautiful bride. I need to go to Ash's after work to grab my suit. DON'T take Bruno on his long nighttime walk until I get there.

Princess: You do realize that I have been taking Bruno on nightly walks alone since I got him right?

Me: Don't remind me

Me: OR TEST ME

Princess: Yes Daddy *eye roll emoji*

Me: I mean… I'll be your daddy *wink emoji*

Princess: OH MY GOD! Go tattoo somebody!

Snickering, I lay my phone down on my station and pick up my sketch pad to continue to work on the sketch for my client's sternum tattoo. Sternum tattoos are one of my favorite pieces to do on a woman, and it's in a completely non-perverted way. The vast majority of the sternum tattoos I've done on a woman have been a work of fucking art. If it's on their chest, women tend to want it to be very intricate, and intricacy is where I really shine. When I am tattooing, I hyper-focus and you will leave my table with the best of the best. This particular client is getting lace cupping the underside of her breasts and a gemstone in the middle. It's going to be big, colorful and probably exactly what I'm going to need after a weekend with Ren's parents.

Poor Ren has been sick over this party. It's a little insulting, like she thinks I will purposefully fuck up her dad's party or something. I'm a nice guy, I'm funny and charming. I'm freaking adorable to look at. Sure, I'm not some super posh doctor or lawyer, but fuck, I make more money than most of those pretentious assholes do anyway! I'm a famous fucking tattoo artist, I know I don't have the look of some rich fuck with his khaki shorts and shirt with the sweater tied over his shoulders, but that's because I don't feel a need to show off that I have money. It doesn't mean I'm broke. I mean, I am no multi-millionaire, but I, like the rest of us here at Hel's, are comfortable. It confuses and frustrates me that she is under the assumption that I'm going to fuck things up. It also is causing a bout of anxiety I can't seem to shake because, am I going to fuck it up?

"You alright, bud?" Derek's voice startles me and I snap my gaze to him and cock my brow.

"Yeah, why?" Derek motions to my hands and I see my broken pencil in my death grip.

I sigh and toss the pencil in the trash and put the sketch pad on the table before running my hands over my scruffy face. "I think Ren is afraid I'm going to embarrass her this weekend in front of her parents."

Derek grabs a bottle of water and sits in Fox's chair. Fox and Janie took off for a couple's spa retreat or some shit. It's frightening the amount of pull that tiny woman has over Fox. But, he's happy and they're in love, so I'm happy for them. Envious as fuck, but happy.

Ash continues to clean up his station. "Dude, there is no

way Ren is worried about you embarrassing her. We all know she's got a thing for you."

Derek snorts, "Which pales in comparison to the boner you've been rocking for her for...how many years now?"

I glare at the man. "Listen Virginia," I smirk as the muscle in his jaw ticks. He hates being reminded of his home state, and I love nothing more than to remind him when he starts riding my dick. "I understand that for an unfeeling robot like you, it can be hard to understand why I never jumped in with her."

"Ha!" He barks out a laugh, though his eyes look furious. "First off," Oh yeah, his Virginia accent is becoming thicker. I pissed him off. Good, I could use a fight. "You don't know fucking shit about me, so sit and calm your dumbass down before I am forced to calm it down for you. Second, it's not hard for me to understand shit. You were a step above a criminal before, but now you're on probation. You have zero to offer that woman, besides health insurance. Which leads me to my third point, you married her before you ever even took her out on a date, so don't talk to me about jumping in. It's sad really, because Lauren deserves a man that cares enough to have the balls to tell her why he really wants to be with her instead of some pussy ass coward."

"Enough!" Ash's voice yells out as I am about to come across the room to deck Derek in his stupid fucking face. "You know, you two could be really good friends if you would stop with this pissing contest. Jesus, why do I have to be the mature fucking adult around here when Papa Fox is out? You are both older than me, fucking act like!"

Letting out a breath, I back up and continue to clean my station so we can close up, when I get a text. Looking down at my phone, I instantly feel my anxiety starting back up, but this time for another reason. I open the message and read over it.

Mom: Atty? Is this still your number?

I stare at the message, reading it over and over again. Why? Why is she texting me? Bypassing her text, I pull up a group chat that hasn't been active in months.

Me: Mom is texting me

It doesn't take long before I get a response.

Amelia: So? Be a good fucking son for once and answer her.

Alex: Fucking calm down Millie, Jesus, are you going through the change or something?

Me: Look, I'm at work. Amelia, I saw that the check I sent to you was cashed, so I know she got the money for her bills. Please guys, handle her.

Amelia: I can't, I don't have gas money to check on her.

Me: You live 10 minutes from her

Amelia: I don't have gas money to check on her.

Me: Fine! I'll send you $20

Amelia: $65 or no deal

Me: $65?! I am paying for gas not to get you through the night!

Alex: Millie, stop being a bitch. Atlas, send her the $20. I'll send the rest AFTER we have confirmation that mom is fine.

Amelia: Fine.

The feeling I have is all around unpleasant. Amelia and Alex are my older sister and brother. Alex lives in Washington D.C. around our father and hasn't been in our lives minus the text messages in fifteen years. Amelia lives about twenty minutes from me in the shittiest area of the city. But, that is where she prefers to be. She is a registered nurse that just couldn't get her shit together enough to hold down a job, so she hops from one man to the next and when she's extra desperate, I give her money to run errands for our mom.

Mom is unstable. She's emotionally manipulative and only cares about herself and her needs. My father left her when I turned eighteen–stating that he only stayed with her for the kids. A ridiculous statement considering my father was never home except to drop off money to Mom. Mom has and will always be a hateful woman, but guilt makes me, at the very least, continue to make sure she has money for food, bills and *medicine*.

My phone vibrates again, and I feel dread as I pick it up. My body relaxes as I read ***Princess*** on the screen. Tapping on the message, I instantly let out a short laugh and my heart rate quickens. She sent me a picture of herself sitting on the floor with Bruno licking her face. Her mouth, nose and right eye are scrunched. She's adorable. She's perfect and Derek is right, I have nothing to offer her besides good insurance. And my words, I can and will continue to remind her how beautiful she is every chance I get because Ren deserves it. She deserves to have a man worship her for the goddess she is. And that's what I will do, as long as she lets me.

"You following me?" Ash asks as he slings his backpack over his shoulder. Nodding, I tuck the phone back into my pocket before following him out of the shop.

"INDY!" ASH CALLS WHEN WE ENTER OUR, WELL NOW HIS apartment. "Atlas is here to grab some clothes." I hear the padding of feet before the petite young woman appears in front of us. Her black hair is as wild and curly as Janie's, and her eyes are an ice blue that is almost unnatural looking. It's a weird contrast between Ash's dark as night eyes and then hers.

"Hey At!" She gives me a wide grin before grabbing her phone and walking over to me. "So, I was wondering," Her voice is light and airy as she speaks. I often think about Indy as a cartoon Princess, just smiley and musical. She flips her phone to show me the screen and my face falls as I'm staring at a chest tattoo of a lace bat nestled perfectly between this model's tits and the wings spread out over the tops.

"W-wondering what?" I laugh nervously, already knowing what the question is.

"Well, when can you do this on me?" She asks, like she doesn't know my laugh is one hundred percent due to surprise and possibly fear as I see the dark eyes staring at me from the hallway. Ash is beyond over-protective of his little sister. Like, think about touching her and die.

"Why not ask your brother?" I say nervously as Ash

shoves my suit into my chest with a little more force than necessary.

Indy rolls her eyes. "He won't do it!" She stamps her foot down in a huff. "What's the point of having world famous tattoo artists in your life if none of you will tattoo me!"

Ash lets out an exhausted sigh. Evidently, this has been a recurring argument between them. "Indy, you know you can't be tattooed right now, and do you really think I'm going to let your first piece be a massive tattoo across your chest? Have you lost your mind?"

"I am an adult!" She growls before spinning around and storming off, slamming her bedroom door when she reaches it.

I give Ash a sympathetic smile. "I'm sorry man, but just know I would ne–"

"I know." Ash interrupts before scratching the back of his head. "I know you wouldn't. She's just," He pauses as if trying to find the right word. "She's fragile right now, and I know she hates me, but I'm just trying to keep her safe."

I have no idea what Ash is talking about. He doesn't talk about Indy much except to say she works at the children's hospital downtown and he was having her live with him so their mom could travel the world with her fiancé or some super romantic thing that I could not imagine experiencing. "If you ever want to talk man, you know I'm here."

Ash waves me off. "None of that heart to heart shit. Get your ass out of here."

I chuckle and look at my phone. "Fuck, I really do need to go. I told Ren to wait for me to walk Bruno." I flip my friend the bird as he makes kissing noises before I head out the door and towards the elevator. Once I hit the main lobby button, I quickly tap out a text.

Me: Hey my beautiful Princess, I just left Ash's, I'll be there in ten minutes and we can walk Bruno.

Princess: It's starting to drizzle. Be careful on that stupid motorcycle.

I don't even try to hide the stupid grin on my face that her words of concern cause.

Me: Awww! I think someone has a crush on me *heart eyes emoji*

CHAPTER 8
LAUREN

Why did I pick this dress?

I stare at myself in the mirror. The high neck of the green dress feels like it's trying to cut off my airflow. I feel like crying, like hurling my lunch up. The dress is form fitting or "too tight for a woman of your size" as my dad will surely say when he sees me. While my mom more or less stays quiet about my weight, my father likes to remind me that men prefer their women slender.

I poke my squishy hip dips that are front and center in this dress, along with the soft pouch below my belly button.

Why did I pick this dress?

"Hey Princess, are you re–" Atlas peers in my room and stops speaking as he looks me up and down. "Wow." He breathes out.

I feel heat rush to my face, not because of his comment but because...holy shit, he looks gorgeous. He is wearing all black–trousers, shoes, shirt and suit jacket with a green tie that...oh my god, it matches my dress.

"How?" I ask, pointing at the tie.

Atlas laughs sheepishly as he rubs the back of his neck. "I took a picture of your dress while we were at the mall and after community service the other day, I went to the suit shop and found one that closely matched. You look really pretty, Ren."

I give him a forced smile. "Thanks, I hate the dress."

Atlas nods before muttering, "Yeah, I'm not a fan of it either."

I jerk my head back and furrow my brows. "You just said I look pretty!" What the hell? I have to spend the entire night in this damn thing, and now I know the hottest man I've ever met hates it too?

"Oh you do, you're fucking breath taking." He states firmly, as if it's the most obvious observation. "But I'm not thrilled about every other man at this party getting to see what I'm looking at right now."

My breath hitches in my throat and I meet his heated gaze. "Atlas?" I whisper, confusion filling me at the sound of his possessive words. I watch him blink and his eyes refocus, his signature grin replacing the almost primal snarl that plagued his full lips.

"You're a goddess," He says softly before reaching into his pocket and pulling out the two wedding bands. I decided to get the cheapest ones they had. Mine is a silver-colored tungsten band that is thin and dainty, while Atlas has a much thicker version.

I go to put the ring on, but Atlas gently taps my hand. "It's my job to put it on for the first time." He states as he slowly slips the ring down my finger. When the band reaches the end of my finger, Atlas slides his hand over mine, allowing the touch to linger longer than necessary.

I take his ring and grab his left hand, allowing my

fingertips to run across his knuckles. I hear his sharp intake of air and it sends a bolt to my lower abdomen. I steady my hand as I slip the ring down his long, thick finger, all while trying to ignore just how dry my mouth is becoming. Once the ring is in place, I mimic his previous actions by running my fingers over his hand. I notice how much I'm beginning to shake. How his closeness is wreaking havoc on my body.

Wait...

"Lauren!" I blink and look up at Atlas. The worry etched on his face. "Where is your phone? What is your level? You're shaking."

My level? Oh fuck.

I sit on the edge of my bed as I smack myself in the head. "Shit, my sensor. I took the old one off and was going to change it and then I got distracted." I look up at Atlas and flinch. Pissed isn't a powerful enough word to describe the look on Atlas' face.

Without speaking, I watch as Atlas walks to my drawer where I keep my supplies for my monitors. He grabs my pouch with my strips and meters. "Check your sugar." He growls while tossing the case on the bed before grabbing my new sensor and the supplies I need for it. I try to load my lance with the needle to prick my finger, but my hands are shaking.

Atlas sighs as he kneels in front of me and loads the lance for me. I watch as he puts the test strip in the meter while simultaneously massaging the tip of my middle finger. I am so focused on him that I don't feel the prick. He places the strip next to the bead of blood on my fingertip and once the meter beeps that it is reading the blood, Atlas cleans my finger and wraps a bandage around it. I want to tell him I don't need one, as it's just a prick, but when he casually kisses the bandage before looking at my meter, I nearly choke on a sob. No one has ever been so sweet to me.

"God damn it," He curses as he sets the meter down and stands up. "You're low Princess, I'll grab you a juice." He leaves and I sit in stunned silence. What is happening? How does he know what I need? How does he know how to read a meter? I rarely change my sensors in front of him.

Atlas returns and hands me a juice while prepping my sensor supplies.

"How do you know all of this?" I finally manage after chugging half the small bottle of juice.

"I've been reading, well listening to audiobooks a lot since you passed out at the chapel. I still probably only know enough to fuck something up," He smirks as he hands me my vial of insulin to inject into my pump. "But I'm trying to figure it out. The children's hospital has a class for families to learn about diabetes in two weeks I'm signed up for as well. I mean, I know you're not a kid but mmf–"

I couldn't listen to another word. My lips crash onto his as I pull his head to mine. I feel his hands grip my hips as he pulls me back from him. Staring into his wide eyes, I immediately get ready to apologize for my outburst when he backs away and takes a deep breath.

"You uhh," He lets out an awkward laugh. "You need to get your pump ready, pretty girl. I'm gonna run Bruno out so that he is good until Stevie gets here." I give him a painful smile as he leaves the room and as soon as he is gone, I smack myself in the forehead.

Really Lauren! You freaking assault him with the tightest lipped kiss imaginable? What the hell?

I groan and stomp my foot in annoyance before going over to my supplies to put my pump in.

GOD, THIS CAR RIDE MUST BE THE SINGLE MOST AWKWARD RIDE OF my life. Atlas didn't speak besides asking me what my sugars were, forty-seven times. Does forty seven seem too specific? I promise, it's not. It takes fifty-three minutes to reach my parents' home according to the GPS that Atlas insisted on using and he has asked me every single minute since we were three minutes into the ride. Besides that, it's been nothing. His hands have been wrapped tightly around the wheel of his Tahoe and his eyes focused on nothing but the road ahead. Every time I glance over, I see his jaw working.

Biting my bottom lip, I see the hill coming up that we have to drive up to reach my parent's luxury estate. "Okay look," I force out, unwilling to allow there to be tension between us. I need him to be on his game tonight or my parents will tear this marriage apart. "I'm super sorry I gave you that weird kiss. I think it was just the nerves and the low blood sugar, plus you were just being really nice to me." I continue to stare down at my hands that are painfully twisting my fingers. "Either way, I shouldn't have done that without consent. I'm sorry."

There is a beat of silence before Atlas snickers lightly. "Ren, I'm not upset over the kiss. I'm mad at you for being so irresponsible with your medication. I'm terrified to see you the way I did in that bathroom. That look on your face will haunt me for the rest of my life. So when you forget, I just... I worry, alright?"

Flinching, I glance towards him. His jaw is looser and I

can see the worry lines on his brow. Shit, I did worry him. "I am really sorry At," I say, feeling that all too familiar feeling of being a disappointment. "R-really, I just," I exhale deeply through my nose, "Things have been crazy and I know it's no excuse, I know better but, I just have a hard time remembering everything when I'm stressed like this." He must hear the waver in my voice because he pulls over in front of a large, ornate metal gate and parks his car.

"We can't stay here." I mumble, concerned that the owners of the driveway we are in will call the police.

"Hush." He states as he removes his seatbelt to look at me. "Pretty girl, you don't have to apologize to me, and please, don't be upset over this. I was irritated but I will be fine. I just wish I could know you're okay without having to ask you eight hundred times." I chew on my bottom lip until I feel his thumb run across it and pull it out of my mouth. "And for the record," His voice is soft and captivating as he stares at my mouth before glancing back to my eyes. "You have my consent to do *anything* you want to me. Anytime, got it?"

I nod, stupidly, because that's all I can do. He goes to move his finger away from my lips when I grip his wrist to hold him there. Without much thinking, I press my lips against his thumb before taking the tip into my mouth.

"Holy fuck..." He hisses. A horn sounds behind us as a car heads up a hill, causing us to jump. *Holy shit, what am I doing?* Atlas clears his throat and returns to his side of the vehicle. I notice his other hand tugging at the crotch of his pants, as if adjusting himself before we back out of the driveway and continue our way up the hill.

ATLAS CLEARS HIS THROAT UNCOMFORTABLY. "SO," HE HANDS HIS keys to the valet. "Who all lives here?" Standing outside the French palace inspired home, I can understand his apprehension. My parents both came from extremely wealthy parents, and both are at the top in their careers, so of course they have a home that looks like a small palace with a massive water fountain in the front that my entire apartment could fit into.

"My parents and my brother and sister, unless they are traveling. My brother's name is Henry, my sister is Adeline." I say while walking up the stone stairs to the large doors.

"That's it?" Atlas laughs in disbelief.

I give him a shrug. "I mean, there is the help as well, but yeah, that's it. My parents like to make sure you know they have money."

The door opens before I can grab the large, ornate knocker and an older man stands in his butler uniform.

"Good evening, Miss Lauren." He drawls, and I give him a familial smile.

"Good evening Ferguson, it's been a while." Ferguson bows his head slightly as he gestures for us to walk in.

"They have a butler?" Atlas mutters out the side of his mouth. "You grew up with a butler?"

Unease continues to churn in my stomach as I scan the massive home. It hasn't changed since they had it built forty years ago. After all, *"Wealth doesn't go out of style,"* as my dad would say every time it would be mentioned that we wanted to decorate. The home looks like someone robbed an 18th century castle in France and threw it in here. Antique, ornate furniture and tapestries, white floors with specks of gold in them, and so much artwork you feel as though you are in the back storage of a museum.

We follow Ferguson as he leads us to the back of the house where the party is being held on one of the massive terraces. We walk outside and I cringe at the curse I hear under Atlas' breath. An olympic sized swimming pool, a tennis court and a matching smaller castle sat off in the distance. That was the spa house. Even thinking it makes me squirm nervously as I think of how this must look to Atlas. Oh god, he probably sees this and is wondering why on Earth he had to marry me.

"Birdie!" I flinch as I hear my younger brother's voice. I watch as the sandy blonde haired man runs over to me and wraps his arms around my waist. "Woah!" He laughs and squeezes my sides. "I can barely get my hands around you anymore!"

"Excuse you?" Atlas snarls, and I slap my hand on his chest.

"He's kidding," I laugh nervously. "Atlas, this is my little brother, well I guess not so little brother, Henry. Henry, this is Atlas, my husband." The wide smile that always got my brother out of trouble growing up vanishes and his hazel eyes glare at Atlas. Henry is taller than I am, but Atlas still towers over him, and with my brother's slender build, he looks like a pencil next to the almost feral man at my side.

Henry juts his hand out. "Pleasure to meet you, At-las." I want to hit my brother at the way he enunciates Atlas' name. Atlas grips Henry's hand in a firm handshake. Henry lets out a hiss of pain before pulling back.

"Might want to work on that grip, kid." Atlas smirks.

"Is that a skull tattoo?" Henry asks, pointing to Atlas' hand. Fuck not now.

"Oh bird!" I hear the booming voice that can only belong to one man, my father.

"Daddy!" I force a smile as I walk over to hug him. "Happy birthday!"

"Thank you, love." He kisses my forehead, the grey whiskers from his full beard tickling my face. "How are you feeling? Your mother seems to be under the impression that you got married. Oh bird, are you cold? Maybe you should go inside and grab a jacket."

I furrow my brows and blink as my brain tries to register all of his questions. "No Dad, I'm fine, it's pretty warm outside."

I watch my father's brown eyes glance over me, before clearing his throat. "I just think it might be in your best interest."

Ah, there it is. "Right..." I say, my voice small as I cover my abdomen with my arms to try and hide myself.

"Are you cold, pretty girl?" Atlas' smooth as silk voice asks as he slides up behind me, his arm snaking around my waist.

"N-no, I'm fine. I'm actually a little warm." I whisper, earning an eye roll from my father.

Atlas smirks, "Well then, I guess she's made her decision then, hasn't she?" Oh god no Atlas, not him.

I look fearfully at my father, who raises a thick salt and pepper brow. "And who are you? Valet?"

My mouth drops open in shock. My dad knows he's here with me. He watched the man put his arm around me. Atlas doesn't seem dissuaded. Actually, his smile widens as he sticks his large, tattooed hand out. "Atlas Hart, I'm your beautiful daughter's husband."

Never have I ever wanted to disappear so badly in my life. Is that my monitor I hear? Is this terrace about to collapse? Do I need to be anywhere other than where I am at this moment? Am I looking for any opportunity to leave this conversation? Absolutely and unequivocally, yes.

I watch my father's face redden and a snarl form. "Husband?" He asks as his fire like stare finds me again. I shrink slightly under his gaze and look away. My eyes land on Atlas' hand. I notice the slightest of trembles in his hand and instantly I grip it into mine and give him a reassuring squeeze.

You're not alone Atlas, I promise.

"Yes Daddy," I state, firmly, "he is my husband."

"So your mother is right," My father slams the drink down he had been holding, creating a loud bang and causing the guests to look towards us. "You have gone mad." He steps into my personal space and snaps his hands in my face, causing me to flinch. "That fast Bird, your inheritance is gone. You think I'm going to let you give my money to some drug dealer because you had a momentary lapse in intelligence and didn't get a prenup?" He snarls and shakes his head. "You are a lawyer, for Christ's sake. You are too damn smart to be this stupid. We had a plan, and you just went and ruined it."

I feel Atlas tense, but I squeeze his hand, signaling for him to stand down. My father has to get it all out before he will calm down enough to reason with. I am more than used to these blows, though I have to admit, the shame and embarrassment feels worse with Atlas standing right here listening to it.

My father laughs dryly, "So, my new son-in-law," His voice drips with disdain. "Please enlighten us. What lavish job do you have to help support my now unemployed daughter who has lost her trust fund?"

Oh god.

I glance up at Atlas and I pray he can hear the apologies I'm screaming at him. He doesn't deserve this.

"Well," Atlas shrugs and scratches the back of his head. "When I'm not smuggling drugs across the border, my whores keep me pretty busy downtown." He gives my now purple faced dad a wink, and it's here that I think my earlier pleas of my monitor acting up are being answered. I stagger slightly as my vision blurs and I hear Atlas yell my name before my world goes black.

CHAPTER 9
ATLAS

Well, this is going great. I had always wondered how I would be meeting my partner's parents. And here I am, fucking killing it.

I follow Mrs, or ***Dr.*** Locklear into the house while holding an unconscious Lauren to my chest. She is drenched in sweat and she looks so clammy.

"Set her here." She states, all business. I lay Ren down on the burnt orange couch thing. I have no idea what it's called, but I've seen fancy paintings of naked women laid across them. I shake my head, trying to focus as Ren's mom speaks. "Did she never get the damn watch?"

I blink, my confusion apparently evident. She growls in frustration. "The smart watch, so that her meter would show up on it. I can't see into her phone with it locked."

"Uh, no, she never mentioned it. But that butler guy at the door was given her bag, her kit is in there, I double checked." Dr. Locklear yells for the butler just as Mr. Locklear walks in from his place in the kitchen.

"She would have that watch," He grumbles while sipping on his drink. "Had she not gotten herself fired from her job. Now she probably can't afford it. Especially if she's carrying you, too."

I stand up and take three long strides to meet the man. "In the last two decades, the only person taking care of me has been me. If she needs that watch, I'll have seven on the counter by tomorrow morning. I may not be some billionaire, but I can and will take care of *my* wife."

A humorless laugh escapes his lips. "You're doing a hell of a job so far, kid. And wife," he scoffs into his glass of what I'm guessing to be scotch, "Boy you've known my daughter for two minutes. You haven't earned the right to use that term." I resist the urge to punch him, though I feel like it would be justifiable. I can't though, hitting a lawyer was bad enough but a judge, I would never get out of prison.

"Well, you've known her for twenty-nine years and she's been having panic attacks about coming over here, so what's that say about you as a father?" I snap back. I watch his face redden again and I begin to fear the man is going to have a heart attack if he doesn't calm down.

"It tells me," His voice booms and echoes off the walls as he slams his drink down for the second time in fifteen minutes. "That my daughter knows she did the wrong thing and was afraid to tell me."

I raise a brow. "Really? And why would a fully grown woman be afraid to tell her father–who she is not dependent on, that she *"did the wrong thing"*? Unless, when said fully grown woman was once a young girl, she was severely punished for making mistakes."

Mr. Locklear is about to scream at me. I can see it, but Dr. Locklear's sharp voice cuts in. "Enough! She's waking up!"

"Atlas..." Ren's weak voice grabs my attention, and all

the anger I was feeling washes away as I run over to her, falling to my knees.

"Hey pretty girl." I smile as I brush the fallen strands from her face. "You feeling okay?"

Her face scrunches as she has me slowly help her sit up. "Yeah," she manages to get out as her mother looks at the meter.

"Your levels look fine." She says it as though she doesn't believe the meter.

Her father coughs before speaking and I grit my teeth to stop me from saying something else that will get me in trouble.

"Maybe high blood pressure." He mutters. "You're looking flush."

"Right." I scoff and roll my eyes. Because she's bigger it must be high blood pressure.

"Atlas," Ren hisses and grips my hand with hers. Her hands are so clammy. "Please, take me home."

She doesn't have to tell me twice. I stand and help her to her feet as she says her goodbyes and apologies to her parents before we leave.

Once we are out of the driveway, it becomes easier to take a breath, that is until I look over at Ren. Her head down, eyes staring at her folded hands in her lap. She's upset.

"Princess–"

"Please Atlas." She interrupts. "I'm so sorry about all of this but, I don't want to talk about it."

"Well too fucking bad." I let a snort out, causing her to glare at me. "What the fuck was that? Your family treats you like shit and you don't stop them? Ash once made a comment about your cleavage and you threatened to take cutters to his fingers below the knuckles." She doesn't speak, her head just stays hanging and I feel a jolt of anger run through me. I whip the vehicle into the first parking lot I find and slam it into park, causing our seatbelts to jerk us back.

"I'm sorry." She whispers softly.

I bang my hand on the steering wheel. "Stop being sorry!" I snap and watch as she flinches away from me. Instantly, the anger subsides and shame replaces it. I made her flinch...*me*. Fucking hell.

Tentatively, I reach over the console and rest my hand over hers. I take a deep breath as I push the darkness back down.

"I'm sorry pretty girl." I say calmly as I squeeze her hands. "I'm angry with your family, not you."

"Can you take me home now?" She asks, removing her hands from mine. I deflate, feeling as though I've completely fucked up everything.

"Baby, please," I whisper and instantly, the most heart wrenching sob comes out of her.

"I am so sorry!" She cries out as she bends forward. I rip my seatbelt off and get out of my vehicle before running to her door and ripping it open. Before she can say anything more, I unbuckle her seatbelt and pull her into me. She sobs hard, all while whispering she's sorry.

Each apology is a knife in my heart. All I want to do is fix this for her, to take all of the hurt she is feeling and absorb it into me so she never feels like this again. I feel her fingers digging into the fabric of my dress shirt as she buries herself deeper into my torso.

I press my lips on the top of her hair while I shush and lull her the best I can. "It's okay, you don't need to be sorry, Princess." I kiss her head again, enjoying the warm vanilla scent of her shampoo. "I am so sorry I scared you." I manage to get out, even though it feels as though I am cracking. Watching this strong woman break like this, it puts me into fixer mode. But this time I cannot fix it. This time there isn't someone I can beat nearly to death.

"I'm sorry," she chokes out, while trying to get control of her breathing. "For the party, for my dad. You,–" her voice squeaks and the sobs start again. "You didn't deserve it. You are so wonderful and any woman would be lucky." She sniffles in a less than attractive way, but it doesn't matter, she is the most adorable creature I've ever seen, snot and all.

"Any woman, huh?" I say with a small laugh, wishing anything I had the balls to ask her what I really wanted to.

What about you?

HOWARD SNORTS LOUDLY, "SOUNDS TO ME LIKE THEY DESERVE TO be hit with a bat." He states as he drops his playing hand. He wins, again. I have been sitting here for forty-five minutes losing all my snacks to Howard. I think it's because I'm distracted talking about Ren. She and I haven't really spoken since we got back to the apartment a couple of days ago. Ren has been staying in her room or she is out with her friends. She won't answer my texts unless it's a yes, no or thumbs up, and it's beginning to wear on me.

"Yeah, trust me," I mutter as I fork over the candy bar. "I was ready to knock my new father-in-law's lights out. When he said she might have high blood pressure. I just," I growl in frustration as I run my hand through my hair, tugging on it slightly. “I can’t believe that none of them see what I see.”

I pull out my phone and hand it to Howard. I have exactly two pictures of Ren. The one she sent me of her and Bruno, and the other was one Stevie took when she got there to stay with Bruno while we were at the dinner, when we had thought we would be gone longer.

Howard holds the phone like it's a fragile crystal as he stares at the photo. “Now there is a beautiful woman.” I see the corner of his mouth twitch up in a rare smile as he stares at her. He goes to hand the phone back, but his finger slips and the photo of her and Bruno comes up. Now he is full on smiling. “That one...” He says handing the phone back. “That’s the one you’ll remember when you look like me.”

“Is that so?” I give a small chuckle as I look down at her scrunched up face. I can’t lie, it is my favorite of the two.

“Yep, anyone can get all dolled up and plaster on a respectable smile. But that photo, well son you have true happiness and beauty captured in there. Treasure it. And you had better do right by her and stand up for her.” His voice grows serious as he points at me. “A man never lets his girl feel less because some fucker isn’t man enough to realize what a prize she is. Father or not.”

“I know you ain’t over there cussing Howard!” Betty scolds as she drops her folders at the nurses’ station.

“You know I fought in the war, right? I should be able to say fuck every now and then.” He grumbles as I help him clean up the cards.

“Alright Howard,” I chuckle as I motion towards the hall, “Let’s go get you shaved up.”

Howard stares up at me in confusion. “What? Boy, is this some sort of sex thing?”

Letting out a surprised laugh, I take him out to our spot outside where Betty has laid out some towels and a bowl of water next to the shaver and shaving cream. It's raining so we stay under the covered awning, allowing the rain to act as ambient noises.

"You know," Howard starts as I place a damp towel over his face to soften his skin. "My wife used to complain about the way I shaved. I always missed some here and there. Said it was because I was always in a rush to get moving, get to work." His eyes go distant and he gets a small smile on his face. "She called me Patch because of it."

My lips pull upwards as I apply the shaving cream, the nickname is sweet. Made me think about Ren and my names for her. I thought about the nickname her brother and father called her...*bird*. Why was that? Did she like to sing, and it was a term of endearment?

"It's funny," Howard's chuckle is forced, and I know it's to hide the sadness coming. "I missed a spot once when we were in our thirties, and that's when Patch started. So every couple of weeks, or whenever she was sad, I would miss a spot again, just so she would rub my jaw there and say *'Nice to see you again, Patch'*. I haven't had a patch since she died until now. Heh... maybe that means I'm getting closer to seeing her." I want to tell him no, that he shouldn't think like that, but who am I to tell him not to want to be with his wife?

"Atlas?" My name sounds like a song and I know there is only one person that can sing it that way. I turn my head and see Ren standing outside of the awning under her blue umbrella. She's wearing a long black maxi dress with poppy flowers all over and a light denim crop jacket.

"Hey Princess," I smirk as I turn back to wipe Howard's face off. "What are you doing here?"

She walks under the awning and closes her umbrella. “Well, it’s raining outside, and you drove that silly death trap over here because you’re a man and know better than the weather channel.”

Howard lets out a hearty laugh as he smacks my chest. “I like her.” I chuckle at Howard’s words. Yeah, I like her too.

“Hi, I’m Lauren, most call me Ren.” She smiles politely and offers her hand to Howard, who graciously accepts.

“I’m Howard. I’m the one that your husband was assigned to babysit by the courts.” Ren laughs lightly as she sits on the bench next to Howard.

“Yeah, well, had I known he was keeping such handsome company, maybe I would’ve tagged along.”

Wait, is she flirting with Howard? What the hell? She never even flirts with me!

Cool it Atlas, he’s in his nineties.

Howard claps his hands together and barks out another raspy laugh, obviously enjoying Ren’s affection. I can’t blame him, if she flirted with me like that I would melt. But again, ***she doesn’t.*** And it really sucks because she’s apparently really good at it.

Shaking my head, I grab the towels and bowl to take inside. “Are you two going to be able to behave while I’m gone?” I tease as Howard raises a brow.

“Are you still here?” He grumbles, and Ren laughs while waving me off. I shake my head while walking away. Just as I’m about to go inside, I hear Ren as she speaks to Howard.

“Hm, looks like he forgot a patch.”

"WHY *BIRD*?" I ASK.

By the stunned look on Ren's face, evidently I might've been a little abrupt. It's possible, I was silent all the way back to the apartment. But only because I was thinking about how sweet she was, and how pretty she looks in her dress with her hair in a messy ponytail. I wanted to tell her that. I still do. But I know she will roll her eyes and brush it off like I'm being silly. It's annoying when she does that. Like I'm blind or something and have no idea what I'm saying.

"Bird?" Ren asks as she slides her jacket off and I'm left to stare at her long, soft arms. An urge comes over me that I must resist. I ***cannot*** lick and bite her arms like a fucking psycho.

"Uh yeah, bird." I say, trying not to continue to stare at her like she is a full fucking meal and I've been left for weeks to starve. "Your dad and brother called you it."

I watch as her demeanor changes and her hands go up to cover her arms. "Yeah, when I was younger I um...wasn't proportional, I mean I'm still big, but it's everywhere now, back then I had skinny legs and my weight was mostly in my middle and arms. Like a bird." I watch as she goes to grab her jacket again to put it on. Quickly, I snatch it and toss it behind me. No way I'm letting her cover up because of those fucks.

"Do you have any idea how fucking beautiful you are?" I ask, with not one hint of humor in my voice. I need her to know that I'm being serious. I watch her shift to move her body from my view. Not happening. I walk towards her, standing in front of her face. I pull her chin so her gaze meets mine. I repeat my question, this time slower and more deliberate. "Do you have any idea how fucking beautiful you are?"

She glares at me and shifts her face away. "Stop it," she mutters.

"Stop what?" I ask defensively.

"Stop with the beautiful shit, the pretty girl, the princess, just stop! Look, I know I'm not some swamp creature. I'm confident enough to not completely hate myself. But you saying those things, especially in front of people, it's uncomfortable." Her cheeks redden and I hear the shakiness in her voice.

"Why is it uncomfortable that I call you those names? Why do you smile when they call you "bird" but you roll your eyes when I call you beautiful?" Why is she so resistant to me being nice to her?

"Because I know why you do it!" She sighs, in what appears to be deep frustration. "I know all about the "player handbook" and how you call the girls you're around nicknames so you don't get them mixed up. I am not one of your damn one-night stands though! You don't have to flirt with me and you don't have to worry about calling me the wrong name. This is a fake marriage, so just knock it off."

I tighten my jaw and stare at the floor between us, allowing her words to continue their stabbing in my chest. After a moment, I look back at her and I see the regret on her face, it's too late though, there's no going back. I hold her eyes in mine.

"I have never." I cough to clear the tightness in my throat, "and I mean ***never*** called another woman a pet name. Not once. You want to know the nasty truth, Lauren?

My "player handbook"? I will learn their names, their signs, favorite colors, aspirations, and I would work off of that. Is my list of names longer than others? Absolutely. But I dare you to call any of them up right now and ask them if I ever made them feel like a fling or one-night stand. I dare you to call any of them and ask them if I ***ever*** forgot their names. Not one of them was called princess, pretty girl, baby or anything. Just. Fucking. You."

"Well, what makes me so special?" I feel a rush of something that I have to push back down. She's being an asshole and I'm having a hard time not biting back.

"Because I like you, you fucking butthole! I fucking like you a fucking lot and I was trying to make you feel special!" I snap as I run my hands through my hair. "A while back, you were at Hel's talking to Janie, and Fox called her baby doll, and you said in that dreamy voice you get sometimes 'that you hope to find a man that will call you sweet pet names instead of your 'ugly' name'. Which is stupid, by the way, because Lauren and Ren are absolutely beautiful names. But you said that, so I started calling you Princess because you are one to me...Why are you looking at me like that?"

Her misty eyes are wide, and her mouth is hanging open. "Did you just call me a butthole?" She whispers, a sad smile on her lips. I shrug my shoulders, still mad at her but feeling a little less heated now that I see her lip wobbling.

"Well, you're acting like one. What you said fucking hurt." Her face drops as her hand goes to her chest.

"Atlas," she breathes. "I'm so sorry. I-I didn't mean to."

I wave her off, beginning to feel itchy and claustrophobic. "It's fine I get it, I have a long list of women, but that doesn't mean that I don't care about you Ren, and that I don't think you are absolutely the prettiest woman I've ever seen."

Her cheeks redden again and I can't help but smirk. "Shut up," she says half heartedly.

"Make me." I challenge her while taking a couple steps forward, stopping short of touching her as I watch panic wash over her and I realize I've backed her into a corner. I take a step back and to the side to allow her space just as Bruno trots into the room and whines before nudging Ren's hip. "I'll take him out." I mutter, but before I can move, Ren grabs my hand.

"I got it. I need some air anyway." Ren gives a small whistle and goes to the door, grabbing Bruno's leash before walking out of the apartment. As the door clicks, I begin kicking and punching the air. I'm freaking out, completely losing it.

Walking over to my phone I see I have two unread messages.

> Papa Fox: Busy tonight? I gotta get out of this house. Janie is on her period and if she asks me why I haven't proposed ONE MORE TIME, I might kill her.

I snicker and go to the other unread message and instantly feel sick and full of rage.

> Amelia: Look what he did to mom!

I stare at the photo of the side of my mother's face where a large bruise was.

> Me: What in the FUCK happened?

Amelia: Donny clocked her, fucker needs to get a dose of karma.

God damn it. Donny. Donny is my mother's on again off again drug dealer boyfriend.

Me: Thought she was done with that shit

I shouldn't be a dick like this. Addiction is not something you can snap out of overnight and I realize that. But families of the addicts suffer too, sometimes more and there is no escape for us. Just constant guilt and worry.

Amelia: Way to care about our mother. Fucking spoiled much? Anyway, it's going to be $300 for dr and the pain pills are $50.

I stop myself from throwing my phone across the room and take a breath. Opening the messaging app backup and type out a quick message.

Me: I'll be there in fifteen.

CHAPTER 10
ATLAS

This is it. This is the moment where I die. I fight for a breath as I fall to my knees and then collapse onto the hard ground.

"I'm done...it's over..." I pant.

"Stop being a pussy." Fox lets out a laugh as he swings his axe into the stump next to him. "That's what you get for getting those muscles in the gym."

I groan against the ground before rolling over onto my back. "This, ugh fuck, this isn't what I had in mind when I agreed to hang out with you."

Fox grunts as he sits next to me, leaning against the stump. "Yeah well, you came over here looking like a fucking maniac. I knew you needed to get that shit out before we could have an actual talk."

I scoff as I try to prop myself up, but my arms are limp noodles. It's fine though, I prefer the hard, dirty ground anyway. "So what, Papa Fox is going to get all emotional with me? How many years did I get classified as the "bitch" of Hel's for talking about feelings?"

Fox winces and shrugs his shoulders. "Yeah, that might've been a dick thing to do. Look, I'm not asking you to cry on my shoulder or some shit. I'm just saying, you are not the usual Atlas, and I'm worried about you, man."

His words give me the boost I need to stand up, despite the screaming protest of my entire body. "Oh right, you mean because I'm not the happy-go-lucky idiot of the shop?" Fox stands to speak, but I stop him. "No man, I'm fucking sick and tired of always, *always* having to have the fucking grin on my face. To be okay. To be happy. I'm fucking NOT okay and I'm NOT happy!" I scream out as I grab his axe and pound it into the stump again and again.

"She thinks I'm a skirt chaser! I'm on this fucking probation. I have to go to these stupid fucking classes, and probate officers and community service." I slam into the stump again. "I have Millie and my mom, all over the worst parts of downtown, doing god knows what to get a hit, and then sending me photos of their marks to get more money for drugs." ***SLAM.*** "I'm a loser in Lauren's parent's eyes, meaning I will never be accepted." ***SLAM.*** "I'm never accepted. Atlas is good for a laugh or a lay, but he isn't relationship material. He isn't a good boyfriend, husband, son, brother, friend." ***SLAM SLAM SLAM.***

I drop the axe as I pant over and over, my body beyond done, as well as my mind. Fox stares at me for a moment before I manage to croak out, "Why doesn't anyone want me Fox?" I watch as my best friend closes the space and pulls me into a tight hug. I try not to cry, I really do, but as he pats my back and tells me it's going to be alright, I will admit that I began to cry silently. It's all just too much, and I'm just too alone.

I GROAN WITH EACH PAINFUL STEP AS I WALK FROM THE ELEVATOR to the apartment. I go to unlock the deadbolt, only to discover it's already unlocked. Walking in, I see a flash of blonde hair turn around and head back to the kitchen. Raising a brow, I make my way towards her.

"How many times have I told you not to leave the door unlocked? Hey, what's wrong?" I ask as I see her hunched over the sink. She shakes her head rapidly but doesn't answer. Walking up behind her, I rub my hand over her back.

"Lauren?" I ask and she sinks lower.

"I don't," her voice cracks and she sniffles. "I don't want to be Lauren."

"Okay?" I say, slowly. "Well, who do you want to be?" Whipping her head, she looks at me with her bloodshot eyes, bloodshot eyes that I'm sure match mine.

"Princess," she squeaks. "Pretty girl...everything you said." I give her a soft smile before pulling her into my embrace.

"You will always be my Princess." I whisper as I hold her tighter. We stay like that for several moments and something begins to feel different. I feel like I'm in a dream state. Everything is real, but not quite. The anger, the sadness, the stress and worry, it is gone. I pull her face to look up at me and when I do, I notice she has a dreamy look on her face.

"Are you okay?" I ask and she nods.

“I’m the calmest I’ve felt in I don’t know how long.” She murmurs as she hugs me again. I rest my cheek on the top of her head.

This is the calmest I’ve felt too.

CHAPTER 11
LAUREN

"Alright ladies and reach up with your leg." Sunday's voice echoes over the speakers as she demonstrates the next move on her pole. She wraps her very toned leg around her pole with ease before beginning her oblique crunches. I groan inwardly and Janie groans outwardly, but we both – far less gracefully than Sunday–wrap our legs around our poles and begin crunches.

"Why did I let you talk me into this?" Janie pants and I can't help but roll my eyes.

"You know you feel better after, and I need someone worse than me so I don't feel as self-conscious." I grunt as my side burns. Janie hates exercising, unless it's a fifteen minute light yoga session followed by a trip to Nuts About Dough. The girl lives her life like a sloth, just laying around and eating. There are times I'm envious. Janie has a slim waist and petite curves, but eats like a teenage boy, yet never gains weight. I, on the other hand, work out, eat a rather balanced diet and can look at a milkshake and my ass gets bigger. But, as much as I feel uncomfortable in my body, lately I've found myself wearing blue colors, and shorts or tank tops without jackets.

"I am going to die." She wheezes as we switch sides. "So, how are things on the job front? How are things with Atlas?" I hear the suggestive undertones in her voice, but choose to ignore it. Atlas and I haven't spoken much in the last two days. I've been busy with check ups and he's been busy with some big tattoo appointment he's been working on at night. A model, getting a tattoo under her boobs.

"I was supposed to go into the office, but I think my dad had his assistant go to get my stuff in order to save face." I sigh as I lower my leg down. "Though whose face, I'm not so sure."

"Do your parents not know what happened?" I shoot a hard look towards my red-headed friend as I press my lips together. She knows better than to ask that. There is zero chance I would willingly tell my parents what had happened. Mainly because I'm scared of what they might say. What if they think I deserved it? Or I provoked him somehow? What if they think I was too hasty and should've given him another chance because of his name? I could never look at them again if that happened, and I'm not ready to roll the dice and bet on them siding with me.

"How's the tattoo going?" I ask as we sit on the floor, preparing to stretch.

"What tatto–oh my ass!" Janie whines as she rubs her butt cheek. "I either need to come more or stop altogether because this is brutal."

"The model." I state, trying to sound uninterested. She isn't buying it.

I watch as Janie's grin slowly spreads, and she reminds me of the Grinch. "Oh, you mean, Valentina?" She says the name in a husky, sensual way that makes me roll my eyes.

"Shut up." I grumble as I reach for my toes.

She smacks my arm before attempting to reach her toes. "I'm kidding, my god you're flexible. But umm, I guess it's going fine. I haven't really been staying late there. I've been busy trying to find someone to run the front of the shop full time and I need to find a piercer. You wouldn't want to run the front of the shop, would you?"

"God no," I shake my head quickly. "I mean, it's an awesome job, but not me. I can't handle the people. I could barely handle my clients." I am only partially aware of Sunday turning the music off and dismissing the class, but Janie and I stay on the floor to wait for Sunday to come over. "So is Atlas there, alone?"

"Oh my god! You think he's banging the model!" Instantly, my face turns red. I lean over and hit Janie in the arm, making her whine in mock pain.

"Shut up!" I growl as my heart rate increases. Obviously, that isn't what I'm thinking. Not entirely.

"What you said fucking hurt."

Atlas' wounded voice echoes in my brain and I feel guilty all over again. I hadn't meant to shame him for his history, and really, did I have any right to be upset if he did have an interest in the model? After all, this is a fake marriage. But how fake was whatever this feeling is? Or that feeling when he hugged me that way. I had never felt so calm, so quiet.

"He's not," Janie says, matter-of-factly. "You don't need to worry about him."

"You know what he and I are," I mutter as I watch Sunday heading over. "I have no right to worry about him."

Janie shrugs, "I know what you are, and I also know what you both *wish* you were. So again, no reason to worry."

"Hey there's my new lady friend." I giggle as Howard gives me a small wave while I walk towards the awning outside that he seems to favor.

"Hey handsome," I grin as I sit on the bench. "What are you doing out here by yourself? Where's Atlas?"

"Ah, he got in trouble and is inside talking to the overlords." Howard waves a dismissive hand. "It's all bureaucratic bullshit."

My heart sinks as I look towards the entrance. "W-what happened?" Did he get into a fight? Was he late?

Howard scoffs, "What happened is, once you live past your utilitarian date, they prop you up in a corner like a damn plant. Water, sun, rotate and repeat. You get no say in your life anymore. Do me a favor, no matter how much you dislike someone, never send them to a home, there is nothing worse than having the freedom you fought so hard for, stripped from you by a thirty-year-old pencil pusher whose worst work injury consisted of a stiff back from sitting on his ass too long."

I am still at a loss. Thankfully, Atlas comes storming out of the building, but halts when he sees me.

"What are you doing here?" He asks while making his way over to us. I can tell by his tense jaw and pressing lips he's pissed.

"I knew you were going to be working late again." I say while reaching into the bag I have across my body, I pull out two energy drinks and hand them to him. I hate that he drinks them, but the way his demeanor changes and a smile forms on his scruffy, unshaven face, I wish I had a palette of energy drinks to give him.

"Thank you Princess." *Princess.* It occurs to me we haven't seen each other hardly at all and he hasn't called me Princess since our hug. I miss it, more than I think I realized until just now.

"So," Howard's voice chimes in. "Are you kicked out?" I whip my head around and fix my panicky gaze on Atlas. His green eyes look from Howard to me and I have a tightness in my belly.

"No,"Atlas blinks before sitting on the bench with an exasperated sigh. "I'm not kicked out, as long as I don't take you. If I take you, I'm disobeying orders and my probation officer will be called."

"What are you guys talking about?" I cross my arms over my chest. They look so defeated. What has been going on that I wasn't told about?

There is a brief silence before Howard takes a shaky breath. "It's Clara's birthday." I furrow my brows at the name, but he continues. "My wife, she's passed away. I've given her a sunflower every birthday for seventy-three years." His mouth trembles and he clears his throat. But is unable to continue.

Atlas looks up at me. His eyes are sad and lost. "They won't let him go on his own. And, because they are understaffed, no one here can take him today, and since I am here on probation orders, I'm not allowed either."

I look from Atlas back to the heartbroken man and feel a sense of determination fill me.

"Okay," Letting out an anxious breath, I pull my phone out of my bag and hit the dreaded contact. There is only one person I can think of with enough pull to help us out and it kills me to even ask.

"Hey mom?"

SHADY SPRINGS MEMORIAL PARK IS NICE AS FAR AS CEMETERIES go. There are several ponds you can sit around, and there are trails to walk through. Though honestly, the thought of walking through a cemetery for any reason other than to visit a grave creeps me the hell out.

We park in front of the designated section as Atlas gets out of the driver's seat to grab Howard's wheelchair from the back of the Tahoe. My mother's lackey, David, sits nervously in the backseat with me.

David is an overly anxious third-year resident with short blonde hair and thick-lensed glasses. He is sweating profusely, and I know it has everything to do with whatever my mother warned him about before he met us at the nursing home. Mother denies it every time she is questioned, but she enjoys riding those residents as hard as possible. It's like a never-ending hell week on steroids. But, even though her reputation is less than positive, and her drop-out rate is higher than any other learning hospital in the state, the doctors that she turns out are the best of the best. And the waiting list to be under her teaching is longer than Santa's good list.

I pat David's hand and try not to grimace at the clammy, sweaty skin. "Listen," my voice comes out calm and reassuring. "I know she's my mom, but I'm not going to give you a bad review or anything, okay? Stop being so nervous. You just need to be here if anything happens."

"He's like a hundred and twelve." David attempts to

whisper.

"Hundred and thirteen last Tuesday," Howard says as he maneuvers himself into his wheelchair. "And I could still beat your ass, sweaty." Atlas snorts at the nickname as he motions for me to grab the sunflower wrapped in brown paper and follow them.

I grab the flower and smile politely at David. "Just relax and stay here. If I need you, I'll yell." I get out of the car before David can say anything and walk briskly to meet up with Howard and Atlas.

"Should we have left him in the car alone?" Atlas asks as we stop at the top of the hill.

"Windows cracked," Howard grunts. "He'll be fine."

Stifling a chuckle, I hand the flower to Howard, who looks conflicted.

"What is it?" Atlas asks, obviously sensing Howard's shift as well.

"I've never," Howard grunts and I watch his weathered hand grip the brown wrapping around the flower tighter. "I need to walk to her."

My gaze snaps to Atlas, who looks nervous, but is not about to tell Howard no. Howard hands me back the flower, and with all the strength he has in his tired body, he begins to push up from his wheelchair. Atlas is at his side, holding the man steady. It's now that I see how deceiving that wheelchair is. Howard is a large man, even at his age. He's shorter than Atlas now, between the hump in his back and deterioration due to his age, but it's not hard to see he was once at Atlas' height. I wonder what he looked like back when he was our age. His square jaw and blue eyes and that cleft in his chin, I'm sure he was a lady killer. Though, it seems that he only had his heart set on one lady.

Howard and Atlas walk the few steps to the dual plot

sight. One side of the dark grey granite is filled in with Clara's information. "Beloved Wife, Mother, Grandmother, Friend" is written under her name and then her birth and death dates. I glance over to see Howard's name, "Beloved Husband, Father, Grandfather, Friend" and then his date of birth. Above both their names is a short quote that causes a lump to form in my throat.

My misty eyes travel to Howard as he places his hand on the headstone.

"In every life, it will be you."

"Happy birthday, baby."

His soft, raspy words are a knife to my chest, and I glance over to see Atlas clenching his jaw tightly as Howard continues to speak to his wife.

"I'm sorry I didn't get to celebrate it with you this year," He lets out a shaking laugh. "You remember when you turned forty, and you cried for days because you felt like you were too old and we were never going to have anything to look forward to again? We made that plan to do something new every year, so we had at least one amazing story each year. I remember taking you across the country in that damn truck one year. The piece of junk quit on us in South Dakota in the middle of the night. We fell asleep in the cab of the truck and come sunrise, we saw we were almost to the Badlands. Which is when you had to remind me in your 'I told you so' way that everything happens for a reason and we may not like the journey, but the destination is worth it." He sets the flower on her headstone.

"Baby, I loved every second of our journey, even the bad times...and there were many. I wouldn't trade them for anything. I miss you..." Howard's voice breaks and I see him crumple slightly but neither me or Atlas move, this moment is too personal, too real and raw and neither of us have the right to disrupt him.

"Clara, it should've been me sweetheart. The kids and grand-babies, they adored you. You had a lot more good to offer this world than my crotchety ass. I can't wait to see you again, and I can't wait to make you fall in love with me all over again in the next life. You won't have to do anything, of course, I know as soon as I find you, I'll be in love with you instantly, just like every time before." He puts his hand to his lips before pressing them over her name.

"I'll be there soon, baby." He whispers, and I feel the tears rolling down my cheeks. Glancing at Atlas, I catch him rubbing his face before going over and helping Howard back to his wheelchair before we make our silent descent back to the vehicle.

I OPEN THE DOOR TO MY APARTMENT, AND WE ARE GREETED BY A very happy Bruno. Atlas has an appointment tonight with the model, *Valentina,* but needs to grab his backpack that he forgot. The ride to take Howard home was quiet, save for David asking a hundred questions about how Howard was feeling and Howard screwing with him to make him more nervous. Once Howard was delivered safely back to the nursing home, Atlas and I drove our respective vehicles back to the apartment, which I am so thankful for because the second I was safe in my own car, I broke down like a baby. The love that man has for his wife, even after five years of her being gone... what's the point in looking for a man if the perfect one is in his nineties and already taken?

"Hey bud." I scratch Bruno's head. "I'll take you out in a minute." I head to the kitchen to grab some juice.

"How's your sugar?" Atlas asks, his voice startling me. It's then I realize he hasn't spoken a word since he helped Howard out of his wheelchair.

"O-oh." I tap open the app on my phone. "I'm alright, a little low, but the sugar should–" I can't speak, I can't think. Atlas' firm, large, strong and oh so warm body is wrapping itself around me, pulling me into his chest.

"A-Atlas?" I squeak, unsure what is happening.

"I just, let me hold you for a second, okay?" His voice is desperate and pleading. I find the edge of the counter and set my juice down before wrapping my arms around him and squeezing him back. We stay like that for a long minute. I can feel his heartbeat and it's oddly soothing. I feel tension loosen throughout my whole body and when he goes to pull away, I nearly cry out in protest. Until his hand moves to my neck and his thumb runs over my jaw. My breath stutters and I'm starting to wonder if Atlas can hear how loud my heart is pounding.

Atlas looks at me, and a small, sweet smile graces his beautiful face. I hold my breath as he leans down, but am slightly disappointed when his lips land on my cheek. He pulls away and takes a step back.

"I'd better get going before I'm late." He juts his thumb over his shoulder towards his bedroom. I give him a stiff nod as he turns and heads to grab his backpack. Once he is out of earshot, I exhale loudly before grabbing my juice and downing the rest.

Glancing over at Bruno, I see him waiting by the door expectantly. Rolling my eyes, I grab his leash and head towards the door to get his evening walk over with.

CHAPTER 12
ATLAS

"Hey At!" Fox calls from the back room that is being remodeled and turned into a piercing area, something all of us are excited for, though Janie refuses to tell us who she's hiring. I think it's because she doesn't have anyone yet. I set my machine down and give Valentina, my client, an apologetic smile.

"Sorry, I'll be right back." Her slim, sharp face turns to me and she gives me a sly smile.

"I'll be counting the seconds." She purrs in her Americanized Russian accent. I watch as her blue eyes look me over, and I give her an awkward smile before walking to the back room. Tonight is the last night and this tattoo will be over. In the beginning, I was so excited to do this tattoo with the intricate lines and lacework, but Valentina is relentless in her quest to fuck me, even though she knows I'm married. After the first night, she tried to kiss me and I put a stop to it, letting her down gently, apparently too gently because she keeps trying. Like moaning when I wipe the ink off her.

Luckily, the guys have noticed my discomfort and have

been staying late with me, so I'm not alone with her in the shop.

"What's up man, I am trying to get her out of here....Millie?" I stare in weary surprise as my sister stands next to Fox. She looks really fucking terrible. Her once long black hair is snarled and faded with grey streaked through it. She's thin, too thin. I can see her hip bones protruding out of her filthy jeans. Her skin is pale, and her eyes and cheeks are sunken in, adding to the skeletal look, and then there are the sores that cover her bare arms and face.

"Atty," she smiles, and it sends chills down my spine. "Atty, I need help." I feel a wave of embarrassment wash over me as I see Derek and Fox watching off in the corner. My family has never come to visit me at the shop, and this is why. My mom and sister are addicts. Amelia is more functioning, usually, than Mom. But when my sister is bad, she's really bad.

"Amelia, you know better than to come here." I state as I try to push her towards the back door.

"You won't answer your phone!" She shouts, and I flinch at the abrupt shrill noise. "I need money! I'm going to get sick if I don't get money, Atlas!"

Derek clears his throat and walks over, patting me on the shoulder. "Why don't I tell Valentina you need to finish up tomorrow?" I run a frustrated hand through my hair, while fighting the urge to both cry and punch something. I nod my thanks to Derek, though I'm a little thrown at the change in him. He and I are constantly at each other's throats, it's weird to have him trying to help me. But right now, I need it, and I am not too proud to admit it.

"Amelia," I sigh, already exhausted from this ordeal. "You know I can't do this. I gave you money–"

"For mom's hospital you selfish ass!" She shouts, and I

watch Fox tense up. I give him a look, telling him to stand down before turning back to her. "You live such a puffy-cloud life, Atlas." She spits out as she starts to head to the door. "I am so glad that you and that other waste of space brother got to go off and live such amazing lives while I sacrificed everything! All I am asking for is a little bit of money, so I don't get sick! I gave up everything for you! All you two did was feed off of me and now, when I need help, you throw me away? How do you sleep at night?"

She begins to sob and, as usual, I feel like absolute shit. I know what she's doing, I've been to enough meetings for the families of addicts to recognize that she is about to go through withdrawals and she will hurt anyone and anything she has to in order to stop it from happening, and I happen to be the "anyone" today. I lower my head as I reach in my jeans pocket and fish out my wallet. I hand her the few twenties I have in there, and she leaves without a thank you or goodbye.

"Do you want to talk?" Fox asks after a long silence.

I shake my head no. I know Fox wouldn't judge me. He had a rough family life, his father was terribly abusive, and his mother and sister were both mentally ill. But still, talking to Fox isn't what I want right now. My mind goes back to Ren and that hug. I nearly broke down when she started hugging me back, like she knew I needed to feel closer. I almost kissed her, like really kissed her. In that moment, she was it. She was everything I wanted and needed.

"I think I'm going to head home." I state as I scratch the back of my head. Thoughts of my sister using that money and what could end up happening are consuming my mind as I head to clean up my now vacant station. I look up in surprise to see my station is clean and sanitized.

"Just shut up and go home." Derek mutters, while removing his gloves and tossing them in the trash bin.

"I am..." I cough and try to muster up enough strength to put my happy mask back on. "I'm deeply concerned with what is happening between you and me. Are...are we about to fall in love?" I bat my lashes as Derek gives me a deadpan stare before flipping me the bird and turning to clean up his own station. I grab my backpack before giving Fox a small wave and heading out the door.

It's about eleven thirty when I walk into the apartment. Bruno pops his head up from his place on the couch and wags his tail.

"Hey bud," I whisper and scratch his ear. "Is your mom asleep?" I look around the empty living room before walking down the hall. I see Ren's bedroom door is open, so I peer in to find her curled on her side under her blankets, sleeping. Quietly, I back away and head to my room. I start disrobing when I feel a vibration from my phone, followed by another. Halting, taking off my clothes, I pull my phone out of my pocket and look down at the screen.

> Mom: Atty

> Mom: Atty baby, it's your mommy. I need money. Please, son, I am in trouble.

I grip the phone so tight in my hand I am stunned it doesn't break. But as the phone buzzes again, I lose my cool and chuck it with all my strength against my dresser. I hear the satisfying crunch of the electronic before storming out of the room. I feel it, the violence, the rage...it's forcing its way up like a volcano and I'm seconds from erupting. It'll never be enough, I will never be enough. I know that right now my mother is sending messages to my broken phone, telling me how terrible I am. How I only care about myself.

I need to get out of here., I need to go hit something. I need to drink. I need...

I glance at Ren's open door and something pulls me to her room. Walking in, I stare at her slumbering figure and I feel alone. Thoughts of her hug come to mind and I wonder if that calming effect would happen a third time.

I hear a faint vibration. My phone evidently is still working, and it causes my anxiety to begin to choke me.

Without thinking, I slip out of my jeans, leaving me in a shirt and boxers, and I slip into Ren's bed. She shifts and groans before she gasps and jolts awake.

"Atlas!" She breathes in relief when she realizes it's me. "What in the hell are you doing?"

I don't know how to answer her. I don't know what I'm doing. All I know is I'm breaking and I know if I walk out of this apartment, I will do something that I will regret.

"I know you're sleeping," My voice is cracking as I speak, but I don't care right now. I slipped into my dream girl's bed while she was sleeping because I'm scared, and my alpha male points have flown out the window. "But I–Ren, I really need to hold you, please?"

I wait for her to tell me to stop being weird and get out. Ren is protective of her personal space. Something I've become very aware of since moving in. But she surprises me by propping herself up on her arm and staring down at me. The lights from outside cast a cool glow over her.

"What do you need me to do?" Her sleepy voice holds

no annoyance, no judgment, just genuine concern and it's too much. I feel the tears come out before I can stop them and she is on me in an instant.

Ren grabs my shirt and pulls me onto her chest. I'm nervous at first that I'll be too heavy, but she is insistent. She guides my head to lay on top of her chest, allowing me to hear her lulling heartbeat while she runs one hand through my hair and the other over my arm. Her lips press to my head and I feel like someone is going to revoke my man card, but I don't care. I need this. I need her.

"Ren..." I manage out through my not so silent tears.

"Shh..." She whispers as she holds me tighter to her. "I don't need to know right now. Just lay here as long as you need, okay?"

I let out a half laugh, half sob as my hand grips her side tighter, as if I'm afraid she might float away. "What if I need to be here forever?" I mentally punch myself at that comment. *Really dude? Could you sound any weirder or desperate?*

"Then I'm going to need snacks." She jokes as she kisses my head again, causing my nervousness to subside, at least a little. "You're safe with me, Atlas, okay? Cry, scream, sleep, do what you need, I'm here."

"Why?" I ask as I look up at her. Her face, so soft and comforting as she continues to run her nails over my scalp. Fuck, it feels amazing. If I died right now, I would be one hundred percent okay with it.

"Because you have done the same for me," she states softly, with a light shrug. "Because I know what it's like, the feeling when you're falling and wishing, just once, that you didn't have to try to catch yourself." She lets out a light, breathy laugh. "I mean, you did beat up my abusive boyfriend for me."

I tense and I feel the heat rushing through me again. “Don’t call him that.” I say through gritted teeth.

“Call him what?” She drops her hands and I bite back a growl in protest.

“Don’t call that fucker your boyfriend. He’s a useless, worthless waste of space who doesn’t deserve that title.”

She mutters something under her breath that I don’t quite catch. “What was that?” I ask, sitting up.

Ren sighs as she rests her back against her headboard. “I said he is not much different from the others.” I feel myself shorting out at the realization. This is it, the volcano is erupting. There are others? Others that hurt her?

“You’re telling me that other men have hurt you?” I ask slowly, and she winces, possibly regretting her decision to say anything. I start to get up, but she grabs my shirt, trying to pull me down. It’s no use though, I had allowed her to pull me into her before. I had given her the control, but I am too strong for Ren to move on her own.

“Where are you going?” She asks as I try to gently pry her fingers off my shirt.

“Ideally? To find every single fucking man that has ever hurt you and beat them with a baseball bat.” She grabs my shirt tighter, so I twist myself and slip out of the shirt and stand up. Ren reaches over and turns her bedside lamp on before glaring at me.

“Stop it Atlas, you are not going to find any of them. You’re going to leave here and do something stupid and end up in prison.” While she’s one hundred percent right, I feel the sudden urge to fight her.

“Oh, so if I’m doing something, it must be stupid? Why? Because everything Atlas does is stupid?” She rolls her eyes, annoyed but unwilling to fight me. “I’m waiting for your response.”

"Oh, I know you are." She says calmly, her arms over her chest. Now that there is light, I can see she is in blue plaid pajama shorts and a white tank top, oh god not now. I am in my fucking boxers and I can feel my treacherous cock, once again trying to be part of a conversation he wasn't invited to. "Come here." Ren orders, but I stubbornly hold fast. She growls in frustration and my fucking cock twitches in response. That's just perfect.

"Atlas Hart, come here or I will pull you here by your nipple piercings." My hands instinctively shield my nipples, and I wince at the thought as I cautiously make my way back to her. Sitting on the edge of the bed, I discreetly adjust myself before looking at her.

"Okay Lauren, I'm here, now what?" At my words, I watch as her eyes narrow and her mouth purses.

"Don't." She warns, and I raise a brow.

"Don't what?"

"Don't call me Lauren. You are trying to poke me because you're upset and you want to fight. Stop it." How dare she be absolutely correct and rational right now? I don't need logic. I need her to scream at me.

"No, I'm trying to find out the names of the assholes that hurt you. And then after I beat them all, you and I are going to have a long talk about your taste in men."

"Atlas." Her tone is warning. I'm going too far and I know it, but I can't stop myself. She is right, I am poking her to fight because I have no one else. I have no one else to throw these emotions I'm feeling at. So turning them into anger, into a fight, that seems to be the most logical choice.

"I'm just saying–"

"Well, stop!" She snaps and glares at me. "I'm not fighting you, so whatever you say, whatever remark you are about to make, to try and light a fire under me, it's not going to work. You and I both know that in the next day or two, you are going to feel shitty for doing it, so stop now."

I clench my jaw as I stare into her chocolate eyes. She's so pretty. Even annoyed, hair all messy and smudged make-up under her eyes, she steals my breath. "I'm sorry." I whisper without realizing it.

Ren lets out a long breath before giving me a short nod. She then, holy shit, she's crawling on her hands and knees over to me, god DAMN IT.

"Listen," She sits next to me on her knees and places a hand on my bare shoulder, if she thinks I'm going to be able to listen to a fucking thing she says to me while she's like *this*, I'm about to disappoint the fuck out of her. Her touch is fire and ice at the same time, and it's sending chills all over my body. I want to both move away and press into it. I want her and I want to run, and FUCK this fucking boner just keeps going.

"Atlas, I don't know what's going on, but I am here for you, alright? I'm not going to fight you though. You are a good, kind, sweet man that does so much for me. You just cried into my chest." She gestures to the wet spot on her tank top. Fucking. God. Damn. It.

Do not do it. DO NOT look at her nip–

"I care about you." Her words stop my perverted thoughts and when her hand moves to my cheek, I'm completely and utterly consumed.

I stare at her lips briefly before putting my hand on the back of her neck. I know I need to ask her first, though every part of me is screaming to claim her. "I really want to kiss you." I breathe out my desperate plea, our lips only inches apart. I watch as she rolls her lips into her mouth before popping them back out.

"I really want you to kiss me."

Sounds like a green light to me. My lips are on hers in an instant. She gasps against my mouth and I take full advantage, slipping my tongue inside her delicious mouth, earning the most sensual moan that goes straight to my already throbbing cock. Her tongue slips, twists and battles against mine before slipping into my mouth and I growl in pleasure as she presses herself closer to me. I grip her thighs, under her ass cheeks and am about to lift her onto my lap when she presses her hand to my chest.

"Easy tiger," she laughs uncomfortably. "You might hurt yourself lift–"

I shut her up by kissing her again and because I'm fucking tired of her talking about herself the way she does, I grip her and put her on my lap before gripping her ass cheeks in each of my hands and standing up.

"Atlas!" She cries out and wraps her hands around my neck. "P-put me down! You're going to drop me or hurt yourself." I walk her up to a wall and press her against it. She likes it. She is scared and unsure, I see that. But there is a spark of excitement in her eyes as well and, even though I know she will deny it, I felt her rocking her hips ever so slightly against me.

I slide my hand up her neck, my thumb running across her bottom lip. "Now, what did you say?" I whisper out while raising a brow at her. She runs her hands down my chest and I hiss when her fingertips run over my nipples.

"Sorry!" She jerks her hand away. "Does it hurt?"

I blink and shake my head. "F-Fuck no." I moan as I lean in to claim her mouth once more, my fingers gripping her thighs in a way I am sure will leave marks in the morning. I press my erection against her center and I feel her loosening body become stiff once more..

"What's wrong?" I ask, pulling back. The look of lust is gone, replaced by...fear, maybe?

Ren tries to shake her head and force the look off her face. She reaches to kiss me again, but I pull back before she is able to.

"Nope, not until you talk to me. What are you thinking?"

Wincing, Ren looks away as if she is ashamed, "I'm...I can't...I mean if you want–"

I place her on her feet and grab her chin to make her look at me. "Look at me, pretty girl." Ren slowly shifts her gaze to meet mine and the watery sheen in her eyes breaks me. "Baby, we are not doing anything tonight, and I am not doing anything with you that you don't want. You got it? There is no pressure here. Whatever you want, you got it?"

I watch her chew on her bottom lip nervously before nodding. "Can..." She looks over towards her bed. "I liked laying with you, like we were."

I smile softly at her. "I liked that too."

She wraps her arms around my bare waist, nuzzling against my chest. Fuck, this feels like what I would imagine a home feels like. "Can we do that some more?" She asks and I nod while leading her back to her bed. Once we climb in, I turn the light off before laying back down on her chest, letting her slowing heart beat lull me into the calmest sleep of my life.

CHAPTER 13
LAUREN

"Oh, my god..." I moan in pleasure as my eyes roll back in my head. "This is the greatest thing I've ever tasted."

Stevie and Janie snort as I take another bite of the cake. We all sit around the small table at Nuts About Dough while trying Stevie's mom's cake recipe, which I'm pretty sure is an orgasm in cake form.

"Seriously," I say, pointing at the cake while swallowing my mouthful. "This is better than sex."

Janie barks out a laugh. "Speak for yourself! Fox and I went camping over the weekend and I swear to God, he was cutting wood and bent me over a log...I felt him in my chest he was so deep."

"Ugh, shut up..." Stevie whines as she slumps back. "My poor vibrator is on his last leg. I need a man so bad."

I shrug as I take another bite. "I'm fine with cake." I mutter.

"Well yeah," Stevie scoffs. "You're married to Atlas, you get it whenever you want." I have to stop myself from flinching. It's really difficult to hide that Atlas and I are in a fake marriage to my friends, but we only allowed Janie and Fox to know. Well, it was supposed to be only Janie and Fox, but ***somehow*** Ash and Derek found out as well. The more people that know, the more likely our lie will come out and if the wrong person finds out... I shake my head. Insurance fraud is something that I'm sure I could get a slap on the wrist for. Atlas, however, is on probation. It's so hard though, having to lie to my closest friends.

"Lauren?" A cold chill runs over me, and my body stiffs at the familiar male voice. Looking up, I see Andrew at the entrance staring at me, and I feel cold and heavy all at once.

"Oh HELL no," Janie's tiny body jumps over the chair and she marches right up to Andrew. "You get the FUCK out of here." She yells and I see Stevie frantically tapping away on her phone. Oh god no, who is she texting?

"Lauren," Andrew's voice is pleading. "Listen, can we just talk for a minute?"

Before I can respond, there is a loud bang. Looking up to the counter, Stevie's seventy-something, five-foot nothing, on a good day, Croatian grandmother, Nika, stands with her hand on the large knife she just drove into the cutting board.

"You," she barks at Andrew in her thick accent, "get the fuck out of here before I cut your testicles off and feed to the rats." I watch as Stevie smacks her face with her hand.

"Baka!" She cries out and looks at her grandmother before saying something in what I'm assuming is a mix of Croatian and English as she walks over and grabs her tiny grandmother, ushering her into the back room.

Andrew looks back to me. "So?"

"So?" Janie huffs. "So get the fuck out!"

"I wasn't talking to you, you little bitch!" Andrew snaps

at her and I stand up, not willing to let Janie get talked like that.

"Don't you speak to her that way! You heard her." I wish my voice was half as confident as Janie's.

Andrew walks up to me, roughly brushing by Janie and gripping my wrist tightly. I let out a small cry in pain when he jerks me.

"Hey!" Atlas' near roar causes my heart to stop. I turn to look as he, Fox, Derek and Ash all enter the suddenly very tiny-feeling front of the bakery.

"Get your fucking hands off my wife." I watch in horror as he clenches and unclenches his fists. Oh my god, he is going to prison. This is it.

Andrew chooses to be smart and lets me go. I instantly run to Atlas and touch his chest.

"Hey...Hey look at me." I say frantically, while gripping his tight jaw. God, he's tense and his eyes are locked on Andrew. I run my hands over his neck, and pull him slightly to try and snap him out of his trance. "Hey baby," I whisper. His eyes snap down to me and his expression softens. I give him a soft smile and reach up to kiss him on the lips softly. He claims me in a possessive kiss, gripping my hips with his hands. When we break, I'm lightheaded and stumble against him.

"Come on," I whisper, while holding his face. I need him to stay focused on me. A task that is thankfully becoming increasingly easier. "Take me outside."

"Go on, At," Fox states. He looks just as pissed as Atlas did. Though it's understandable, he did walk in to see my abusive ex towering over his girlfriend.

I pull Atlas outside and to the parking lot. Breathing is becoming increasingly easier with each step we put between us and the restaurant. Atlas stops a few feet from his vehicle and I see it, it's like he changed his mind. "Nope." He growls as he turns around and starts back towards the shop. "I need to kill him first."

"No no no no!" I run and place myself in front of his massive body. "Come here." I say and pull him back to the parking lot. I get us to his Tahoe and open the back door before climbing in. He looks at me confused as I motion for him to get in.

"Why are we in the backseat?" He asks as he shuts the door.

"Less likely you'll turn the car on and run him over if he walks by." I say simply and he nods as if that was probably a good idea.

"I think," He laughs lightly, his mood softening slightly. "I think I was nineteen the last time I was in the backseat with a girl."

"Oh, do you take them all home? Very gentlemanly of you." I say dryly, and he laughs again.

"What can I say? If I'm spending hours making a woman feel good, I need space. I'm a little large to be doing too much in a car."

I can't decide if I'm annoyed and jealous, or aroused by his comment.

"You called me baby." He states with a smirk that causes me to blush.

"I was trying to get your attention so you wouldn't end up in prison." I huff. It's starting to feel stuffy in here.

"Hmmm..."Atlas hums as he glances towards the bakery. "I wonder what else you would do to 'distract' me."

"Fuck off Hart." I snap, and he shrugs as his hand goes to the handle.

"Well, okay then." He starts to climb out, but I grab his shirt and pull him back, ripping the collar in the process.

"Oh my god." I breathe out while covering my reddening cheeks. "I'm so sorry. I'll buy you a new one." Atlas stares at the tear I ripped diagonally across his pec.

"If you wanted me shirtless, you just needed to say so, Princess." I open my mouth, but no sound comes out. He smirks and leans closer to me as I lean back into the third row of seats. "I'm going to kiss you now." He whispers and I manage half a nod before his lips are on mine. He maneuvers between the two captain's seats and situates himself in between my thighs and I groan, loving the weight of him on me. His buttery soft tongue slips into my mouth and I run my hands up his neck and into his hair, tugging softly on his messy locks and getting a growl in response.

Atlas moves slightly and the bulge in his jeans rubs against my center, and I thank every god that I wore my thin leggings so I could feel it. "Fuck," He hisses as he starts to move away. "Sorry."

Gripping his torn shirt, I pull him back. "Do not stop." I pant. He smirks and rubs against me again.

"Oh—Oh God..." I moan as I feel the sensitivity rising between my legs. God, just this feels almost too good.

He lifts his head up from where he is nuzzling into my neck and looks at me with an intense heat in his eyes. "Unless I am your God, you better start moaning the right name, Princess."

Did I just come? I swear if it were physically possible, those words in that deep, gravelly voice would've done it.

Without thinking, I rip his torn t-shirt the rest of the way and begin peppering his tight, firm chest with wet kisses. I reach his pierced nipple, the piercing is a simple bar with two silver-colored balls. Feeling intoxicated with lust, I stick my tongue out and run it over his nipple.

"F-Fuck!" He breathes out. I smirk as I wrap my lips

around his nipple, playing with the piercing in my mouth. Altas lets out a moan that causes my panties to become even more wet, something I thought only happened in the books I read. He slams his palm against the headrest and I hear the leather being gripped under his massive hand.

I slide my hand over the waist of his pants and make short work of his belt and zipper before reaching my hand in and holy shit.

I pull back and stare up at him. "You're kidding."

He gives me a cheeky smirk, but he's not nearly as collected as usual. His body is nearly vibrating, his pupils are blown, and this fucking log between his legs is pulsating in my hand. I give his shaft a squeeze and watch his green eyes roll back.

"Ren..." He groans as he thrusts into my fist. "Holy fuck..." He shutters. I reach up to kiss him as I continue the movement, squeezing a little more. I want to pull him out, to see him, to feel his head, but all I can seem to find right now is his massive shaft. Trying my best, I give him another stroke. "Fuck! Ha...right...right there...fuck that's it princess..." His panting increases, as does the grip he has on the headrest.

BANG BANG

We both jump and Atlas whips his head towards the loud noise to see Fox standing by the hood of the vehicle.

"Oh my god." I groan, feeling the heat of embarrassment as I watch Ash laughing hysterically.

Atlas looks back at me, growling in frustration as he begins zipping himself up, muttering about murder or something.

"Can I give you a ride home?" He asks and I shake my head. No way I want to be anywhere around him or the guys right now.

"No, I am actually meeting Sunday." I lie as I get out of the car, marching past Fox and the men without a second look. I cannot believe I just did that, in public, with Atlas.

I look down at my hand and notice it's a little wet. Oh my god it's got to be his pre-cum. HE was about to blow. Fucking hell, have I lost my mind? In front of everyone? Me? The person who is unsure what constitutes as appropriate PDA was jerking her fake husband off in the back of his Tahoe.

And fuck me. I want to do it again.

I PULL ON THE DOOR TO SUNDAY'S DANCE STUDIO AND FROWN when it doesn't open. I knock on the door and after several seconds: I see her running up the hallway. She unlocks it and looks at me nervously.

"What are you doing here Ren?" She asks and I raise a brow.

"Just came to talk, I figured I'd catch you after your last class. Am I interrupting something?" I motion to the hallway she just came from.

"What? No! Not like Janie and the boys were interrupting you and your hubby." She winks and I groan.

"She already told you?!" I lay my head on her front counter.

"You're lucky she didn't send pictures. You know Janie ain't holding back goss-"

"Hey Mom,"

I hear a young male's voice call, followed by footsteps. I

look at Sunday, who is now ghost white, and her honey-colored eyes are as wide as saucers.

I look behind her to see a preteen boy walking up. I'm sure that he is tall for his age, standing about my height. His hair is sandy colored and messy, hanging in front of his eyes, the same eyes as Sunday.

"Mom?" He repeats again, snapping Sunday out of her trance.

"Y-yeah bud?" She asks nervously. Why hadn't she said anything? Why is she so nervous?

"Mamaw is here. I'm going to go now." He says slowly as he looks at me with suspicion. "Are you okay alone?" Something in his protective tone squeezes at my heart. Sunday nods and gives the boy a hug before watching him go out the back door.

Once inside, she lets out a breath and stares at me. "I guess I need to explain."

"Only if you want to. You kept the matter to yourself for a reason, you know I don't pry." I shrug, though inside I'm dying to know.

Sunday pulls herself up on the counter and gives me a pained look. "That's Wade, he's my son. He's eleven."

Sunday is twenty-four, I do some quick math and then try to hide my expression, but I'm not quick enough.

"I was thirteen." She states firmly, her brows creased. "But I wanna make it clear, I have worked hard my whole life to graduate early, to raise him, have a job and my dancing career. I was young and got taken advantage of, but I do everything in my power to take care of my son." I flinch at the sharpness in her tone., I can't blame her, though. Having a child that young, she has probably had to defend herself on more than one occasion. Walking up to her, I place my hand on top of hers.

"Sunday," I start softly. "I'm not judging you. Yeah, the age is startling, but you don't have to justify yourself to me or anyone. I have no doubt you're a good mom. It was just shocking, since you've never mentioned him."

"I know..." Sunday lets out a tired breath. "People have always been so...temporary in our lives. No one stays around long and it's been hard on him, so I keep him separate from the rest of my life."

"Well," I lean against the counter. "If you ever decide you want to change that, you know me and the girls would love to meet him." Sunday rests her head on my shoulder.

"Thanks Ren, I kind of love you right now."

I laugh and pat her cheek. "I kind of love you too Sunday."

There is a moment of peaceful silence between us before Sunday lifts her head and chuckles. "So, sex in the car while his buddies are beating up your ex?"

I groan. This is going to be a long evening.

CHAPTER 14
ATLAS

"I mean," Derek shudders as he preps his station for a tattoo. "Do ya'll not own a fucking bed? All three of you! Fucking in cars, the shop, that water fountain..."

"Hey!" Ash stands up and points at Derek. "Vegas, man! You don't break the Vegas code."

"My point is," Derek looks back at me but I don't care, I'm alternating between being deliriously happy because holy shit Ren's hand on my cock was the greatest feeling of my life, right next to her sweet mouth on my nipple. As well as being pissed the fuck off because these three idiots interrupted the best sexual encounter of my life. My balls are so blue right now it's painful.

I look up at Derek and realize everyone is looking at me expectantly. "I'll be honest, I heard nothing that was said after Vegas." They all groan and go back to their work. I hear the door alarm chime, followed by the clicking of heels on the tile. I whine in annoyance, knowing exactly who those heels belong to. Slowly, I spin my chair around to see

Valentina standing in the doorway, a tight black mini-skirt with a red cami that ended above her belly button.

"There's my guy." She purrs and I want to cry, but I'm a professional, so I give her a smirk and pat the table, ready to finish this last session with her.

"ALRIGHT," I SMILE AS I CLEAN HER TATTOO UP. "YOU ARE ALL done."

Valentina smiles and stands up as she walks to the mirror and looks at herself. "It's beautiful. Atlas, you are magical."

I laugh as I remove my gloves. "Well, I'm glad you like it. I'll head up front to start getting the checkout going while you get dressed."

I'm so exhausted. Valentina drug the session out again with multiple stops. I had hoped to get to the apartment to talk to Ren about the car thing and find out if she's okay. But I haven't even had time to text her yet.

Valentina walks out and smiles at me. "I hope your wife won't be mad." I raise my brow at her as I flip the screen to show her the total.

"About what? She's used to me having to work weird hours." Valentina hands me the cash, allowing her fingers to run over my hand.

"That you are doing art on someone like me." Her smile is confident and I am instantly irritated, though I don't have it in me to tear down a woman's confidence, even if she deserves it.

"My wife is the most beautiful woman I know." I say

simply as I hand her the receipt and the aftercare instructions. "I only have eyes for her, so she has nothing to get mad over."

Valentina's very full lips purse and she gives me a long, hard stare as if she's waiting for me to tell her that I'm just kidding. I get the feeling she isn't used to getting turned down. Valentina gives me a tight smile and a sharp nod before elegantly spinning on her spiky heels and walking out of the shop.

When she leaves, my whole body collapses onto the counter. I hear Ash snickering behind me and flip him off without moving my head. I am so ready to go home.

Walking into the apartment, Bruno runs into the entryway and begins whining and huffing. At first, I think he needs to walk until I hear the faint alarm going off.

"Fuck." I rush into Ren's room and see her sitting on the floor, her head resting on her mattress.

"Holy shit, Ren." I rush to her side and kneel next to her. She's barely coherent, and she's drenched in sweat. I turn on her light beside her bed before getting up and going to her drawer where her supplies are. I grab her testing kit and run back to her.

She tries to look at me but can't lift her head. "Princess, stay still. I got you." I check her sugar and cuss as the low number appears. It's too low to treat with just a juice box or sugar, and I know I need to take action to treat her to prevent her from going into a coma. I see her eyes rolling and I slap her cheek lightly. "Lauren!" I bark out, trying to keep her up. Going back to her drawer, I pull the small red case out that holds her emergency glucagon. As I walk back, I call 911 and put them on speaker.

"9-1-1 what's your emergency?" The operator asks as I open the case.

"Princess, I've only watched one video on this." I say nervously. "Y-Yeah, my name is Atlas Hart. My wife is type one diabetic, and I just found her on the floor. She's low and fading in and out of consciousness. I'm about to give her a glucagon injection." I give the operator the address before following the instructions that I remember on the instructional video. Luckily, it's pretty straight-forward.

"Flick...it." Ren whispers weakly as she fights to keep her eyes open. I tap the side of the syringe to remove the air bubbles. I grab Ren and lay her on her side, remembering that she might throw up, before piercing her thigh at a ninety-degree angle and injecting the medicine.

"Mr. Hart?" The operator says. "Did you give her the glucagon?"

I furrow my brows as I stare at her. "Yes, why isn't she better?" Did I do it wrong?

"Sir, it takes about fifteen minutes, the paramedics are on their way to you now, alright." I sit down, putting Ren's sweaty head in my lap as I run my hand through her messy hair. She lets out a small whimper.

"Shh, just rest, pretty girl." I say softly, while trying to swallow the hard lump in my throat. I can't do this. I can't keep finding her on the ground, dying and alone. I'm going to be in constant fear of her going low whenever I'm away.

There is a knock on the door and Bruno, who had been laying next to Ren, stands up to investigate. He comes back a few seconds later with the paramedics. After fifteen minutes, Ren is not where they want her after the glucagon and is not coherent enough to swallow any food or drink herself, so I tell them to take us to the hospital.

"WELL, WHAT WERE YOU DOING?" DR. LOCKLEAR HISSES WHILE looking over Ren's chart. We've been here for six hours, and I'm exhausted but I refuse to go to sleep, I'm terrified something will happen. I keep looking at the clock, knowing that in about three hours I have to be checked-in for my community service, and I would give anything not to have to go.

"I was at work." I sigh as I rub my face. She has been in here interrogating me for the last fifteen minutes since she got out of a surgery she was performing.

"Right, the doodler." Let it go, Atlas. Let. It. Go. "Well, does your job pay you well enough to afford things like a phone? Or a smart watch?"

I glare up at her, "Dr. Locklear, I am exhausted, I am stressed, and I am trying to be a good son-in-law and allow you to take your frustrations out on me. But I'm giving you one more try to talk to me like I didn't just smear shit on your face and flip you off before I shut down."

Her eyes narrow and in an instant, the woman is in front of the chair I am sitting in. She leans down and stares into my eyes.

"That girl, your 'wife', is *my* daughter. And you, a grungy tattoo artist with a family full of addicts and a criminal record... oh yes, we know all about you, Atlas. You somehow thought you were good enough to marry *my* daughter? I know what you are, son, you're a tumor." She raises back up and rolls her neck. "And lucky for Lauren, I am the best of the best at removing them." I look down, unable to say anything to fight her.

"Now," She brushes the sleeves of her white coat before staring at me again. "Until such time as I remove you, you may as well be of some use to me. Can you afford smart devices?"

I don't verbally answer, instead I glance at the iPhone sitting on the tray. Dr. Locklear nods and pulls a pad of paper out of her pocket and begins to write something down before handing me the paper.

"That is the app, the username and the password. That's the monitoring app for her device. Set it up on your phone so that you'll be alerted if something goes wrong again. And then, go buy you and her a smart watch so that she can monitor it there as well."

I take the paper and look down at her instructions. "If you know all of this, if you know she needs a watch, if you know the app and the login information, why aren't you monitoring it? Or your husband? Someone should've gotten alerted that she was going low."

Dr. Locklear stiffens and she turns to go out the door. "Lauren is an adult. It's not my job to bail her out every time she messes up. She'll never learn that way. I have countless diabetic patients and they seem to manage just fine without their mother alternating between watching their monitor and trying to run a hospital. If she needs a keeper, she should get married... oh wait." She gives me a hard look before walking out of the room, leaving me alone with my sleeping wife.

"YOU SHOULDN'T BE HERE. GIN." HOWARD STATES AS HE LAYS HIS cards down and takes his winnings. I scratch the back of my head as I sip on my energy drink.

"I like you Howard, but today I wouldn't be here if I didn't have to be." I look at my phone, no messages yet. Sunday and Janie are at the hospital while I'm here with Howard. They are supposed to text me when Ren is up. But so far I haven't received a message.

Ren woke up right before I left, but was confused and combative. I found that to be an overstatement. She was scared and freaked out, but I guess it doesn't matter what I think because they put medicine in her IV and she's been out since. I already went to get her and I new watches, and I downloaded the app on my phone. Now I just need to hear her voice.

"I'm scared." I whisper out loud without realizing it. Howard hums as he slowly nods his head.

"That's understandable. The person you love is ill and you can't fix it." I wince at his words. *Love?* I don't think I'm at the point that I'm ready to look into the process of love. Fuck, I haven't even taken her out on a proper date.

An idea pops into my head so fast I have to reach for a pen on the table and write it on my hand before I forget it. This is perfect. I am going to ask Ren on a date.

I REST MY CHEEK ON MY FIST AS I LAZILY TRACE THE VEINS AND lines in Ren's hand. There isn't a word for how tired I am. But even if I mentally told myself it is okay to fall asleep, my body is so jacked up on the energy drinks I've been shotgunning all day that I'm practically vibrating.

"Atlas?" Ren's weak voice reaches through my exhaustion and brain fog and rips me back into the real world. I whip my head up and stare at her. She looks at me and winces. "You look like shit." I can't help the laugh of relief that forces its way out.

Standing up, I lean over her bed and cup her cheek softly. "You scared me." I whisper before glancing at the monitor, her heart rate is increasing. I smirk as I turn my gaze back to her. "Something got you excited, Princess?" I watch cheeks redden as she glares at the monitor as if it ratted her out.

"I'm sorry." She says weakly, and I feel her nuzzle into my hand. Fuck, I'm a goner with her. My obsessive crush with Ren is nothing new. I've been trying to fight down those feelings, playing them off as casual flirting for a long time. But this last year, it's become harder, probably because she's been in my life more since Janie took over Hel's with Fox. And now, we live together, and...

"The person you love is ill and you can't fix it."

Howard's words hit me again. Love. Maybe I might be falling, I don't know. But I am sure of one thing, Dr. Locklear is right, I haven't proven myself to be worthy of her, yet. But that will change.

I lean down to kiss her but stop myself. I can't just take a kiss from her, she's not my–

"Are you going to kiss me or just stand there?" She huffs out with all that fucking attitude that I adore. I chuckle as I place my lips onto hers, fully expecting a chaste kiss. But apparently Ren has other plans, and those plans include seeing how high she can get her heart rate to go.

Her sweet, warm tongue slips between my lips to explore my mouth and I groan into the kiss. She grabs my hand from her cheek and I freeze when I feel my hand traveling down her throat towards her chest.

Ho..ly...

"W-wait!" I hate myself for saying it, but I need to. Ren freezes, and I want to scream when I notice how close I am to her tits. "I– Holy God, I want this but, please, not here." It's at that moment I notice I'm talking to her chest, not her face. Glancing up I notice the look of rejection that she is in the process of masking. "No." I state firmly as I grab her chin. "You knock that off immediately. Listen, if you want me to touch you," I let out a breath at the thought while trying to get my hard as fuck cock under control. "I will gladly touch you everywhere, Ren–once you are out of here and feeling better. But don't you dare take this as a rejection, you hear me?"

"I'm never going to be better, Atlas." Her voice is tired and distant as she stares at her lap. "This is my life. Sure, there are days that I'm not unconscious on the floor, but hospitals, blood sugars, insulin, possibilities of transplants in the future. This is my life, and it's a lot to handle. It's a lot to ask anyone else to handle. Which is why I've never done that before."

"So what are you saying? You don't want anything with me because you think you are a burden?" I furrow my brows as I stare at her face, she rolls her pretty brown eyes and shakes her head.

"Of course I am a burden, Atlas." She snaps while pulling herself up into a sitting position. "Look at you, you look like absolute shit, and it's because of me. You don't deserve that. You don't deserve to be worried. I just thought, if I could make it up to you–"

"Stop." It comes out harsher than I meant it to, but she hit a nerve and I feel myself becoming pissed off. I stand up and back away from the bed. "Let me explain something to you, Lauren. I am a fucking grown ass man, fully capable of making my own fucking grown ass man decisions. Now, you are not a burden, I never want to hear you say that again, and I don't know who made you believe that because you're sick you are a burden, but you tell me who they are and I'll beat their ass. Also, yeah, you are a lot to handle. I mean fuck, you're too fucking smart and quick-witted, you're fucking gorgeous as hell, you're opinionated and your sense of humor is as dry as sand." She snorts at the remarks, but says nothing as I continue.

"You ***are*** a lot to handle, but that's not a bad thing. I would give my left nut right fucking now to have the honor of being the one to handle you." I say as I walk back over to her bed.

"Wait..." She looks up at me, uncertainty pooling in her eyes. "What are you saying?"

I take a deep breath as I try to hold on to this little bit of courage I have. "Ren, can I take you on a date?"

CHAPTER 15
LAUREN

"I cannot believe you're going out!" Janie squeals as she bounces on my bed. Her excitement is infectious, or it would be if I wasn't so damn nervous. It's been three days since I got home from the hospital and agreed to go on a date with Atlas, and I've only thought about backing out a hundred times.

Rubbing my hand over my queasy stomach, I look over at her. "I'm going to throw up. Are you really sure you have no idea where he's taking me?"

Janie gives me a sympathetic look. Everyone knows I hate surprises, like I detest them. I need to know exactly what is happening so I can plan accordingly, but Atlas wouldn't budge. Only saying to dress comfortably and casually, no dresses, and no nice shoes. Atlas is very fit and enjoys sports and chasing adrenaline highs. I don't, at all, and the last thing I want is to find out we are rock climbing and I have to tell him no.

"He didn't tell me," Janie shrugs while tossing me a pair of jeans. "Just wear jeans and that cute cropped hoodie." I go to make a face but stop at the warning glare Janie is shooting me. There is no body shaming in front of Janie.

I wiggle the ripped black high waisted jeans over my hips before grabbing the thin blue hoodie. It's November, but in southern California it's never really "sweater weather" so a light long sleeve shirt will be comfortable. I look in the mirror, the sliver of skin showing is small, less than two inches for sure, but it may as well be my entire torso in my mind.

"You look so adorable!" Janie claps her hands as she waves me over. "Now you do your makeup and I'll do your hair. Atlas will be back soon."

I SAY ONE LAST GOODBYE TO JANIE BEFORE HEADING OUT MY DOOR. Janie volunteered to spend most of the day at my apartment to hang out with Bruno while she works on going through applications for a body piercer and front of house manager, but not before asking me again to consider the position, which I once again declined, though I promised to help her vet the applicants once Atlas and I were back from our date.

I step into the elevator and hit the downstairs button to meet Atlas, who sent a text earlier saying he had pulled in. I rub my stomach, willing the butterflies to go away, only to have them increase at the feel of my bare flesh. God, I'm about to make a fool out of myself.

The elevator dings once it reaches the lobby and I step out, finding Atlas leaning against a pillar near the entrance, staring at his phone. He's wearing a pair of dark wash blue jeans that hug his large thighs in a *very* pleasing way, a reddish brown henley hugged his broad chest and large biceps and, oh shit, the wedding ring. I reach into my purse and quickly pull out my band and look back up, thankful he didn't see. I really need to be better at wearing this damn thing.

"Hey," I say, jerking him from whatever is causing the angry expression on his face. He looks at me, smiles, and then something weird happens. I don't know how one can do a double take when they are still looking at the person, but he does. Atlas' eyes widen and his mouth opens slightly. "Is– this okay?" I ask nervously. "I can go back up and change if it's not." I point over my shoulder at the elevator.

Atlas blinks and shakes his head. "W-what? No! You look, um, wow." He breathes out and smirks. "Princess, you're...fuck...you're beautiful." I smile softly, not quite sure how to accept the compliment. My ex's rarely gave them and if they did, it was because they wanted something. Even though Atlas has never shied away from giving me a compliment, I have always made sure that my walls were up, deflecting those compliments. But now, I'm trying to let him in, I'm trying to allow him to see the parts of me that I never let anyone see, and it's scary.

Atlas grabs my hand before leading me to his Tahoe that is still idling under the portes-cochères. He opens the passenger door for me and I smile awkwardly as I climb inside. The interior is freshly cleaned, I can smell the cleaning solution that must've been used, and I can't help but feel a little giddy that he is trying to think of all the little details.

"So how long are we going to be gone?" I ask as we pull

away from the apartments. "Because I may need to stop and get some extra snacks, I only brought–"

"I got you Princess." Atlas smiles and taps his center console. "Open it up." Raising a brow, I do as he says. What I find makes me want to cry. It's a refrigerator, with snacks and juice, glucose tablets and the area next to the fridge has his own emergency kit in case I need, holy shit in case I need ***anything.***

"That's where I was this morning," He smirks while merging onto the expressway. "I had someone take out my old console and put this fridge one in."

"That must've been so expensive." I whisper, unable to speak any louder for fear of sobbing.

Atlas shrugs lazily. "Doesn't matter. Besides, part of it is in trade, I'm going to give him a half sleeve next month."

I know what the guys' hourly rates are. I also know how long a half sleeve generally takes. "Atlas I– this is too much, I'm not wor–"

"I dare you," he says, his playful voice now lowered as if he's warning me. "Tell me you're not worth it and watch what absolutely stupid shit I do."

I can't help it, I burst out laughing, which causes him to laugh as well. "Atlas, this is seriously the sweetest, most thoughtful thing anyone has ever done for me." I lean over and kiss him on the cheek. "Besides you marrying me so I could steal your health insurance, which, by the way, thanks." I giggle and he shrugs.

"If you need it, I'll find a way to get it for you, princess."

THE CAR RIDE IS PLEASANT. WE PLAY THE GET TO KNOW YOU GAME. Atlas is a lover of puns, which I didn't see coming, enjoys musicals–again, didn't see coming, but the real kicker is that he is the baby of his family with an older brother and eldest sister. I knew he had siblings, but he never talks about them. His brother lives across the country with their dad, while his sister and mom live a city over. I tried to ask more but saw his souring mood and decided to push it onto the back burner for right now.

I told him about my love of books and wanting to be a narrator when I grew up. I don't know why I did, but when I broached the subject, I couldn't stop myself. Atlas hung onto every word, asked really important questions as if fully engrossed in the subject, and told me I should try it since nothing was stopping me. I gave him the song and dance about it's too noisy in my apartment, equipment is expensive and most importantly, I needed to get a paying job soon because my savings were dwindling.

Staring out my window at yet another field I raise a brow when I notice Atlas turning onto a completely dirt road. I whip my head to him, he's grinning widely as he continues to drive. "Where are we?" I ask cautiously as I look out the window again and that's when I see them. Cows, tons of them, and as we get closer, I see their shaggy brown hair and I make a completely embarrassing squeak. I don't care though. They are Highland cows. He's taking me to look at freaking Highland cows.

"Oh my god!" I am vibrating as he parks and we get out of the car. "Oh my god, I get to spend the day looking at Highlands!" I bounce as I grab his hand and we head towards the farm. There is an older couple standing at the entrance. Apparently, they are waiting for us. The older woman smiles. "Mr. and Mrs. Hart?" She asks, and I can't stop nodding. I need to see the cows.

"She's excited." Atlas laughs while squeezing my hand softly. The old woman's weathered face crinkles as she smiles. "Aww, well, what a nice husband you are to let her do this. Alright sweetheart, now they are gentle, and more likely than not, you'll end up with one in your lap if you let them. When you are ready to leave, if you can't move them, holler out and one of us will come help you, alright?"

I stop bouncing and look from Atlas to the old woman several times. *On my lap?*

"I'm sorry, but what are we doing?" I look up at Atlas, who shrugs.

"Cuddling cows all afternoon."

Holy shit, if I wasn't already married to him, I would propose.

I'M IN HEAVEN. AND, IF THIS ISN'T HEAVEN, THEN I DON'T WANT to go there. I am resting under a shady tree against Mocha while her calf, Moose, rests on my lap. I've only cried and hugged every cow I could reach four, okay, maybe five times. I'm filthy, I stink, I'm tired and I've never been happier in my life. The sun is setting, and besides a small break for lunch and my multiple pee breaks, we've been in the pasture.

Atlas hasn't talked as much as I thought he would. He's just been taking pictures and letting me enjoy this moment. I have no idea how to thank him. I will probably have to start by detailing his car after the long ride home in these clothes.

As we say our goodbyes to the cows and the lovely older couple that allowed me to live out my greatest dream in their pasture, I head to the Tahoe, only to feel Atlas' hand on mine.

"If you want to say no, it's completely fine but, I did rent out that cabin over there for the night. I thought at the very least we could get cleaned up and some fresh clothes on." I blink at him and look at the small, lit cabin behind the farm. It's cute, quaint and I can see from the window it has modern upgrades inside. Though, I guarantee it only has one bed. I am tired though, and god, do we stink.

"I didn't bring any clothes." I sigh apologetically, even though I couldn't have known.

"I got you covered." He squeezes my hand. "You wanna stay? Because if so, I'm calling for food and then I'll rock, paper, scissors you for a shower." I laugh at him and nod quickly. I really, really did want to stay. Atlas seems pleased with my answer and tugs my hand as we begin the walk into the cabin.

I was right; it is small. A very tiny, but modern kitchenette, a flatscreen tv and oversized loveseat–or undersized couch, I'm not quite sure what to call this in-between piece. If you climb a small wooden ladder, there is a loft with a bed. I win the game of rock, paper, scissors, though I think Atlas lets me win, so I take the shower first. I don't stay in there long as I'm feeling a little shaky and need to get some juice or something in me and I know Atlas has to want a shower, too.

A knocking on the door startles me as I shut the water off.

"Hey princess," Atlas says as he cracks the door. "I'm

not coming in, listen your sugar is dropping, I brought you an apple juice from the Tahoe, and our food will be here soon, alright?" He cannot be real. How is he *this* perfect?

"O-Okay, let me get dressed and I'll be right out. Thanks." I slip my grey pajama shorts and blue tank top on that Atlas had packed for me and put in the Tahoe this morning, and groan upon staring at my reflection. I really need a bra if me and my very generous chest are going to be in Atlas' company while eating. Reaching over, I grab the bra I had been wearing all day and bring it to my nose.

"Oh god, no." I hold back a gag as I place the offending garment and my clothes in the towel I used to dry off before walking out. "Hey, does this place have a washer?" I ask as Atlas looks up from his phone. His eyes go wide and his phone falls from his hand, landing on the floor with a thud.

"Fuck," He curses as he reaches under the table for his phone. "Y-yeah in the kitchen- ow fuck!" He growls as the back of his head hits the underside of the table.

I wince as he stands up, rubbing the back of his head, a pink hue over his cheeks. Is he blushing? Why is that the cutest fucking thing I've ever seen?

"Are you alright?" I giggle lightly.

"Yeah, I'm going to go shower," Atlas mumbles, while grabbing his clothes. "There is your juice, also that bag there is for you."

"What is it?" I ask as I stare at the blue gift bag.

"Nothing much, it's just some stuff that made me think of you the other day when I had to run to the office store to get more markers for the shop." He shrugs as he walks to the bathroom, cheeks still red and muttering about his head.

I grab the bag and look inside and I nearly cry at the contents. Annotation tabs, highlighters, and post notes. All in muted colors. He remembered I hate the neon colors. My bottom lip pouts out as I bring the supplies to my chest. Why does this bag of office supplies touch me almost as much as him bringing me to pet the cows?

I go to put the items back in the bag when my hand hits something hard. Pulling the item out, I realize it's a picture frame. I turn the frame over to look at the front and I gasp. It's a picture of him and I when we were married. Our first kiss. My eyes are wide and I am sure I am in mid-squeak while Atlas has his arm around my waist, eyes closed and he's laughing against my mouth.

I pull the frame to my chest and hug it like I did the supplies. This day, this man, it's all so overwhelming, but surprisingly, not in a bad way. I've just never felt so cared for before. Everything today has been so meticulously planned in order to make me have an amazing day.

There is a knock on the door, pulling me out of my thoughts. I stand up and open the door, smiling at the delivery man before taking the pizza from him and telling him to have a good night.

Atlas walks out just as I finish my small bottle of juice and I spit the contents in my mouth out in a comedic mist all over the kitchen.

Atlas is shirtless, in grey pajama pants hanging low, very low on his hips, and his tattooed skin is still damp from his shower. Water droplets slide over his pecs, down his chiseled abs and get lost in that fucking dark trail of hair that I am so desperate to–

"Are you gawking at me, Princess?" I scream at his voice. Literally, scream. I was so deep in my fantasy that I forgot I was laser focused on his crotch.

My face heats up, and I look away. "No!" I snap and walk to grab a piece of pizza as he laughs.

"I knew you found me hot." He beams as he grabs a slice, too.

"Obviously, I find you attractive, Atlas," I roll my eyes before shoving a large mouthful of pizza into my mouth. "I jerked you off in your car, sort of."

Atlas temporarily chokes on his pizza, and after several coughs, he settles down and looks at me. "Must you be so vulgar?" He asks, his voice full of mock indignation.

I bark out a laugh as I finish my piece. "Me? Vulgar? Really, Hart?"

"Yes! That was a beautiful moment between us! And you call it 'sort of jerking off', I'm honestly hurt." I shake my head as I throw my plate in the trash can and start washing my hands in the sink.

"What would you refer to it as, Atlas? *Love Fisted*?" I cringe as soon as "love" leaves my lips. Before I can turn around, I feel Atlas' hard body against my back. I see his hands gripping either side of the sink, caging me in.

His lips skate across the back of my neck, and goose-bumps erupt over my flesh. "Atlas..." I breathe out as he runs his fingertips over my pebbled arms.

"It's alright," he whispers as he inhales deeply. "I'm not expecting anything. I'm just happy I got to spend the day with you and make you smile. I don't want to make you uncomfortable, I'll back off." Atlas takes a step back and I'm cold instantly. I turn around, and my perverted eyes can't be stopped as they zero in on his, oh holy shit. He is *much* larger than I thought. I felt him in the car, but not all of him, and he was crammed in his jeans. Now, with nothing constricting him and his grey pajama pants doing what they do best. Well....

"Wait." I say a little louder than I mean to. "I ummm... I don't know if I want you to back off." God, this is awkward.

I stare at his tight sculpted body and then look at mine, and feel like hiding.

"Oh no you don't." Atlas steps back towards me and pulls my face up to his. "That thought, trying to wiggle its way in, squash it." His voice is low and his hooded eyes are locked onto my lips. He presses his hips against me and I gasp at his hard erection pressing against me. "You, princess." He leans in and brushes his lips over mine. "You and only you cause me to feel this way. So don't doubt yourself for one second."

"I don't, Atlas. I don't look like you." I whisper as I fidget nervously.

Atlas lets out a surprised laugh. "You don't say? I have eyes Ren, I know you don't look like me. It's actually one of the things I find the most attractive about you, physically. I'm not turned on by myself."

I roll my eyes as I head to the ladder to go up to the bed. "That's not what I mean, ass." I grumble as I lay on the large bed that overlooks the tiny house. Atlas jumps and grabs the railing around the bed and, oh my god he's pulling himself up. I watch his muscles tense as lifts himself up and swings his body over the railing.

"Can't use a ladder?" I ask dryly, though I'm pretty sure the cotton in my pajama bottoms is completely flooded at this point.

Atlas smirks as he crawls across the bed towards me. "I mean, I could've, but then you would've missed out on that impressive move I just did there."

I snort and tsk in fake annoyance. "Yes, you're so amazing."

He lies on his side, propping up on his elbow. "You know I really am attracted to you right?" I instantly heat up at his blunt words as my eyes meet his.

"Atlas, I think you like me because I challenge you."

"Oh no," Atlas laughs as he sits up. "I adore that about you, but that has nothing to do with being attracted to you." He leans in and goes to brush his lips against mine, but I stop him.

"What if I said okay? What if I said show me? Then what?" Atlas' pupils dilate and a wicked grin spreads across his face.

"You say show me Princess, and you will need to be carried down that ladder in the morning." I give him a "yeah, okay" laugh until I notice he's not laughing.

"Oh..." I begin to chew on my bottom lip and watch his gaze rest on my mouth, his tongue slipping out to run over his lips. "Okay." I breathe. I watch his eyes snap up to me and a brow raises.

"Okay what?" His voice is a low growl as he crawls towards me, causing me to lie back on the mattress. "I need specifics, Princess. Use your words."

I take a steadying breath. "As long as I can say stop if I need to, I'm telling you to show me."

Atlas is on top of me in an instant, but he isn't groping and pinching me. Instead, he cups my cheek and presses his forehead to mine. "Pretty girl," he purrs before kissing me. "You say stop and I'm off instantly. You are in charge, okay? Never forget that." I choke on a sob as I nod dumbly at his perfect words.

My sobs transform into a moan almost instantly as Atlas nips on my neck. He pulls his head back and stares at me in amazement. "Oh Princess, it's going to be a short night if you moan like that, holy fuck." He groans before kissing my lips again. I groan as I wrap my arms around his neck to hold him close while spreading my legs so he can get closer.

Atlas grunts as his large hands slide up my bare thighs before he grips the sides tightly. "God, you're so soft." He whispers as his hand starts to head towards the hem of my tank top. Instinctively, I grab his wrist, lifting his hand and begin to guide him to my breast. Atlas takes his hand back and gives me a disapproving stare.

"I'm all for switching the dominant roles, Princess, but not when I'm trying to get to know your body. I need to see what makes you feel good." I block him from touching my stomach again.

"There's nothing good there." I state nervously. "I could maybe slip my tank top down so that my breasts are out."

His lip curls up, and he shakes his head. "What the? That sounds uncomfortable to have the neck under your tit–uhh..breasts." I chuckle at how sweet he is being.

"It'll hide all of the... less fun parts, really it's–"

"Has a man ever touched your stomach?" His voice has no humor in it, so I simply shake my head.

"No, it's always been covered."

"Would you take it off and let me touch you?" His question is so soft, but feels so hard. I look at him, he knows my body. He has lifted me, he knows. I take another shaky breath as I take the tank top off and squint my eyes shut as I lay on my back.

"Holy fucking shit." Atlas breathes and I wait for the *"You are bigger than I thought"* line. But it doesn't come. I crack open an eye to see Atlas, staring at me, mouth slack.

"What?" I ask, feeling like I want my shirt back.

Atlas blinks and shakes his head. I notice him adjusting his "holy shit" erection before clearing his throat. "Lauren..." He breathes out my name. It sounds like a plea and a prayer all wrapped up in his smooth, yet gravelly voice, and I feel myself tightening in my belly.

"Princess you are, please, can I touch you?" I nod slowly and close my eyes as his hands run up my thighs and over my hips. I tense as he runs up the sides of my waist, but then relax and groan as he finds my breasts. His hands are as gifted as I thought they would be. He massages and kneads my breasts while running his thumbs over my nipples. My eyes shoot open when one of my nipples is suddenly inside something warm and wet.

Looking down, I see Atlas latched on my left nipple while his hand takes care of the right. "A-Atlas!" I gasp as his teeth graze over the bud.

"That's my girl." He growls as his mouth moves to assault my right nipple. "Get ready to start screaming my name."

My body goes stiff as a rod as Atlas runs his tongue over my stomach. It feels so good, and wrong. Almost shameful. He then slips his tongue in my belly button and I roll my eyes into the back of my head and let out a moan whimper hybrid as my back arches.

Atlas chuckles against my skin as he bites the waistband of my shorts with his teeth. He looks up at me and I lean up on my elbows to see over my breasts. I nod my consent and he grips them at my hips and slips the garment off, leaving me completely nude.

"Holy shit, " he looks up at me in shock before looking back down.

"W-what?" I ask nervously.

"Your pussy is really pretty." I am cackling at his words. I don't know what else to do. I hear him grumble something about being unappreciated and I'm about to say something smart, but am silenced by his tongue tracing the floral tattoo that takes up my thigh and hip.

"Oh god..." I moan loudly. Atlas stops and shifts slightly. I then feel a finger tip sliding up and down my slit.

"I'm sorry, who is the one giving you pleasure?" He asks as his middle finger slips inside my slick center. I hear the growl he is trying to suppress.

"Y-you!" I whisper and moan louder as his ring finger slips in and he curls his fingers upwards. The cool metal of his wedding band meeting my center and making me see stars when I close my eyes.

"Oh... my g– Atlas!" I correct myself. I hear him chuckle as he nuzzles my mound and inhales.

"Fuckkk, you smell amazing." He groans.

"It's just the s-soap." I pant as I try to grind against his palm.

"I know I smell soap," He laughs before kissing my lips, right by my clit. So fucking close. "But ***your*** smell. The smell of your arousal, of you–that is what I'm talking about. I need to taste you, Princess." He doesn't let me respond, instead he removes his fingers before assaulting me with his tongue. He drags his tongue up and circles my clit before sucking, causing me to scream his name while gripping his hair. Atlas slides his fingers back inside me, pumping in and out, curling upwards and hitting my perfect spot.

"Right there," I whine as I try to stop myself from grinding against his face. "Shit, fuck, damn it, I'm so close."

"Let go," he growls against me. "Use me Princess. Fuck my mouth and let me consume every drop." He takes my clit between his teeth and flicks his tongue against it, and I'm done. I have no control of my hips as they thrust and grind against his mouth while I scream his name over and over. He doesn't stop. He slows his tongue but keeps the same pressure inside me, causing another orgasm to start back up.

"What the fuck?" I pant as I begin to shake.

"Relax." He groans as he licks my clit before sucking it.

This feels different. The fire is hotter, the tension tighter, and right before I come undone, something unimaginable happens. I feel something shoot out of me. The sensation is too great, and I scream out as I come and feel another burst.

"Oh my fucking christ." Atlas groans as he sits back once I come back down. I look at him, he's dripping with something.

Oh my god, did I just pe–

"You can squirt?" Atlas asks in amazement and I just look at him in horror, embarrassment and confusion.

"Squirt? Not... never before." I've heard of squirting. I've seen it in porn, but never experienced it for myself. I just figured it wasn't something I could do and moved on. I watch as my fluids run down his chin and chest. "Sorry?" I question meekly.

"Oh, the fuck you are." He growls as he situates himself between my legs before trailing kisses up my stomach, over my breasts and on my lips. "That is the fucking hottest thing I've ever experienced. And now, I want to see it happen on my cock."

I can taste myself on him as I feel him slip his pants down. I stare at his cock and...

"Atlas, is that a piercing?" I stare at his massive erection and see the two silver balls on the top of his tip. How had I missed that in the backseat of the car before? I kind of remember something, but everything was so rushed.

"Uhh yeah..." He laughs shyly. "I got the dydoe when I got the nipples done. If you want me to take it out, just give me a second."

"No," I say firmly. "I ummm...I'll try it." I can't imagine

it really doing much and I fear if we stop, I'll lose my nerve and I *really* wanted to continue this.

"Shit, condom." Atlas curses as he goes to get up. I grab his wrist.

"I'm clean, and I have an IUD."

Atlas inhales sharply and his eyes almost brighten. "Uhmm...I get checked regularly. I'm completely clean. I promise, I think I have the picture in my phone."

I chuckle and grip him. "I trust you. Come on." I pull him towards me as I lay back down. Atlas exhales slowly as he grabs my hips. I squeak in surprise as he lifts my hips and angles his cock against my entrance. I gasp at the pressure of him sliding in, filling me completely.

"Shit," He hisses as he stills. "God damn it, you feel so good." He nearly whimpers as his breathing goes ragged.

I shift to look at him, and he puts a hand on my stomach. "I refuse to be your shortest fuck, Ren. Give me a second." He states, and I stifle a laugh. After a moment, Atlas moves in and out slowly, and we both moan in unison. Okay, I was wrong, those two balls are adding such a firm pressure to my g spot, it's almost too much.

"You ready, princess?" He whispers as he thrusts in me again.

I let out a cry before squeezing my walls around his cock, earning a ragged moan. "Ready." I smirk.

Atlas grips my ass and lifts my lower half up as he drives into me. I cry out as my nails dig into his back.

"That's my girl." He praises, slamming into me again. "Dig those pretty nails in. Leave your mark on me."

I wrap myself around his shoulders and squeal when he rolls us so I'm on top. "Crap, I'll hurt you."

"Oh no you don't." He bucks his hips, throwing me off balance. "Ride my cock." He orders.

"Atlas, I don't want to crush you."

"Princess, I'm only going to say it nicely one more time: Ride. My. Cock." I hesitate for a moment too long because he sighs in frustration before grabbing my throat and pulling me to his face.

"Whatever you are thinking," his voice is deep and primal, and I feel it in my core. "Stop. Be a good girl and ride my fucking cock. Now."

No one else could pull off saying that to me. But Atlas does, and very well evidently because I completely obey. I grind against him and bite back a cry of pleasure as that piercing presses against my inner wall.

"Look at you," He marvels as he grips my hips tightly, helping me bounce on him. "You're so fucking sexy, my god, your tits, your curves, this tight perfect pussy, and this sweet fucking ass." He swats my ass and I moan while moving faster. "Are you going to come for me, Princess?" He asks between pants. I nod, unable to verbally communicate. "Good," He smiles. "I want you to soak me."

I whine out his name and then cry as he begins thrusting up into me while he does some magic with his knuckles on my clit.

"Oh no," I cry, feeling the buildup, this time so much more intense.

"That's my girl. Show me how good it feels. Come on Princess, ride it." I cry with every thrust before I feel the explosion again, following Atlas praising me before I throw my head back and scream as I am given the most intense orgasm of my life. I feel my toes curling as I grab his throat without realizing it.

"That's it," He gasps. "Take charge, choke me princess. Make my cock yours." I squeeze my hand on the sides of his throat and I feel him pulsing inside me as I grind against him. He doesn't last ten more seconds before he roars out my name and I'm filled with his hot cum.

I release his neck and remove him from inside me after a moment. I lay next to him and smile when I feel him pull me to him.

"Give me a minute." He pants and kisses my jaw. "Let me remember how to walk, and I'll get you cleaned up."

I SHOOT UP, GASPING FOR AIR. I LOOK AROUND THE UNFAMILIAR, dark room as panic fills me. Where am I? Where is Atlas?

"Bruno?" I call out. "Atlas?"

"Hey, hey!" Atlas' shadowed figure climbs up the ladder and rushes to my side, both his hands on either side of my face.

"It's okay," He whispers. "What happened Princess?"

I take a deep breath as my eyes adjust to the dark room. "Bad dream," I get out though I can't remember the dream, just the feeling of drowning.

Atlas crawls into the bed with me and pulls me to his chest. "It's alright," he coos as he kisses my head.

"Where were you?" I ask as I feel his body stiffen.

"I..." His voice is strained as he speaks. "I got a message that I needed to respond to."

I push myself up from his chest and ignore his protests. "A message? In the middle of the night? That you had to answer away from the bed?" *Away from me?*

Atlas sighs and sits up. "It's not what you think. It was my sister."

I feel slightly relieved but not completely. "What's wrong? Why did she–"

"Ren," He sounds exhausted as he speaks. "Please, we've had such an amazing time. I don't want my family to ruin it."

"Oh," I say, my voice small. I can't lie, it hurts that he doesn't want to open up to me but, I won't force him. "Okay, well I'll leave you alone then. If you need to go back down, go ahead. I'm sorry like I said, bad dream."

"Stop it." He warns from behind his palm.

"Stop what?" I ask, genuinely confused.

"Stop being understanding." I let out a laugh of surprise as I reach over and turn on the bedside light.

"Atlas, what do you want? Me to demand answers?"

He shrugs but doesn't look at me. He's sitting right beside me but may as well be a thousand miles away.

I crawl up to him and straddle his lap. I watch a smirk appear on his face. "Princess, I am a drained man. I mean, if you can get him up, he's yours for the taking, but– Ow!" He cries as I pinch his forearm.

"Look at me." I say, my voice holding no humor. He looks at me with his cocky face and then crosses his eyes. I flick his nose and narrow my eyes. "Stop that."

"Stop what?" He whines, rubbing his nose. "You're the one beating me up, and not in the sexy way."

"You don't have to be this way with me, you know that, right?" I watch his mask slip ever so slightly.

"I don't know–" I press my finger to his mouth.

"Don't insult me with that lie." I sigh, and I watch as his eyes soften and he kisses my hand.

"My sister sent me a text," He said softly while running his fingers over my hand. "She and my mom are sick."

"Oh no, I'm so sorry. Do they need help? Should we go?"

I ask as I start to get up, Atlas clamps his large hands on my thighs to stop me.

"Not that kind of sick, baby." His voice is full of pain and he still refuses to look me in the eye. "My mom and sister have a drug addiction. They are in withdrawals because they've been without for a while and they want me to give them money. I was texting Millie, my sister, to tell her I'm not around to give her cash tonight and she, well, she wasn't happy."

I sit quietly as I let it all process. "You give your mom and sister money to pay for their addictions?"

Atlas sighs as he leans his head back against the headboard. "No, yes, I don't know. It's not intentional. I'm not going around like 'Hey mom, here's enough for a hit.' I just, yes, it's a disease that started because of something they chose to do. But they still might decide one day to get better. My dad and Alex left a long time ago and left me here with Millie and Mom. Mom was... ***is*** a very sick woman that never went to get the help she needed. She thought that self medicating was better. And the pills went to harder pills, then went to snorting and now..." His voice trails off and my heart begins to break for him. "I know that the money I give them goes to getting high, but what am I supposed to do? They need help and everyone else has abandoned them. I just, I don't want to be the selfish prick that thinks they are too much and writes them off."

I grab his face and pull him to look at me. "Oh Atlas, there isn't a selfish bone in your ridiculously attractive body." I give him a small smile and lean in to kiss him. I go to pull back after a second, but Atlas grips the back of my neck and holds me there as he deepens the kiss. I moan as his tongue runs across my lips and I part to give him access to my mouth, which he eagerly accepts, and the sweet, chaste kiss I started has been replaced by something deeper, something more raw. Something real. He let me see something in him, something he doesn't show others. He lets me look behind his mask of smiles and playful flirting to see a little piece of his darkness. Like a test to see if that little sliver would send me running. But I'm not going anywhere. I will accept his darkness as my own. I will show him that he doesn't have to hide anymore, not with me.

CHAPTER 16
ATLAS

"Oh my god," Derek groans as I twirl Janie around while singing *My Girl* in the middle of the shop room. "We get it, you got your dick wet. Can you fuck off now?"

I stop mid dip to shoot Derek a glare. I would neither confirm nor deny the magic that happened last night between Ren and I, or this morning before I had community service. But saying "got your dick wet" when he refers to Ren pisses me off.

"You know, Virginia, maybe your dried up mini sausage is why you're in such a foul mood." I grumble as Janie smacks my chest.

"Stop being a brat, Atlas." She scorns while walking over to Derek and flicking his ear. "You too. He's married to my best friend, don't you be talking about her like she's one of your common lays."

"Sorry Mama J." Derek mutters under his breath as Janie walks away. "Tiny fucking tyrant." He mutters, once he is sure she is out of earshot.

I laugh lightly and shake my head. Fox and Janie have

somehow become the honorary mom and dad at Hel's. Fox always had the nickname *"Papa Fox"*, so when Janie became his girl, it only seemed right she became our mama. Or that's how I explained it to her when I gave her the nickname. Just like I had given Fox his.

I hear the door chime and go up front to help the customer when I see Ren walking in. Her hair is pulled back in a high ponytail, wearing tight black workout leggings and a ripped grey sweater that hangs off her shoulder, showing me her collarbone that I now want to run my tongue over and bite.

"Well! How is my pretty, sexy hot as fuck Princess wifey doing this afternoon?" I grin as my loud voice causes her to instantly blush. "It had better be amazing because fuck girl," I growl as I look her up and down. "Someone walking around looking like a goddess deserves nothing but the most amazing of days."

"Okay, okay!" She laughs uncomfortably and covers my mouth with her hand. "Will you stop— AH! Atlas!" She squeals as I lick her palm. I go to say something, but her playful eyes narrow when the petite redhead walks into the front of the shop.

"You bitch!" Ren growls at Janie, causing her to freeze and my eyebrows to raise.

"Oh pleasssse, girl fight." I whisper, earning a slap from Ren before her attention goes back to Janie.

"How could you! I was there alone! I had to partner with Luca!" Janie winces at Ren's voice before holding her shaking hands up.

"Ren, I'm so sorry. I have had a bad couple days with my tremors and I didn't think I could handle the heels or the pole." Ren's eyes soften, but now I'm intrigued.

"I'm sorry what? Pole? Heels? *Luca?*" I have never been

as equally turned on and pissed off as I am right now. I remember the name Luca. He was Janie's date to her father's remembrance party that Ash and I held at our apartment over a year ago. Tall, muscular, tan... *Italian...*

"*Luca?*" I question again, more forcefully this time.

Ren looks over at me. "You know about Sunday's pole dancing class?"

"Pffft, the fuck I do! I vaguely remember Janie saying she was going to a pole dancing class once as a joke to piss Fox off."

Ren gives me a half shrug. "Okay well, it wasn't a joke. I go twice a week and have for well over a year. And this one here," Ren grumbles as she glares at Janie. "Should've texted me so I didn't end up having to go to a partner's class with no partner, so freaking Luca had to come out."

"I'm sorry! I am a shitty friend! But..." Janie gets a mischievous look on her face. "Did he lose the shirt? I heard he's been bulking up."

I go to brush by the girls, but Ren stops me. "Where are you going?"

"Oh yeah, I was going to go in the back and drive a hammer into the walls, and then I was going to go find Luca and do the same to his face." Ren and Janie both stifle a laugh, which only annoys me further.

"I'll leave you two honeymooners alone." Janie winks before walking off. Ren turns her attention back to me and smiles shyly.

"Hi," she says coyly, and I find the cooling effect she is having over my boiling, raging body slightly irritating.

"Hi pretty girl," I say back as she walks towards me and grips the waist of my shirt, pulling our bodies together. My thoughts go to last night, and this morning. Her arching, screaming and coming underneath me. Her squirting...

fuck, I cannot believe she does that. And now it's become a goal of mine to make her squirt as often as possible.

"Are you mad at me?" She looks up at me with her eyes wide and her bottom lip out and, oh, this little brat.

"Yes, so stop being cute." I state while using my finger to push her pouting lip back. Ren seizes the opportunity and captures my finger between her teeth and teases it with the tip of her tongue. My sore dick instantly becomes very alert. "Unfair." I grumble.

Ren raises a brow, "All is fair in–" the chime for the door sounds and I am ready to tell them to fuck off as I come face to face with my sister and mom. The good, playful mood I had is gone now. My body goes tense and I stand up straight.

"Amelia, w-what's going on?" I feel Ren's body stiffen and she begins to pull back, as if she is going to leave. I don't want her to see whatever is about to happen. But I also don't want her to leave me alone. After opening up to her last night, I need her to be here.

"Lauren, this is my sister, Amelia, and this is my mother. Guys, this is Lauren, my wife." I feel Ren relax slightly back against me, but both my sister and mother are wide eyed.

"You're married?" Mom's gravelly, weak voice croaks out, full of hurt that I am sure I will pay for later.

"Yeah," I affirm softly. "A few months now."

My too thin mother walks up to us. Her salt and pepper hair is pulled tight into a ponytail, which is how she wears it when she hasn't showered in a while. Her too big for her clothes are full of stains and holes and I see once she is closer, her body is shaking. She's withdrawing, meaning they didn't get money after I said I wasn't home last night.

"Got enough money for some fancy wedding, but not to

help us out?" Amelia sneers as she glares Ren up and down. "Or is all your money going to feed this one?"

"Hey!" I shout, startling the three of them. Ren places her soft hand on my forearm and gives me a squeeze.

"It's okay," she reassures me.

"Atty," Mom's voice is wavy as she starts to produce tears. "Son, I need just a few dollars, Millie and I, we need some food."

I'm about to say no, feeling like maybe I could talk them into a rehab with Ren by my side, but before I can speak, my sweet girl steps forward. "Oh, if you guys are hungry, my friend works at this awesome bakery across the street. They have great lunch items, I would love to take you both."

Mom and Amelia both look at Ren like she's speaking another language, and it guts me that she's trying to be polite, thinking that these people must matter to me. She knows they are addicts, yet she is trying to get them food. As if that is really what they are after.

"Uhh no," Amelia scoffs and looks at me. "Why would we want to go to lunch?"

"Because you said you were hungry and Ren is trying to be a kind person." I state through gritted teeth. "Much kinder than you deserve."

"Atlas." Ren hisses and gives them a soft smile. "I understand that you may be wary of me, what with the marriage being sprung up on you–"

"Princess," I give Ren a squeeze on the hip and kiss her temple before reaching in my pocket. Mentally, I scold myself, I forgot to go to the bank this morning to get any cash out as I spent all but twenty bucks at the farm with Ren. I hand my mom the twenty and I may as well spat in her palm by the way she is looking at it.

"W-what are we supposed to do with this?" She growls

loudly as she crumples the money. "So that's it, huh? I give you life and all I'm worth is a twenty? How typical, just like your father and brother. You just leave, get married and want nothing to do with us. Be careful girl, he will do the same to you."

"Mom," I snap, feeling the guilt, anger and anxiety mixing together. "Knock it off. All I have is twenty on me. If you wait until after work I can–"

"We need it now!" She shouts, this time getting the attention of the guys in the back. "We are sick NOW!"

"Here." I look to see Ren's outstretched hand and before I can stop it, Amelia snatches the folded up money and pockets it before pulling mom with her towards the door.

"You're a selfish man, Atlas Hart." Mom breathes as she stands in the doorway. "Forcing your wife to take care of your family because you can't be bothered."

The door shuts and I feel everything intensify. The lights, sounds, smells. I'm too hot and I can't breathe.

"At," I hear Fox's voice, but I ignore it. I need to get out of here. I head into the back and grab my backpack.

"Atlas wait," Ren grabs my hand, but her touch is like a zap of electricity and I pull away. I see the flash of hurt on her face and shake my head. I can't be here. I can't let her see me like this. I give her what I hope she takes as an apologetic look before bolting out the back door and to my motorcycle that I've been leaving here since moving in with Ren. Firing her up, I sigh as the loud engine drowns out the rest of the noise around me and I take off down the street to put some distance between myself and the humiliation I just encountered.

CHAPTER 17
LAUREN

I listen to Atlas' motorcycle race off; the engine getting fainter every second until I can no longer hear him. He left, and I don't know where he went. I try to hold the hurt and rejection back as I stare at his station. I was trying to help, I thought that if I gave them the money, they would be happy and leave, then he and I could have a discussion about them. Maybe try to find them help. I don't know much about addiction, but one of my former classmates in law school runs a sober living non-profit, and I was thinking maybe I would contact her.

But he ran. He pulled away from me and ran. I faintly hear the door chime and Ash talking to a client. Not wanting to disrupt the guys and their appointments, I begin to head to the back door to leave. Only to have Janie grip my wrist and yank me into a new room of the shop. I look around the area, it's not finished yet as there is no equipment or furniture, but the room is sectioned off, two rooms with no doors and then an open area with a sink and several unopened boxes. The walls are done white and I can tell the guys are taking turns coming back here and painting different images all over. It's an eclectic look. All of their strikingly different styles mix together and at the center is a mural of the goddess Hel, a drawing that Janie did sometime ago after Fox turned her on to digital artwork to allow her to continue her passion for drawing despite her tremors.

"Wow," I breathe, looking around. "Your new piercers are going to be so excited to work here." Janie snorts and rolls her eyes.

"Yeah, if I can find some who aren't douchebags. I had one guy tell me that he would love to work here, as long as I remember my place." She deadpans as she motions for me to follow her into one of the rooms. She sits on one of the stools and motions for me to do the same.

"I would rather not." I whine, knowing where this is going.

"I didn't ask." She states as she arches a brow. Sighing, I grab the stool and sit down. Janie has the *"I will sit on you"* look and after the beating I got at pole class as well as last night's events, I'm too tired to try and fight her.

"Good girl." Janie states and we both stare at each other... eyes wide before busting out in laughter. "Good to know we both share a similar kink. But seriously, we need to talk because my bestie is not about to leave the shop and go have a car cry alone."

"Janie..." I whine again before sighing in defeat. "Okay, so he and I had sex last night."

"I knew that extra happy Atlas was not a facade! Damn, so Derek was right," I blink at her comment but shake it off.

"Anyway, it was..." I bite my lip as I remember last night. "Uhmm, moving on. Last night after... that... he and I had kind of a deep conversation about his mom and sister. And I don't know, I guess I thought we made it over an obstacle and then that just happened and he shut down and ran off. So maybe I read too much into everything last night."

Janie nods and stays quiet for a moment. She pushes her mass of red curls out of her freckled face while rubbing her chin. "Ren, you know I love you, right?" Oh god here we go.

"Yes Janie. I love you too, currently." I shoot her a warning look that doesn't faze her in the least.

"I would die for you, I would kill for you, but more importantly, I am willing to accept you being mad at me if need be because I'm about to fuck you up with all the truths right now." Just once, just one time, I would like to converse with her without a *"Janie-fied"* television quote getting thrown into the mix. "Seriously Ren," she continues as she crosses her legs. "That man worships the ground you walk on and has for, well, for longer than I've known you. And he doesn't make it a secret. Think about it. With Fox and I, Jesus, we were in love and still telling the other we hated each other. Not Atlas, you are always on his mind, and god, the way he flirts with you."

I blush and tuck a lock of fallen hair behind my ear. "You know he's a big flirt."

Janie looks up at me, giving me the most serious look I've seen from her in a long time. "No Lauren, he isn't. He is a big flirt with you. If you think he is here acting that way with other women, you are very wrong. Jesus, look at his station! He has photos of you two and he always has ***his*** wedding ring on." She states, and I subconsciously cover my bare hand. "My point is, you are closer to him than anyone, and it would hurt him to hear you say you thought that what you two shared last night wasn't genuine. Because if Atlas showed you himself, you know it was real. I don't know a lot about Atlas' family. But I know with Fox, he held a lot of heavy guilt, hell he still does. Fox liked to keep a certain persona up, it kept everyone back. And all of us know how hard it is to break that habit. Atlas is stressed, and I believe he wants to be who you turn to, but fears if he shows his weakness, you won't feel able to. So maybe give the guy a break. I'm not saying he should've run off. But maybe we shouldn't look at this as him trying to hurt you but rather him still struggling to be okay sharing things with you. After all, this is new to him, he's spent his life not having anyone. It'll take time to break that."

I take in her words before nodding and letting out a sigh. "You're right, I know you are. I don't like it, though."

Janie shrugs and gives me a smile. "You don't have to like it. Just accept it."

I laugh, "I feel like poor Fox hears that quite often."

"He wouldn't have to if the idiot would stop fighting me. Now, on to more important matters, how was it?" Janie grins and runs her tongue over her teeth.

I blush deeply as I giggle. "Did you know he's pierced?" Janie's eyes widen.

"Shut up... like... how? Did it hurt?"

"No, it's on the top and it was, it was amazing." I sigh, remembering the balls massaging the perfect spot.

"Wowwww! Atlas is a freak." I laugh at my friend, deciding I would keep the squirting to myself, at least for now.

CHAPTER 18
ATLAS

"Atlas fucking Hart," a familiar, mature feminine voice purrs as I down a shot before signaling to the bartender to get me another. I turn to see the petite brunette make her way over to the barstool next to me. She's attractive, older than me, maybe mid to late forties. Fuck, she looks familiar. What's her name? I run my eyes over her thin frame, and stop when my eyes land on the cat tail tattoo that wraps around her wrist.

"Josie," I smile fondly and watch her relax when I say her name. "How's my favorite pussycat?" She laughs as she sits on the barstool.

"Better than you, I'd say," Her dark eyes look at the shot glass I have pressed against my lips. "Aren't you on probation?"

I down the shot and signal for another. "Yes ma'am. Guess you were wrong about me being too much of a good guy for you, huh?" I laugh dryly as she rolls her eyes.

"Hart, you are a good guy. Why you try so hard to come off as a flake, I don't know."

"I am a flake! You told me you don't do good guys, and I

proved to you what a douche I am by having a one-night stand with you! Never called you back. That is a textbook flake." I go to get another shot, but Josie reaches over and covers my hand to stop me and she gives me a sympathetic look.

"Atlas, you and I had a one-night stand over four years ago and you remember my name. And I bet if you weren't so intoxicated you would remember more than that. You aren't a flake and you are a good man. Trust me, I've had my fair share of bad men, you aren't one of them. So whatever this is," she gestures to my shot glass. "Stop before it puts you in a place where there is no chance of you coming back out as a good man."

"I'm tired." I say while staring at her hand covering my glass.

"Ain't we all, sugar." She chuckles as she sits next to me. "Wanna talk about it?"

I huff and shake my head. "Do I want to unload all of my personal baggage on a woman I was a dick to four years ago? No. I think I'm good."

"Listen, excuse my language but, I fucked you sugar. Remember? It was my forty-third birthday, and I was in the middle of my first divorce and you showed up at the bar looking younger and more fit than any man I ever dreamed I could have and I had my first ummm... what is it? *Cougar moment*?"

I laugh lightly as she continues. "We had a one night stand and I, not you, said bye and no thanks to the phone number. So again, you weren't a dick."

Groaning, I rest my head on my forearm and look at her. "I have a wife." I blurt out, and she smacks my arm.

"That is amazing! About time someone snatched you up." I shake my head and sigh.

"She is amazing, and so smart... like way too smart to be with me. And she's so pretty. She went to law school, she comes from wealthy parents. She's just so sweet and well, she met my mom and sister today who are deep into their addictions." Josie winces, and nods as if knowing exactly what I'm talking about before urging me to continue.

"Ren is so beautiful and sweet and kind, and she doesn't deserve to be around that kind of destruction."

"But you do?" I turn to stare at Josie and raise a brow.

"What?" I ask and she crosses her arms over her chest.

"She doesn't deserve it, but you do? Tell me, what did the big bad Atlas Hart do to deserve being trapped in that hell, alone? And I'm just going to take a wild guess here and say that the addiction started way back in your childhood? Maybe even before you were born?" I wince at her words, the only acknowledgement I give to her very correct answer. "Exactly," she states. "So don't tell me what the big bad adult Atlas did, instead tell me what little Atlas did? What did that little boy do to deserve that hell?"

"Nothing..." I choke out. "He did... nothing."

"Right, no one deserves to have to be in that chaos. But, you have a wife. A partner who is wanting to stand in that with you so that you aren't alone. That's rare, sugar, trust me. If my husband and I, hell if any of them and I had that even once in our marriages, maybe I would've tried to work things out. Lean on the girl some, it might calm the chaos down some."

Josie gives my arm a squeeze before walking off to leave me with my thoughts. I stare down at the empty glass, wishing like hell that it was full, but also wishing I had never come here in the first place. Grabbing my phone, I tap Fox's name. As I wait for him to answer, all I can think about is that look on Ren's face and how much I hate myself for running away and leaving her.

"Jesus Christ." Fox sighs as he walks over to the bar. "You look like shit."

I force a small laugh. "I've been hearing that lately." I slur as I slide off the barstool. "Don't tell Ren I'm drunk, okay?" I mumble as he helps me out of the bar.

"She's going to know when I drop your ass off." I climb into Fox's vehicle with some trouble and curse when I slip and hit my knee on his running board.

"You gotta take me to your place." I grunt. "Please Fox, I can't, she will be so disappointed."

Fox sighs and shakes his head. "If I take you to my place, I have a tiny redhead with a massive mouth. She will tell Ren in a heartbeat." He taps his fingers on his steering wheel while he thinks in silence before he grabs his phone out of his pocket.

"Hey man," Fox says to whoever is on the other line. "I found him. He's plastered, I need to take him to you to keep him away from Ren. Alright, I'll be there with him in about fifteen." When he hangs up the phone, he puts his vehicle in gear and starts driving. "I'm taking you to Ash."

I groan loudly, but don't fight him. Going to Ash is probably the best option, though going there and having to get yelled at because I interrupted his "fun time" with whatever girl he's picked up for the evening is not something that I have the energy to deal with. But it is still better than facing Ren when I'm this drunk. Though, I should probably call her before I pass out tonight.

I GO TO KNOCK ON THE DOOR TO WHAT WAS ONCE THE APARTMENT that Ash and I shared. But before I do, the door opens and I look down to see the tiny little raven-haired girl...woman?

"H-Hey Indy, is Ash here?" I try my best to straighten my posture even though the world is spinning.

"He is." Ash says as he comes behind his sister and opens the door the rest of the way. "You look like shit."

"I've heard." I mutter as I walk inside and sit on the couch.

"Oh!" Indy clasps her hands together and smiles. "I know this great herbal tea that is supposed to prevent hangovers! I'll brew some up."

"Oh Indy no," Ash groans as he flops in the chair next to the couch. "The last time she "brewed" herbal tea, the apartment smelled of death for three days."

"She doesn't have to make it on my account." I mutter as I smash my face into a pillow and curl up on the couch. "I'm totally deserving of whatever hangover I end up with."

"Oh, so we are nose diving into self pity, awesome. I am so glad I didn't miss that portion of the evening." Ash snorts out and I don't have to look up to know he has annoyance written all over his face. Ash is a fixer. He doesn't have time for "deep troubling feelings" -which is why he hasn't had a relationship since I've known him and when asked about any exes, he shuts down until the subject changes.

"Look," I groan as my stomach lurches while I jerk up. "Gross," I mutter before shaking off the nausea. "You were there. You saw how my family acted in front of everyone, including Ren. And then I freak out and leave her."

"So? Stop being a bitch and go apologize. She ain't mad anyway. She was worried about you, but not mad. You know Ren, she's well thought out and practical. She seems like the type that would understand your shit *if* you would be an adult and talked with her." Ash makes a good point, even if I don't want to admit it. Ren isn't a runner. She isn't one to hide and cry. If she were mad, I would know. And she absolutely will be mad if I don't let her know what is going on.

Sighing, I pull out my phone just as a rancid smell fills the room. "Tea is almost done!" Indy nearly sings and I look at Ash in pure horror before putting the phone to my ear.

"I can't drink that." I whisper before I hear Ren's voice on the other end.

"Atlas? Are you okay?" My chest tightens at her voice, filled with fear and concern. I would give any amount of money to be with her right now, to hold her to my chest, to hug her in that special way that makes everything feel better.

"Hi Princess, I'm alright. I'm at Ash's, I uhh, I had a little too much to drink." I give an awkward laugh, unsure what to expect out of her.

"Okay," she lets out a breath, and I hear keys jingling. "I'll be there in about twenty to get you."

"What? Why? Ren, just stay home. I'm drunk and not–"

"You belong in your home in your bed." She states firmly, and I hear the sound of her locking the door. "You don't need to spend the night on the couch, feeling like shit and then have no way to get to your community service in the morning so, I'm coming to get you. I'll be there in twenty minutes, baby."

"Okay," I say softly as I try to decipher the overwhelming feelings I have flooding through me. "Thank you." I end the call and look down at my knees as I try to process everything.

"What's up, At?" Ash asks.

My home. My bed. Baby.

I rub my chest where I feel pressure as I continue to stare at the floor. My home and my bed, that I share with her. Technically, she and I haven't slept in that bed together for a full night, but after the amazing sleep at the farm with her in my arms, I refuse to sleep in a bed without her. I've never felt so calm, so safe or loved

Loved?

Is that what I feel from her? I don't know, but I do know, on my end, what I feel for Ren is so much stronger than anything I've ever felt before. She is my morning, noon, and night. My rainbow and my shooting star. She is all I've wanted for so long, and now I've had her, and I just want her more. I want her mind, body, and soul. I want her heart.

"At?" Ash snaps his fingers, pulling me out of my thoughts. "What's going on?"

I look up at him with wide eyes, "I... I'm in love with Ren."

CHAPTER 19
LAUREN

"Okay, so, in most romance novels, there comes the time where the main character meets the love interest. Typically, that's met with some over the top feeling inside them, some pull they feel towards that character. It's like- "their eyes lock and suddenly her breath hitches as she feels her heartbeat quicken and a warmth run through her". I know, I've written this scene a hundred times. The scene is unrealistic, you cannot meet someone and in four seconds your body has decided that they are your soulmate. It doesn't work this way, and it's only written like this because us authors have to make a lot happen, typically in less than a hundred thousand words. So, to speed things along, certain parts of the story wind up being embellished. Or so I thought."

Closing the book, I can't help but giggle at the chorus of groans that follows.

"C'mon Lauren!" The older woman sighs in a way that reminds me of a teenager. I laugh lightly as I place the book in my bag.

"I'm sorry, guys! Atlas is almost done and I've got a doctor's appointment today, otherwise I swear I would stay." I say apologetically as I stand up, trying to ignore the dizziness I feel. I see Atlas sitting over at the table with Howard and head over. Bending over, I give Howard a hug around his arms. "Howard, you're looking handsome as ever."

Howard laughs roughly as he pats my arm. "You sure you don't want to leave him and come marry me?"

I look over at Atlas. He's horribly hungover and looks like he hasn't slept in days. The poor guy was up most of the night puking his guts out, along with some atrocious tea that Ash's sister gave him.

"I would, but this is what he looks like when he's without me." I say, gesturing to the greenish hued man before giving Howard a kiss on the cheek.

Atlas looks up at us and gives a pained smile. "It's true, I'd die without her."

I feel goosebumps at his comment and have to shake off the fluttery feeling. Reaching in my purse, I pull out a container and hand it to Howard without the staff noticing. "Chocolate and peanut butter fudge." I say low, and Howard beams brightly before looking at Atlas.

"You treat her right or I'll come out of this wheelchair and beat your ass, boy. Don't think I won't either. I got one more left in me."

Atlas chuckles and shakes his head. "Never Howard. I'll lay down and die first. You ready, Princess?"

I nod and we say our goodbyes, and Atlas talks to the woman at the front desk before we leave the building.

"How's your sugar?" Atlas asks as we get into the car. Before I can answer, he looks on his watch and pulls up my monitoring app. He frowns and reaches in my glove compartment, pulling out a little bottle of juice. "You are getting low, princess."

Snatching the bottle from him, I crack the seal and take a drink. "I am aware."

"Okay, I'm sorry, I was just trying to help." His words fill me with guilt, and I let out a long sigh.

"No, I'm sorry. I'm just tired and frustrated. I have to go to the doctor and now I'm low. I shouldn't take it out on you though. Let me finish my juice and I'll take you to the bar to get your motorcycle." I watch as Atlas gets out of the passenger side, rounds the front of the car before opening my driver's door.

"Come on, I'll drive you." I give him a thankful smile as I get out of the car. I go to walk away, but his demeanor stops me. He looks deflated.

"What's wrong?" I ask as I place a hand on his chest. I feel his body lean into my touch, so I place my other hand over his neck.

"I'm sorry," he whispers as he leans in to rest his forehead against mine. "For everything that happened yesterday."

"Atlas, I'm not mad at you. You have no reason to be sorry."

"You shouldn't have been treated that way by them. And then I left you." He goes to look away, but I force him to look back.

"You know what your mother said was a lie, right?" I watch as he flinches as he continues to avoid eye contact. "Atlas! Look at me."

His eyes meet mine, and I waste no time in pulling him to me, hugging him tightly. His body melts against mine, and I need to lean against the car to keep my balance.

"I'm so sorry." He whispers into my neck. "You didn't deserve that. You deserve so much better."

"Well," I pull his head up and kiss the tip of his nose, earning a small chuckle. "I guess both our in-laws suck."

Atlas lets out a pained laugh before bending down and kissing my forehead. "You are, without a doubt, the greatest human I've ever met."

I blush as I hug him tightly. We stay like that for a moment longer before Atlas ushers me to the passenger seat.

WHEN ATLAS OFFERED TO DRIVE, I ASSUMED HE WOULD BE TAKING us to the bar where he left his motorcycle. I assumed incorrectly. Atlas parks my car in front of my doctor's office before turning off the ignition.

"I really didn't mean for you to waste your time here." I mostly mutter to myself as we walk into the building.

Atlas shrugs nonchalantly as he follows me into the office and takes a seat while I check in. I smile at the receptionist as I give her my information, as well as my new insurance cards with *Lauren Hart* printed on them. It's weird, sometimes I forget that he and I are legally married. I mean, we had our first date two days ago.

"Mrs. Hart," the older woman says loudly to get my attention. "Your copay is fifty dollars."

"Oh! Right, here you are." I smile softly as I hand her my card. She swipes the card, and the machine makes a funny noise.

"Ma'am, this card was declined." My stomach drops. *Declined?* I knew I was getting close on my savings, but I thought I had–

My insulin...

I feel my shoulders slump as I remember that my insulin supply is larger this month because it's the holidays and they were insuring I wouldn't have any issues. I forgot about the payment, shit.

"Problem?" I jump at Atlas' smooth voice behind me. I watch as he smiles at the older woman. "I'm her husband. What's up, Princess?"

"Oh!" *Shit, I can't let him know.* "I think my new card is messed up."

Atlas nods and hands the woman his card before kissing my temple. His card goes through and we both go and sit back down.

"Sorry," I wince, feeling uncomfortable.

"It's alright. Though I wonder what's wrong with your card." I shrug and look away as I pray that the nurse calls me soon. I didn't want to discuss money with Atlas. Though it's now official, I have to get a new job quickly. I cannot believe I allowed myself to drain my account that far, I guess part of me thought that I would get my old job back or Atlas would've moved on, and I would be in my parents' good graces again. Well, as good as I've ever been, anyway. Thankfully, I don't have to sit in the uncomfortable silence for long, the nurse walks out and calls my name. I smile and tell Atlas I'll be back soon.

"I can't believe you." Atlas snaps as he shuts the driver's door and starts the ignition. Apparently, while I was in my appointment and Atlas sat in the waiting room, he decided to do some online banking and found that the checks he had been writing me for his parts of the bills were never cashed.

"Atlas, I have my reasons." I groan, while laying my head back on the seat. "You've already given me enough with the health insurance. I don't need more money on top of it."

"It's rent!" He snaps in frustration. "I was giving you money for my rent and bills. No wonder your card didn't work, you have no fucking money!"

"It's fine! You weren't supposed to be paying rent, anyway!" I snap back defensively.

"The fuck I wasn't! When I said I needed a place to stay, that didn't mean a free place! Jesus Christ, Ren! All the food and bills, you've just been paying on your own!"

I sigh loudly, "Atlas, I'm going to find a job and start work. I think the restaurant down from Hel's is hiring." I jerk forward as Atlas slams on the brake at the stoplight.

"Restaurant? You're a fucking lawyer. Why would you work at a restaurant?" I notice he has done a u-turn and is now parking again at the doctor's office. He's angry and needs to move, that is obvious. He slams the car into park and gets out of the car.

I sigh and pinch the bridge of my nose before following suit and walking around to meet him. "Because I can't work for another competing law office for twelve months. It's in the contract I signed when I got the promotion. Once the year is up I am free to do what I want, but until then I have to find other work. Besides, I've been a waitress before, I can do it again. Oh, this reminds me, you're going to Sunday's birthday tomorrow night, right?"

Atlas wasn't taking the subject change. His green eyes glare down at me and I feel equal parts intimidated and turned on. "Cash those checks," He says in a deep, gravelly voice that causes every drop of my stubborn feminism to evaporate. Without realizing it, I run my tongue over my lips and I watch as his eyes laser focus on my tongue. I hear his heavy exhale as I slide my tongue back into my mouth. I watch his nostrils flare as he looks around before he opens the back door of my Rav4 and slides in.

"Get in." He orders and I squish myself in the car next to him, which isn't easy. My back seat isn't big and Atlas by himself takes up a lot of room with his massive body. I untuck my dress from beneath me and before I can ask why we are back here, his mouth consumes mine. I feel his hand grip my jaw as I moan into his mouth. "Fuckkk." He growls before coaxing my tongue out of my mouth and into his. I whimper against him before gasping and breaking the kiss when I feel his hand slipping up my thigh.

"Oh," I laugh nervously. "A-Atlas! It's broad daylight and there is no room."

"You really think daylight is going to stop me? And there is plenty of room. You hop on, face the front and let me make you feel good." He flicks his tongue over my earlobe as I feel his hand slipping to my panties. I almost wore boy shorts, but something told me not to and as he slips the crotch of the garment to one side before plunging a digit inside me, I thank the universe for deciding against the boy shorts.

"Fuck, Ren," He growls as he bites on my shoulder. "Pretty girl, you're so wet and tight. You want this as bad as I do, don't you?" He curls his fingers inside me and I let out a sharp cry.

"Y-yes!" I shudder as he slips another finger inside me.

"Good, now get on my dick." He orders as he unzips his jeans. He leans back against the seat and pulls his fully erect cock free. I look around and don't see anyone, so, with some twisting, I situate myself, facing forward, on Atlas' lap. I feel him move my ass as he slides the head of his thick cock to my entrance and I shiver while he grips my hips and slides me down to fully sheath him.

"God fucking damn it," He hisses and I see in the rearview mirror his head rolling back in pleasure. After he gathers himself, Atlas pulls me up slightly before thrusting–hard–up into me. I cry out in both pain and pleasure as he thrusts again, and again, and again.

Leaning forward, I rest my head on the back of the driver's seat as I scream his name over and over as if it were a prayer that I am singing to the heavens. Atlas reaches around and I feel him slide his hand over my stomach and when his expert fingers find their way to my clit I sink my teeth into the leather backrest.

"Oh no you don't," he pants as he pulls me back against his burning chest. "You let me hear those pretty screams while I fuck your perfect pussy. Are you going to soak me like the other night, princess?" His hot breath on my ear sends shivers all over my body and I lull my head back as I feel the pressure building.

"I think... ah... oh shit..." I cry out as he pulls back and I feel the rush of fluid leave my body, something that I had no idea I could do until the other night, and now I cannot seem to stop, at least not with him. Thankfully, he seems to enjoy it.

"Fuck, that's my girl." He praises as he shoves back into me and I cry out as I begin bouncing on his cock, chasing my release. "Oh god Ren," he growls and I feel him dig his hand into my hip while his other presses on my clit.

My walls tighten around his cock as I feel his hot come shoot inside me. "There..." I cry out as I feel the explosion inside me. "There.. there... fuck... Atlas!" I scream as I frantically bounce, milking him as I come on him.

I can't move, my body is ruined in this moment and I know that we have to. I'm terrified to know what kind of mess I've created, or how on earth I'm getting *that* fluid out of my upholstery.

"I need you again." He growls and I laugh.

"Well, it's going to have to wait, we have to leave here. What is with us and cars?" Atlas chuckles as he bites my neck.

"Ren," He whispers in my ear. His tone sends nervous butterflies fluttering in my stomach. "I wanted to talk to you about–"

His phone rings and I once again am thanking the universe because if he is wanting to talk about us, that is something I am not ready for.

CHAPTER 20
ATLAS

"I don't know, man," Fox says, his voice full of apprehension. Even still, he continues to lay the stencil over the top of my hand. He cocks his head from one side to the other before cursing under his breath and wiping the stencil off my hand before placing it in a different area. "Obviously I will do it, but I feel like you should probably talk to her first." My only response to him is a shrug of my shoulders. He decides the spot is correct and reaches over to grab his glasses.

"If I ask her, she'll tell me no." Fox chuckles and shakes his head as he starts setting his machine. Derek walks over and looks at the outline on my hand.

"Color or black and grey?" He asks, while taking a sip of his drink.

"I was thinking color since my sleeve is black and grey, it'll make it pop." I state, and Derek nods his approval. Fox starts the first line and I hear the back door open.

"Hey fuckers," Ash states, walking in with his sister. "Coffee is here."

"Hey Indy." I say, followed by Fox. Indy beams brightly

at us and waves with both her hands before grabbing two coffees and sitting them next to us. She grabs another coffee and walks over to Derek's station.

"Hi! I'm Indy! Here is your coffee!" She beams as she holds the coffee up to Derek, who looks startled as he fumbles with his phone before clumsily grabbing his coffee that splashes onto his hand.

"Fuck," He hisses and Indy giggles lightly as she takes the coffee back and sets it on his station.

"Nice introduction." She laughs as Derek blushes.

"Dude," I whisper to Fox and Ash. "Virginia is blushing." Ash snaps his gaze up and his lip curls.

"Indiana." He barks out, causing Indy to jump before waving bye to Derek. She comes up to Ash and scowls at him.

"Ash, what the hell?" She hisses and pinches his arm.

"He is nearly twice your age, don't be gross."

"Excuse you?" Fox looks up over his glasses, and Ash, holds his hands up.

"My bad, anyway, there's the coffee. I'm grabbing the merch samples and going to the meeting. Send me a pic when that's done." He says, pointing at the tattoo before they head out.

"Bye!" Indy says, smiling and giving a little wave to Derek on her way out the door..

"Uhh...you too!" Derek says before smacking his face when they leave. Fox and I burst out laughing at him, causing him to flip us both off.

"Alright man, I think we are done." He says, wiping down my hand. "I have to say, I'm fucking amazing."

I would roll my eyes at the arrogance, if it weren't for the fact that Fox really outdid himself. I stare down at my hand and smile at the tattoo of Ren's perfectly plump lips on the top of my hand.

"Pretty ballsy," Fox chuckles as he wraps my hand up. "Getting a tattoo of a woman's lips before you even ask her to be your girlfriend."

"I asked her to marry me before she and I were technically friends. This actually fits perfectly with our journey." I smile as I stand up and stretch.

"Yeah, well, now Janie is going to be all 'Why don't you have a tattoo for me'." I laugh and look down at my phone and see Ren sent me a text about five minutes ago.

Princess: Hey, I hate to ask, but could you pick me up after my pole class? I have a headache.

Princess: Actually, don't worry about it. I'll call an Uber.

Me: Absolutely not, beautiful. I will be there. Do not get an Uber.

I smile at Fox. "I really appreciate this man. I better head out, I got to go grab Ren from class." We give each other a backslap hug before I head out the back door and towards the car.

HOLY FUCKING SHIT.

A literal pained whimper escapes my mouth as I walk into the dance studio and see Ren spinning around on the pole. She stops and does this sexy slither thing as she holds the pole over her head. My dick has never been so hard. I watch in complete awe as she bends down lower and lower.

"That's it, pretty girl," I mutter to myself as I watch her ass slide down.

"Can I help you?" The young male voice causes me to nearly fall over.

"Fucking hell," I pant with my hand against my chest. "No man, I'm fine."

"Look old man," *Old man? What the fuck?* "This is a dance studio. If you want a show, go somewhere else." I admit, the balls on a kid so young is impressive.

"Atlas?" I turn to see Sunday and Ren coming out of the dance room.

"Hey Sunday," I smile. "Hey Beautiful." I kiss Ren softly as I turn back to the boy.

"Wade," Sunday scolds. "Were you yelling at Atlas? Son, I've told you, just because a man walks in here don't make him a creep!"

"Mom, he was looking at Ren's butt and saying 'that's it, pretty girl'."

"Ho-Okay! Well, this has been fun. Sunday, you have a great evening. Princess, let's go." I laugh awkwardly as I pull Ren out of the studio, her cackling the whole way to my vehicle.

"You are such a pervert!" She says between laughs.

"Yeah, yeah, get in." I mumble before walking over to my side. I get in and start the ignition and I hear the gasp.

"You got a tattoo?" She asks, looking at my SaniDerm wrapped hand.

"Yeah, uhh, Fox did it." I say, suddenly nervous. I watch as she looks at my hand, brows furrowed.

"Lips?" She asks. It's a little hard to tell with the ink and everything filling the wrap.

"Yeah... yours." She gasps again, and I look at her anxiously. "Are you mad?"

She's quiet for a moment and just as panic is about to fill me, she smiles and looks up at me. "That is absolutely the most impulsive and insane thing anyone could do, but it's really fucking hot."

I smirk as I look over at her. "Hot enough to get lucky tonight?" I wink and she rolls her eyes.

"If by lucky you mean dinner and Netflix, then absolutely."

"Fucking score." I joke as I pull out of the parking space so we can head back to the apartment.

CHAPTER 21
LAUREN

"Alright Princess," Atlas says as he walks into my room. "Are you ready to head—ho...ly shit." Atlas' green eyes are as big as saucers as he looks me over.

"Do I look okay?" I ask nervously. "I showed Sunday and Janie several outfits, and this is the only one they both agreed on, though I'm not sure they were stoked on it and now I'm second guessing all of this." I make a hand gesture towards my outfit. I have on a black forties style blouse with a high neckline, button fastening and a large keyhole that shows off my prominent cleavage. I paired it with red, high-waisted, wide leg pants that hug my curves and a pair of low black heels. My hair is down and in soft waves and I will be topping it off with my favorite trilby hat.

"Listen," Atlas clears his throat while he tries to look anywhere but my chest. "I understand you are an adult, you are your own woman and fuck the patriarchy. I'm right there with you, sister." His eyes have managed to stay off my cleavage for all of three seconds. "However, you wearing this outfit and showing off those hips is making me want to bend you over and claim you, and then bite every bit of exposed flesh, which, my god," I can't help but laugh as he adjusts himself in his dark wash jeans. "And while I do realize I am not allowed to partake in such cavemen-like gestures, just know that I will murder everyone that looks at you tonight."

"Don't you mean every man?" I raise a brow as I walk with him to the living room.

"Nope, everyone. I'm equal opportunity when it comes to beating someone's face in over you." I place the hat on my head before turning around and smiling up at him.

"That is disgusting." I laugh as he shrugs.

"Only for you, princess. Now, what are the chances I can fuck you while you wear that hat?"

"ATLAS!" SUNDAY BEAMS AS SHE TUGS ON JANIE AND I TO STAND with her and Stevie. "Take our picture!" Inwardly I cringe, I'm not big on getting my picture taken, but it is Sunday's birthday so I squeeze in and smile as Atlas snaps a couple pictures.

"Some beautiful looking ladies!" He grins as he heads over to the bar with Fox.

"Where's Derek and Ash?" I ask Janie, who is currently fussing over her hair. The poor girl has mountains of wild red curls and the weather changing is wreaking havoc on them.

"Oh, you know Derek, he'd sooner shove a rod up his dick hole than be seen socializing." I shake my head. Janie had a mouth on her when we first met, but working at the tattoo shop and living with Fox has definitely made her more comfortable with her *enhanced vocabulary*. "And I think Ash's sister is sick or something, he had to leave work early."

"Good riddance." Sunday mutters, causing us all to look at her in shock. "No! Not that his sister is sick, just that he ain't here. I don't really care for him too much. He's kind of a pig."

Janie snorts into her drink. "Yeah, that's kind of his thing. He's a nice enough guy if you aren't fucking him. Have you met him since he did your tattoo?"

As if on instinct, Sunday scratched her back where a full piece of a dragon with cherry blossoms lay, courtesy of Ash some time before any of us knew each other.

"Uh no," Sunday says quickly. "But from that encounter then and what y'all say about him now, I think I'm good. Hey Ren, who is that talking to Atlas?" I turn my attention from my girlfriends to the bar where I see a thin, scantily clad woman all but straddling Atlas.

"Fuck," Janie mutters. "It's Valentina."

My head snaps towards the redhead. "Valentina?" I repeat, the name is like vomit in my mouth. "The model he worked on?" Janie gives me an uncomfortable look and I take a breath before walking over.

Upon my arrival, Atlas gives me a panicked look as *Valentina* turns to look at me. She looks me over once, twice, and then a third time.

"I love your outfit." She says, and I'm taken aback by the genuine tone in her voice.

"Thanks." I say slowly as I look back at Atlas, who is just as confused looking as me.

"Valentina," He says, remembering he has a voice. "This is Lauren, my wife."

She snorts. This bitch actually snorts and then looks at me again. "Cute." She then turns back to Atlas and places a hand on his knee. "Now like I was saying–"

"Valentina, please stop." Atlas says somewhat forcefully as he pushes her hand away.

"Are you deaf?" I snap, feeling anger and jealousy and fuck, is this that possessive alpha thing I read about all the time? "He said I'm his wife. So back off."

Valentina steps back as I walk up to the bar and she scoffs as if I've insulted her.

"There is no need to be rude. I was simply speaking to a friend. You may want to work on your trust issues."

"Possibly," I state as I grab the shot glass that is sitting in front of Fox. "But I think you need to learn not to touch what isn't yours. And if the wedding band isn't clear enough, let me help you." I step onto the footrest of the barstool, empty the contents of the shot glass into my mouth before leaning over Atlas, grabbing his jaw and pouring the liquor into his mouth.

The bar erupts in catcalls and hoots and as I go to pull away, Atlas grabs me and kisses me, causing the bar patrons to grow louder. When we break, Valentina is no longer standing there. Atlas stands up and looks over to Sunday.

"Happy Birthday, we need to go." He says and I scream as he heaves me over his shoulder, smacking my ass before walking us out of the bar.

"Atlas!" I squeal as I hit the wall that is his back. "Put me down!"

"Not likely, Princess." He chuckles as he smacks my ass again. "Did you honestly think you were going to do something *that* fucking hot and we were going to just continue hanging out? Yeah, fuck no. I'm taking you home and you are riding my fucking face until I'm drowning."

"REN. I'M NOT PLAYING." ATLAS GROWLS AS HE PUSHES ME INTO my bedroom and shuts the door. His expert hands make short work of my shirt and pants while his mouth consumes my lips, tongue, and neck.

"Atlas," I groan. "I don't know if this is going to work the way you think it will." He wouldn't let up on the "me riding his face" fantasy and while I really wanted to, I have to be practical here.

"Princess," He growls as he grabs my jaw to make me look at him. "I am only going to say this one more time. Sit. On. My. Face."

I look from him to the bed while I chew on my bottom lip.

"Stop," He orders. "Whatever you're thinking, stop and fucking suffocate me. Now." Atlas pulls me to the bed and I fall onto him. He pulls the elastic of my panties and snaps them. "Lose them or I rip them off."

I let out a nervous breath as I slip my underwear off while he removes his shirt and lies on the bed. "Come here." I do as I'm told and crawl up the length of his body.

"I'm nervous." I confess in a soft whisper. Atlas smiles softly as he tucks a lock of my hair behind my ear.

"You are the most beautiful creature I've ever seen. You are a goddess. Let me worship you." He kisses me softly before I climb over him. I grip the headboard to hold myself up as I hover over his face. Atlas chuckles as he grips my thighs and bucks me off balance so I'm fully on him. I'm about to scamper off and apologize when his arms become like steel, holding me firmly in place.

"Holy shit!" I cry out in surprise as his tongue licks my entire slit before his lips pull my clit into his mouth. "A-atlas..."

"Mmmhhhmmm..." He moans from under me, running his teeth over my nub.

"Atlas," I pant as my hips buck involuntarily. "Shit, I'm sorry!" I hear him sigh and I squeak as he pushes me back onto his chest. I look down at his face, his lips and chin glisten from my arousal, and the sight nearly makes me moan.

"You see how easy it was to move you?" His voice is full of patient annoyance. Is that even a thing? Whether it is or not, Atlas is full of it. "If I can move you that easily, you ain't going to crush me, hurt me, kill me, whatever. So, for the last time, put that pretty pussy on my face and come in my fucking mouth."

I stare in shock at his obscene language, but also, why is it turning me on?

"Say more." I breathe out, surprising both of us. I watch his expression morph and a sly grin creeps on his face.

"Oh? Does my princess like dirty talk?" He rubs his thumb over my clit as I sit on his chest. Fuck, he shouldn't be this talented, but also, thank whoever is up there for giving this man this ability.

"I'll tell you what I'm going to do." He smirks as he slips a finger inside of me. I whimper as a second follows. "I'm going to make this pink little pussy squirt all over me, and you are going to like it. God, yes you are. You're going to let me consume your sweet fluids while your soft thighs shake and you grind against my mouth. You are about to come in my hand with just me talking about it, isn't that right?" I whimper and nod as his hand continues to work its magic on me. "And then, I am going to flip you over and fuck you so hard from behind you're going to be seeing stars. All while I get to grip and hold onto that fine fucking ass of yours."

Atlas curls his fingers inside of me as his thumb runs over my swollen clit. "Now, are you ready to soak me, pretty girl? Come on Princess, drown me." His mouth connects with my sex again and I throw my head back and cry out as I release all over his mouth, chin and neck.

I hear his moans of approval as he presses up on the roof of my center and I explode around his fingers. I barely have time to register the orgasm as he flips me onto the bed on all fours and pushes my upper half to the mattress. I wince as I hear the crack of his hand meeting my ass, followed by the sting. I moan as he massages the spot with his hand before surprising me and licking my ass cheek.

Fuck...I *really* like that.

"Ass up, Princess." He orders as he pulls my hips back upwards. I tense up as I feel his tongue and lips on my ass cheeks.

"Oh, fuck." I shudder as he bites the flesh. I hear him chuckle darkly while straightening back up and delivering another smack. My body shudders and I whimper as he rubs the tender flesh before he lines himself up and buries his hard cock inside me. I let out a loud muffled cry into the mattress as he fills up my still contracting hole.

"Damn it!" He hisses as he gives me a small thrust. "You feel too fucking good. God, I want to stay buried inside you."

"I want you to." I say through pants as he grips my hips and thrusts deeper and harder into me, his piercing massaging my swollen spot. "Atlas, don't leave me." I cry out as I start matching his thrusts.

"I won't, baby," he grunts as his hand holds my chest to the bed. I gasp as I feel myself squirt again, and his praises fill me with so much confidence and desire.

"Atlas, baby I'm going to–" He pulls me up to his chest and starts massaging my clit.

"That's my pretty girl, come for me." He bites my shoulders as his thrusts become more erratic. "Fuck, that's it... I'm coming." He pants and presses his head against my shoulder. "Shit... ah... Fuck! Ren I... I love you!"

I try to freeze, but I'm already coming as his words leave his mouth.

And all I can think is–*Oh fuck.*

CHAPTER 22
ATLAS

"You told her you loved her," Fox's stupid, annoying voice over the bluetooth speaker in my Tahoe sounds almost humorous. "As you were fucking? Dude, were you a virgin up to this point? Everyone knows that is the big no." I groan as I pull into the parking spot at the nursing home.

"Yeah asshole, I know, trust me. And I said it with her back to me." I cringe, completely humiliated and disgusted with myself. After my confession last night, things were...tense.

Ren instantly got up, saying she needed a shower, and then proceeded to stay in the bathroom for over an hour. I think she was waiting for me to leave the room. I changed her sheets and when I tried her door later, it was locked. This morning I waited as long as I could to try and talk to her, but she never came out, saying she was going to sleep in due to a headache.

"I think I completely fucked everything up with her." I confess, as I take my seatbelt off and stuff my bag with snacks for Howard, along with more fudge from Ren.

"Give it a couple days," Fox reassures. "Ren is practical. I guarantee she will rationalize it and chalk it up to you being a horny idiot in the heat of the moment."

Rolling my eyes, I shake my head. "Gee thanks, I love you too."

"Listen, you need to stop being so damn loose with that word."

I snort at his remark before telling him bye and walking towards the entrance. I wonder if there is a way to talk to Howard about this without coming clean that Ren and I aren't married for the traditional reasons.

Walking inside, I smile at Betty at the counter who looks both sad and shocked to see me. "Hart? What are you doing here?"

I furrow my brows and look at my watch to check the date and time. "It's game day." I state while patting my backpack and smirking."Is the old man ready to get his ass handed to him?" I joke while looking around the common area for Howard. She doesn't laugh, in fact she looks almost as if she's pitying me. My stomach drops and my heart rate increases.

No. Please No.

"Where's Howard?" I ask slowly. She doesn't answer, and that's not acceptable. Whatever is happening right now is ***not*** acceptable.

"Where is Howard?" I ask again, somewhat louder. Betty gives me an apologetic look and I see the tears welling in her eyes.

"H-Hart–"

"WHERE IS HE!" I shout and slam my hand on her desk, causing her to jump. He's not gone. Not yet. I need to talk to him. I grip the desk to hold myself up and as I look around. Everything is blurring together.

I'm mildly aware of Betty coming to my side and sitting with me on the couch. She's talking, but I don't hear most of it. *Went in his sleep last night. Was holding things in his hands*... I didn't hear what. All I keep hearing is my own thoughts.

He's gone. He died here, alone.

I AM ONLY MILDLY AWARE OF THE DOORS OPENING AND REN running inside the lobby. I had texted Fox to tell him what was going on and that I wouldn't be in today. Apparently he contacted her, fucking traitor.

"Atlas," she sighs as she kneels in front of me. I feel her hands on my thighs, but it's almost like I have multiple layers of clothes on creating a barrier between us. "Atlas, look at me." She says and I slowly obey, raising my gaze to look at her. Her eyes are red rimmed and her nose is pink. She must've been crying.

"He's gone." I croak out as I look away again. It's taking everything inside of me not to break down, to not freak out. I should've been here yesterday. I kept saying I was going to start stopping by and seeing him on my non community service days, but I didn't. I selfishly didn't. And he died in this place that he hated, alone. If I had come, maybe I could've been here, I could've said goodbye.

Ren gets up and sits next to me. "Atlas, why don't I take you hom–"

"No." I bark out, causing her to flinch. Instantly I hate myself, but I don't have it in me to fix it right now. "Just leave me alone, Lauren." I sigh, feeling exhausted.

"What?" She whispers out, her voice hitching.

"Leave. I don't need you here. I don't need anyone here. I'm not a child, I don't want to be coddled." I tighten my fist on my thigh as I try to hold back the heartache.

"Atlas, I... I agree that this is heartbreaking because he mattered to you, but Howard hated it here. He couldn't wait to get to his wife again."

"So he's better off dead?" I sneer as I glare at her. "Is that it Lauren? Are you happy for him? Are you happy he's gone? The one fucking person in my life that I could just talk to. No expectations, no judgment He wanted nothing from me but time and fucking snacks. He's gone and I'm left here in this shit hole on probation for another six fucking months and I'm fucking alone."

"I-I'm here." She whispers, and I jerk my head in the opposite direction.

"Yeah, well again, you can go." I hear her breathe in sharply before standing.

"Okay, I will go, if that is what you really want." I look up at her in time to watch a tear slide down her cheek.

"I said I did, didn't I?" I whisper and the tiny sob that escapes her, it wrecks me. I watch her go through the lobby doors and back outside.

I hate myself. Hate isn't a big enough word. But I need Ren to go. I can't let her see me break, and I can't let her see what I'm about to do.

Knock

Knock

Knock

I look at the number on the stained and dented apartment door to make sure it's the correct number. I hear movement inside and when the door opens, I'm taken aback by the foul smell of old food, booze and filth.

"Hey mom." I say softly and she leans against the door frame.

"Ahhh...look at that, too good for me in front of your wife, but now that she's not around, you come crawling back." I slump my shoulders and nod slowly.

"Someone close to me passed. Mom, can I just, please. Can I come in?" I look up to see her staring at me, arms crossed with a contemplative look on her face.

"What do you have on you?" I pat my pockets and pull out my wallet.

"Two hundred." I say, she nods and moves so I can walk in.

"Thirty minutes, then I have to go meet a friend." She sits on the couch and I try not to cringe at the literal filth as I sit at the opposite end. I watch as she downs whatever liquid she has in her cup before looking at me. "Alright, let's hear it."

I explain the situation to her. The fake marriage, the parole, Howard, and how I've grown closer to Ren over these months.

"I think I'm in love with her." I admit as I rub my hands over my face. "And I don't know what to do. She's completely out of my league, her parents hate me and to top it all off, I am terrified that if she does end up loving me back, I'll lose her too."

Mom is silent as she looks at the clock on the wall before letting out a breath and standing. "Well, this has been fun. Now pay up."

I furrow my brows and look at the clock. "I have five minutes. You know the deal, I tell you my issue and you act like a mother for a minute and give me advice, then you get paid."

"Atlas, what do you want me to say?" She laughs while shaking her head. "An old man in a home died, that's what happens. And blondie will stay with you no matter what, you have money and insurance. Two things you said she needs. I'm not seeing the problem. Now I have problems,"

I roll my eyes. "Yeah, that's an understatement."

"Watch your tone, boy, I'm still your mother." She says through clenched teeth.

"Then fucking act like it! I do everything in my power to take care of you. Probably too much! All I wanted was half a fucking hour to talk to my mother about my shit, and I'm paying for it! That old man was more of a parent to me than you ever were. Growing up I would've given anything to have other parents!"

"Are you saying you wish I hadn't had you, Atlas?" She asks, her voice as cold as ice. "Because believe me, son. I tried to get rid of you. I've been trying your whole damn life to get rid of you. But like a damn cockroach, you keep coming back."

I stare at her cold, hateful eyes in shock and betrayal. "You've tried to get rid of me?" I manage over the lump growing in my throat.

"Damn pills didn't work. I smoked, drank, fell down the stairs, nothing. Sent you to the firehouse and your damn father and then later your sister kept bringing you back. When are you going to get it, Atlas? I don't want to be your mother."

I don't want to be your mother.

There has been this tiny hair that has been holding on

to the hope that one day, my mother would want to start over. That one day she would get sober and get her life together. And while I will still hope like hell she does, sober or not–I will never see this woman again.

"I think... I just got it." I said firmly as I turn to head to the door, ripping it open.

"Hey! Where's the money?" I crumple the bills and throw them in a pile of trash before leaving the apartment. Once in my vehicle, I begin beating my steering wheel while screaming.

Once I've broken my knuckles apart, I finally stop hitting the steering wheel and rest my head back.

She never wanted me. These little "mother moments" that I've paid for over the years, I thought maybe that was her and she just was too full of shame now to try and show it. But no...she never wanted me. And Millie has been bringing me back each time she dumped me?

My watch alerts me, and I look to see it's Ren's glucose monitor. Fuck, she's dropping.

I turn the car on and speed out of the parking lot while dialing her number. It rings and rings, but she doesn't answer.

"No, no, no!" I growl and hang up. Thoughts of her unconscious somewhere fill my mind and I begin to panic. I scroll my contacts and call Janie.

"Fuck you." Is my immediate greeting.

"Wait, she's low!" I yell before she has time to hang up. "I'm a shit person but please, I don't know where she is and–"

"She's with her parents, so again– FUCK. YOU." The call ends and I groan as I pull up to a stoplight. I scroll through my contacts and hit another name.

"Oh, hell no." Sunday's southern twang echoes through

my speakers. "Boy, you've lost your damn mind if you think I haven't already heard. I am already headed to Hel's with a bag of sugar for your motorcycle."

"Please, please, please. I know she's with her parents, but her sugar is still dropping. PLEASE call her and check on her. Please."

There is silence, and then a sigh. "Wade!" She yells and rustling follows. "Let me borrow your phone for a second." She says to her son and there are some more noises and muffled voices before Sunday comes back on.

"Ren is fine." Sunday says after several moments. "I talked to her mother, she is with her, they are taking care of it. Now leave her alone."

"Sunday–" The line goes dead and I punch my steering wheel again before driving off to head home.

CHAPTER 23
LAUREN

"Are you going to talk about it? Or just... lay there." Mom asks for what feels like the hundredth time since Bruno and I showed up at their house two days ago. Luckily–if you want to call it that–I had dropped so low the first day that I was asleep most of the afternoon and evening. But since then, she's been very much up my ass. I would think it was concern, if it weren't for the fact that it's my mother and I know she's only asking to be nosey.

"Mom, I really don't want to." I groan as I lay my head on the couch. "Atlas and I are just having a disagreement."

"So? Talk it out. You know better than to waste time on little pissing matches. My god, if your father and I separated every time he and I fought–"

"Mom," I interrupt, rubbing my head. "We aren't separated. Someone close to him passed away and I'm giving him time to process. And since when were you on his side?"

"I'm not," she shrugs while walking to my bedroom door. "I think he is all wrong for you, I think he is going to ruin any potential you had to make something for yourself.

But, you're a grown woman and usually, aren't under my roof. So, I have to accept your very wrong choices." With that said, she walks out of the room, leaving me to lay on the bed.

While what she said is harsh, it's probably the closest thing to a compliment that she will ever give to Atlas.

I look over to the foot of my bed and sigh as Bruno's sad eyes look at me. "I'm just trying to give him space." I justify. Bruno has been completely distraught since we left the apartment and Atlas. He wasn't the only one.

It's funny because the night before, he and I had sex and when he told me he loved me, well, it terrified me, let's be honest. But over that night, I started thinking how much I've grown accustomed to having him with me, and how the anger and jealousy I felt over Valentina, it wasn't fake wife or the unspoken fuck buddies arrangement we had going on. No, it was a woman claiming *her* man. Atlas is mine, and I think I'm falling in love with him too.

There's a knock on my bedroom door that pulls me from my thoughts.

"You decent?" Is that?

"Derek?" I ask as I open the door to see the massive man before me. Derek is a sight to behold, and though I'm sworn to secrecy, Janie confessed that before Fox, she had a crush on Derek. It's easy to see why. Derek isn't built like the men out here. He's tall and broad and rugged, he's got that dark hair and scruffy beard that has hints of grey in it. Plus he's a complete mystery, which adds to his attractiveness.

"Why are you here? In my parents' house? At my bedroom door?" I watch as he grunts in discomfort as he rubs the back of his neck and grabs something off the table in the hallway. A large round box with blue roses.

"I drew the short straw, so I had to bring them to you

for Atlas." He mutters before placing them in my hands and turning to leave. He stops at the top of the stairs and turns around. "It's not my business, I don't want it to be my business and I'm never mentioning it again." It's almost a warning tone in his voice as he looks at me, and I realize this might be the most I've heard him speak at once.

"Some people go through terrible things in their lives and they don't know how to deal with it. It usually goes one of two ways. Your *boy toy* decided to go the "make everyone laugh and believe everything is great" way. But when people go that route, they don't always know how to handle situations when they truly aren't great, and they shut down. He needs you right now. Anyway, have a good one."

"What's the other way?" I ask for an unknown reason. I watch Derek's large, tattooed hand grip the banister as he stops himself on the first step.

"The other way to what Lauren?" He asks, his voice low and distant.

"You... you said there are usually two ways, what's the other?" He looks back over his shoulder and his usually coppery-brown eyes look eerily dark.

"Go call Atlas. He is sick over this and it's annoying as shit." And with that, Derek walks the rest of the way down the steps, leaving me standing at the top of the stairs, holding a giant box of roses and feeling more confused than ever.

I sit the flowers down on my dresser before grabbing my phone and bringing up Atlas' contact. I sigh as I sit in my chair and set the phone against the lamp to prop it up as I hit the video call button.

I'm not even sure there was a full ring before Atlas answered.

"Hey," I say softly as he moves around to prop up his phone.

"Hey," He smiles weakly and his poor face looks so exhausted. He's unshaven, his skin is pale, eyes bloodshot and the dark circles are the most prominent feature on his face. "So," His voice is rough as he clears his throat and I see his signature playful grin appear. "I was going to call you beautiful, but that doesn't seem like enough, so I've acquired five other possibilities. You let me know which you like."

I watch as he reaches over and produces a notepad before coming back to the phone. "So, I have Goddess–of course, and then there's, Radiant, Recherché–yes, I googled a French word and learned how to pronounce it, Bootylicious, and Lavish. Now, Bootylicious, though old school, is my favorite and I really feel like you could make it trendy again but, I am really interested in hearing your opinion."

I stare at him through the screen, my eyes stinging and my mouth open. He's so sweet, he's so perfect... I...

"I loke you." I stare at him in shock and embarrassment.

"Loke?" He repeats with a light chuckle. "Is that like the in-between stage?"

I groan and smack my face with my hand. "I'm such a hot mess."

"Hey Princess, look at me." I peek through my fingers to see his real smile. The genuine heart warming smile that makes my heart do concerning things. "I loke you too." He says softly. "Very, very much."

My stomach twists before snapping open, and I give him a small smile. "I want to come home."

He lets out a long breath. "Thank God, because I can't do this alone. I need you Ren." The desperation in his voice makes me want to reach through the phone and hug him.

"It's probably a stupid question," I laugh nervously as I tuck a stray lock of hair behind my ear. "But how are you?"

Atlas is silent for a moment as he looks me over, his red-rimmed eyes bore into me with such intensity it's hard not to look away. "I'm not okay," He manages, "And I mean that in every way possible Princess." He runs his hands over his face as he lets out a breath. "I feel like my boat has taken on too much water and I just threw my life raft away."

I wince at the pain on his face, the haunted stare, his dark circles. "Atlas–"

"When I am at my wit's end," He interrupts, "When I am at my lowest point, I... God Ren, please don't think less of me for what I'm about to say." His voice is pleading, and it causes my anxiety to rise. What is he talking about? What does he do?

Licking his lips, Atlas continues to speak. "I have, or had this arrangement with my mother. I would go over and talk to her, tell her every thing going wrong in my life for about thirty minutes or so and she would give me motherly advice and then I'd pay her and leave."

"Wait," I blink and shake my head, trying to wrap my brain around what he said. "You pay your mom to talk to you... like a mom?" I watch him flinch and nod slowly.

"It's the only way I can get any sort of halfway decent advice from her, well usually the last couple of times it's been her just patronizing me and then the other day when you went to your parents she basically told me my problems were pointless and that she never wanted me, but that's not the point."

"No," I state firmly, stopping him from pushing away his feelings. "Do not do that, Atlas, that is the point. You can feel hurt by that. You should feel hurt! I feel hurt for you." How could a mother act that way towards her child? How could anyone act that way to Atlas?

"I just," I hear him intake a shaky breath. "I just don't know what is broken in me that makes me unlovable. What did I do wrong?" His voice cracks and I can't handle it anymore. I cannot handle being away from him one more day, hour, minute. I stand up and start grabbing my bags.

"What are you doing, Princess?" He asks as I grab my phone.

"I'm coming home." I state a matter of fact. "You've spent all of this time showing me how much I mean to you, how worthy I am. Now, it's my turn to show you. I'll be home soon." And with that, I end the call and grab the rest of my stuff, determined to ensure that Atlas never feels unloved or unwanted ever again.

As I walk out of my elevator, Atlas is standing in the doorway to greet me. He wraps his arms around my waist and hugs me tightly before falling to his knees and pressing his face against my stomach. "I'm so sorry. I'm so fucking sorry." He chokes out as he grips my hips.

"Let's go inside and talk." I whisper as I lead him to the door. We are in the living room and I'm about to ask what all the papers are that he has scattered everywhere when he turns and kisses me deeply. I drop Bruno's leash and wrap my arms around his neck as he presses me against the wall.

I groan as he grinds against me, but quickly shake my head. "Not now." I whisper, and he looks at me, rejected. "I am not a 'sex to make up' kind of person, Atlas. Please?"

He nods and backs away. "I understand Princess and again, I am so sorry."

"I know you are. And I forgive you, I just, not today. Now, why don't you explain what all of this is." Atlas rubs the back of his neck and groans.

"Yeah, that would be me trying to figure out Howard's funeral arrangements because his kids want nothing to do with him. I thought everything was done, but I need to call the funeral home, order a casket, and everything is supposedly in these papers and they aren't organized and I can't read them and I'm just overwhelmed."

Nodding slowly, I look from the papers back to him. "Well, lucky for you, I know someone who is very good at organizing tasks and making lists." I smile softly as I kiss his cheek before grabbing a pile of paper to begin this painful task.

CHAPTER 24
ATLAS

Is it just me, or does it seem to always rain at funerals? When Tony died, there was a terrible drought, but it rained hard that day. But only that day. And here I am at the grave site under umbrellas as I stand around Howard's matte black coffin. I glance over at Ren, she's red-rimmed and sniffling as she holds my hand, our fingers intertwined. Looking around, I see several of the staff from the nursing home, Betty and a couple orderlies. But no family and no friends. Betty had said Howard's family wanted nothing to do with planning his funeral, so I spent the time doing it, and when Ren came home, she was an angel and helped me figure out what I needed to do to make sure he got a proper send off.

Looking at the headstone, I see the quote written above their names–

"In every life, it will be you."

Howard's words from the last time we were here still ring in my ears.

"I can't wait to see you again, and I can't wait to make you fall in love with me all over again in the next life."

That's all I want with Ren, I want to make her fall in love with me a little more each day.

As the minister finishes his sermon, and every one departs, Ren and I stay still.

"He's so lucky." I whisper as I stare at the black coffin. "To believe so deeply that you've not only found your person in this life, but in every life you may have, I'm envious of being able to love someone that openly." I remove my hand from Ren's as I walk over and place it on the coffin.

"I already miss you, you old bastard. We didn't know each other long enough, Howard, but I felt a connection with you that I had been searching for... forever. I didn't have to be a goofy idiot with you or some kind of Casanova. You were just happy busting my balls and playing gin. In the months that I've known you, you were more of a parental figure to me than my own parents, and I thank you for it." I take a shaky breath as I try to hold myself together. "I hope you've found Clara and you two are happy. I'm going to miss our talks." My voice cracks at the end and I instantly feel Ren's hands on my biceps. My initial reaction is to push her back, to not have her near me while I'm this broken. But I shove that feeling to the side, and turn around and hug her to my chest as we both cry in each other's arms.

"Why don't you go take a shower, Princess." I sigh as Bruno bumps me with his nose. "I'll go take Bruno out."

"Are you sure?" She asks as she places a hand on my face. God, she's so sweet. Leaning into her caress, I kiss the inside of her palm. "Yeah baby, I'll be back in a few." Ren nods before dropping her hand and heading down the hall.

"Alright Bruno, come on bud."

Once back from our thankfully quick walk thanks to Bruno hating the rain, I head into Ren's bedroom to check on her. I smile softly at the sight of her sitting in the middle of her bed, highlighting something on her tablet.

"What are you doing, pretty girl?" I ask as I loosen the knot on my tie, I need to get out of these funeral clothes and a shower.

"Hm? Oh, I'm highlighting different characters in this story so I know which voice to use for the next reading."

I raise my brow as I remove both my button-down and under shirt. "Are you going back to the nursing home?"

Ren looks up from her tablet, and I hear the sharp intake of breath. "Y-yes..."

I smirk as I watch her eyes scan over my naked torso. I flex my pecs and laugh as her eyes dart away and her cheeks begin to redden. "You enjoying the view, Princess?"

Ren huffs as her face goes redder. "Shut up. Just go shower."

I nod as I walk up to the bed, unbuckling my belt and pulling it through the loops. "Better idea," I drag my belt up her thigh while bending over to meet her face. "How about you come shower with me?" I bite her bottom lip and she releases a moan. I see it in her eyes. The hesitance and as I'm just about to tell her it's okay, I'm only playing, she forms a small, shy smile before nodding her head.

"O-Okay."

Holy shit, that small little word just sent a jolt to my cock. I grab her hand and lead her into her bathroom before she has the opportunity to change her mind. I turn on the water in her walk-in shower before turning back and pressing my lips to hers. As soon as we meet, I feel every emotion I've been trying to hold back since Howard died evaporate as her sweet tongue slips into my mouth. Placing both hands on either side of her face, our tongues begin to battle each other for dominance, neither willing to submit.

Finally, I pull back for air and I stare at the hazy eyed goddess in front of me. All woman, all curves and amazing smells and sexy sounds. I'm so in love with her, I want to tell her, but the thought of terrifying her and her running, I can't handle it, not now.

"Where are you?" She asks, and I realize she has slipped her hand down to my dick.

"Hu–oh fuck." I hiss as she gives it a firm stroke. "I... god damn it... Princess I l-loke you."

Ren chuckles lightly as she stares up at me. "I loke you too. Now get in the shower." She doesn't need to tell me twice. Quickly, I remove the remaining articles of clothing as she peels off her pajamas. Fuck, her large, perfect tits are like a siren's song luring me in. I pull her into the shower with me, allowing the water to hit me first so I can be sure it's a comfortable temperature for her. I'm about to move in to kiss her when she stops me.

"Turn around." She says, and I give her a wary look.

"Okay," I say slowly as I raise my hands up and turn. "But my safe world is Batman."

"Batman?" I look over my shoulder to see her looking at me with apprehensive curiosity.

"Can you think of anyone safer than the Dark Knight? Exactly."

"I wanted you to turn around so I could wash your hair, you weirdo, but thanks for that information." She sounds disturbed, but the smile on her face tells me she thinks it's funny and that's all I want, I just want her to laugh.

"Oh, wow." I moan as she massages the shampoo into my scalp. It feels amazing. This isn't my first time showering with a woman, but it is definitely the first time a woman actually wanted to wash me. Usually it's a dangerous game of *"don't slip"*. She pulls me close to her so the water can rinse out my hair and I feel her tits against my back. I have to fight the urge to both stroke my aching cock as well as turn around and suck one of her pink nipples into my mouth.

I jump as I feel the loofa run over my back and shoulders, over my ass and down my legs. She has me turn around, and she does the same to my front until she gets to my dick. I watch as she takes the soap from the loofa into her hand and runs it over the length of my cock. I roll my eyes back as the tight, wet sensation sends waves of pleasure through my entire body.

I watch as she kisses my chest and down my torso. It takes a minute for my sex-filled brain to catch up, but when it does, Ren is on her knees.

"W-what are you..." I can't finish the question because she slides my dick into her hot, sweet mouth and I nearly come at the sight. She is making direct eye contact as she moves me in and out of her mouth. My knees buckle when her tongue starts to play with my dydoe piercing.

"Holy fuck..." I pant as I grip the hair on the back of her head. "Princess... I... I'm not going to–ah shit right there... I'm not going to last long..." God fucking damn it, I watch her look up at me, my dick sliding in and out, her cheeks hollowed from sucking. The image is too much. It's too fucking hot.

She removes my dick from her mouth with a *pop* and I nearly cry out as she licks me from my nuts to my tip before kissing the head. "So," she purrs as she nuzzles against the tip. "Don't last long. Come for me, let me taste it."

Who. The. Fuck.

I watch in complete awe as she shoves my cock, quite literally, down her throat. I hear her gag, but she doesn't stop. One hand grips my ass while the other cups my balls, and all I can do is grip her hair tightly and grunt as she bobs her head back and forth.

"Fuck... Ren... Fuck..." I growl as my hips start to thrust against her. I feel my balls tighten and let out a warning moan. She grips my ass tighter as if to tell me not to pull out while she moans loudly with me down her throat.

And that's it, I'm coming. I'm coming harder than I ever remember coming. I try to pull back, but she doesn't allow it. She swallows every last drop, milking my pulsating cock a few more times until it becomes almost too much. She lets go, and I help her off of her knees and stare at her in wonder.

"Was it o-" I capture her lips with mine while sliding a

hand around her waist and pulling her to me, determined to make her feel just as good as she made me feel.

I JERK AWAKE AT THE SOUND OF AN ALARM. LOOKING OVER, I SEE Ren tangled around me, her face nuzzling into my neck. The television in her room is on, playing the following episodes of the docuseries we were watching before we fell asleep.

I hear the alarm again and this time, Bruno bops my arm with his snout. I look at him and then it clicks. It's Ren's alarm. I look over at the nightstand for her receiver and read the alert on the screen. She's out of insulin.

I peel myself from under her and head to the kitchen to grab her a new insulin vial out of the refrigerator. I give Bruno a quick pat on the head before heading back to the bedroom and getting into her drawer to pull out a new pump. I open the pump, fill it with her insulin and let it sync with the receiver while I slip her waistband down and pull the old pump off. I wait for it to wake her up, but she doesn't move. Once the device tells me it's ready, I place the pump on the outside of her thigh. I have never done this before, but with the amount of reading and the secret lessons at the nursing home with Betty, I am confident I'm doing it correctly–I just hope it doesn't hurt too bad.

I hear the click of the pump inserting itself. I watch as she flinches and lets out a small whimper. "It's okay, princess." I whisper as I reach over and kiss her temple.

She whines and peeks open an eye. "What time is it?" She mumbles as I clean up the mess.

"About three in the morning, baby. Your alarm woke me

up, your insulin was out. I put it on your outer thigh. I hope that's okay?"

Ren shoots straight up and looks down at her leg and then back at me. "Did you put insulin in it?"

I try not to take offense to that. Instead, I smile softly as I come back to bed. "You mean you don't put milk in there?"

She rolls her eyes as she looks at the receiver. "How did you know?"

"Besides living with you and having eyeballs? I researched a lot, and the class. I mean, I don't think I studied that much in fucking high school. I have spent months learning all the ins and outs of diabetes and the tools you need. And then Betty worked with me to teach me how to work the pumps and transmitters since several patients there are diabetic."

"You did all of that? For me?" I lean up on my elbows to stare at her.

"Princess, what do I have to do for you to realize that I'm crazy about you?" In the glow of the television, I see the tear that rolls down her face.

"Atlas..." Her voice cracks and panic fills me. She's about to say something I can't hear yet. Not because I don't want to, god knows I do. But because I need to earn it.

"Shhh..." I pull her to me and kiss her softly. "Just come and lay on me again."

She takes a breath and nods before curling up back into my chest. "Thanks for being such a good husband." She whispers into my neck, sleepily. My heart tightens at her words and I let out a shaky breath as I squeeze her to me.

"Anything for you, Princess."

CHAPTER 25
LAUREN

"Fuck the dinner, I'll just eat you." Atlas growls into my ear as he wraps arms around my waist. I giggle and turn to kiss him.

"Nice try, Hart, but if I have to go, so do you." Atlas deflates and moans, but lets me go so I can finish getting ready. It's the weekend before Thanksgiving and we are heading to my parents' house for dinner. I look myself over in the mirror one last time, I chose a burnt orange single breasted flare skirt, and a black ribbed high neck sweater. I slip on a pair of low heel ankle boots and walk out to see Atlas sitting on the couch, rubbing Bruno's belly.

"You're going to get all furry." I chuckle and Atlas shrugs.

"I don't think Bruno's fur is going to make your parents like me any less. Oh here, I got you something." Furrowing my brows, I watch as he pulls a small box out of the pocket of his trousers and hands it to me.

"What's this?" I ask, though I know jewelry usually comes in these types of boxes.

"I saw it yesterday and I thought of you." Atlas sounds

nervous as he watches me open the box and there is a gold necklace with a sunflower pendant. I look from the pendant to him and then back at the pendant again.

"Atlas," I breathe out and stare at him. "This is, it's too much."

Atlas rolls his eyes and takes the box from me to remove the necklace. "It is not. It looks like you. You needed it." He mutters as he clasps the chain behind my neck.

"I look like a sunflower?" I ask, unsure how to take that. Is my hair really big or something?

"Okay, wait, hear me out. You have those rich brown eyes that are so deep, alluring, soft and nurturing. Your warm golden halo, your strength. It just reminds me of a sunflower." He seems a little frustrated with having to explain his thought process to me. "Look, I'm not one of those perfect book boyfriends in those books who say the absolute perfect thing. But if you give me the chance, I will try to be. I will learn all the right things to compare you to that will make your knees weak."

My smile drops, and I blink at him. "Wait... did you just ask to be my boyfriend?"

I see his cheeks grow pink and my heart flutters, it's adorable.

"Y-yeah? I mean, I know, we are already living together, having sex and married..."

I can't help the laugh that comes out, and I wince when I notice he is becoming uncomfortable. I walk to him, pressing myself against his chest and pulling his freshly shaved face to me. "There is nothing," I say softly as I press a sweet kiss on his lips, "that would make me happier than to be your girlfriend."

His smile could light up the city. "Oh my god," He sounds so relieved. "Are you serious? Oh my god, this is amazing!" He kisses me this time, his hands holding my cheeks. "This means I can cuddle you without sex being involved."

I laugh as I pull back. "What?"

"Well, like, I've never had a girlfriend, so I've never gotten to cuddle on the couch and watch T.V. and stuff without, you know." I cock my head to one side as I think back over the last six months. I guess we really haven't snuggled unless sex was involved.

"Weird confession," I cringe, almost wishing I hadn't started the sentence, but I want him to know this is new for me as well. "I've never cuddled on the couch and watched TV with a guy, either."

"You've had *boyfriends,* though." He doesn't like calling my exes boyfriends, and I have to admit that jealousy in his tone is kind of a turn on right now.

"I have, but they weren't into that. And I wasn't into being close to them if I didn't have to be since they were–" He grips my chin and makes me look at him.

"I'm three seconds from cancelling dinner and murdering those fuckers." I give him a peck on the lips and pat his chest.

"Easy tiger, come on, we are going to be late."

"Oh my god, did I break your ribs?" I instantly try to get up, but his strong gloved hands grab my hips and hold me still.

"I'm grunting because every time you move, the handle of

the shovel hits my nuts. Please... stop... moving." I look down and sure enough, the yellow handle is wedged firmly into his groin. I stare into his eyes, begging him to feel my apology.

"God damn," Atlas groans in sympathy for the character. "Why the nuts?"

I laugh as I close the book I had been reading from and look out the windshield. "God, I don't want to go to this dinner."

"Why? I mean, besides your parents hating me." Atlas runs his tattooed fingers over my knuckles and I feel the goose-bumps erupt. I stare down at his hand, the tattoo of my lips staring back at me. Seeing that tattoo the first couple of times, it made me nervous. I mean, he got a tattoo of my lips before anything was discussed about us. But the more I see it, I don't know, I'm insanely turned on by it. Like it's my mark on him, and it makes me want his mark on me.

Snapping back to reality, I take a breath before answering his question. "It's been six months, they know I'm out of money, they know I don't have a job, they're going to start 'suggesting' places to send in resumes to get in on the entry level until my twelve months are up." I sigh while watching his fingers move back and forth over my hand.

"Do you not want to go back into law?" He asks the question so simply, as if the answer is that easy.

"No, I don't want to go back. I've hated the field since the day I started law school." I try to breathe out my growing anxiety as Atlas makes the familiar turn up the street.

"So don't go back. You should try narrating, take some

time off and take some of the classes you've been looking into last month."

Laughing, I shake my head and pat his thigh. "That's a nice dream, but I can't afford my rent, insulin, food, or anything for that matter. How will I be able to pay for a booth, equipment and classes?" I look over at his expression before punching his thigh. "Absolutely not! Atlas no, you are not paying for anything."

"I could probably–"

"I said no." I interrupt and wave my hand. "I'm not taking money from you."

"You're going to have to eventually or we're going to be out on the street, Princess." I flinch at his all too real words.

"I'm working on getting a job working at Sunday's dance studio–Oof! Atlas! What the fuck?" I rub the spot on my chest where the seat belt tightened on me when Atlas slammed on the brake.

"The stripper studio?" He questions as his gaze becomes hot.

"It's a studio that specializes in pole dancing, and I would be doing the clerical work, not instructing. Not that there should be anything wrong with that." I shoot him my own heated glare, challenging him to go caveman on me.

"Princess, I would support you one hundred percent." He sighs as he begins driving again. "You want to teach people to spin on that pole, you do it. I just don't like the thought of you leaving there alone after closing, but if it's something you want to do, I'm not going to fight you." I relax before he mutters, "I absolutely will be creeping and watching you walk to your car though."

We are quiet as we pull up to the large estate and get out of his Tahoe. Ferguson greets us at the door before we can knock. I give him a warm smile as we walk in.

"I am inclined to mention Miss Lauren," Ferguson says softly as to not bring attention to us from the others in the house. "Your parents have guests."

"Guests?" I ask nervously as he nods.

"Cambridge guests, Miss." My heart drops at the name. No one here knew about Andrew and his abuse, only that he and I had a nasty break up that resulted in my termination. And they definitely didn't know about Atlas being the one to beat his face in, or did they? How did Ferguson know I would want to be warned?

"Ren," Atlas whispers. "I can't be around him. There is a–"

"Lauren!" My mother calls and motions for us to head to her. "Come on in, the guests are in here!"

I must have a deer in the headlights look on my face because my mom's eyes narrow and she gives whoever she had been talking to a smile before walking over to Atlas and I.

"Lauren, if you and your *husband* don't get in there and act like civilized adults." She threatens through clenched teeth.

"Mom," I hiss through my own clenched teeth. "I am not going in there. The Cambridge's and I have nothing to say to one another!"

My mother purses her lips together as she stands poker straight. "The Cambridge's and Andrew are a big influence in your father's career. Next year is an election year and–"

"Is Andrew Cambridge actually in this house?" Atlas interrupts in a stern tone that takes both me and mom by surprise.

"Well, of course," Mom sighs. "Are you telling me you are too childish to have a holiday meal with your in-laws just because Lauren's ex is here?"

"No, I'm telling you that I am under strict orders not to be within so many feet of that fucker and I'm not violating that. Lauren, baby, we need to go. It was one thing at the donut shop when he was intimidating you, but this is different." Atlas grabs my hand and pulls me to the door.

"What? You are under what? Lauren, what is going on? What is he talking about?" I feel the anxiety consuming me and it's enough to make me want to cry.

He looks up at my mother, his eyes narrowing. "You know I'm on probation. You said you looked into me, you know my charges as well as my sentencing." Atlas turns to me and says softly. "Princess, I'm not leaving you somewhere with him where I can't protect you."

Mom scoffs and rolls her eyes. "Please, Andrew is harmless. Which is more than can be said about you."

"Mom," I breathe out and look at her, my eyes filling with tears. "You know Atlas is on probation for hitting Andrew? And you invited Andrew anyway?" I feel betrayed. There is only one outcome if we stay, Atlas is in violation of the protective order, which violates his parole. Anger fills me as I hear Atlas opening the front door. I scowl darkly at my mother, who has the audacity to stand there like we are insulting her. "Did it not occur to you when you found out about Atlas and Andrew–behind my back, by the way, that maybe there was a reason Andrew was hit?"

My mother crosses her arms and rolls her eyes. "It's obvious that he," she points her slender finger at Atlas, "was infatuated with something he had no right having and decided to steal it."

My laugh of shock is garbled as it comes out with a sob. "No, no mom, Atlas did it, after Andrew..." I choke on a sob and Atlas opens the door.

"After I found out that he was beating the shit out of

her. Happy Thanksgiving. Goodbye." He says and ushers me out of the house, leaving my stunned mother behind.

THE RIDE DOWN THE HILL IS QUIET. UNTIL WE REACH THE BOTTOM of the hill, and my phone begins to ring.

"Hello?" I say through a sob.

"Bird," It's my father's voice, but it's different sounding than I'm used to. It's softer, like when he told me my goldfish died when I was seven. "Can you come back to the house sweetheart, I need to talk to you."

"No dad, I–I shouldn't have to be around the Cambridge's and Atlas can't be so–"

"They are no longer here. In fact, they are probably about to pass you if you've reached the bottom of the hill, please Lauren." I sigh and look over to Atlas, who is waiting for my decision. I give him a small nod and he reluctantly turns the vehicle around to head back up the hill once more.

Once we park and head to the front door again, Ferguson ushers us in and I see both of my parents standing in the foyer.

"Why didn't either of you say anything?" Dad asks, looking at Atlas and I. "Boy, I–I could've helped you! Your sentence was bullshit."

"My sentence is fine for what I was willing to talk about. Lauren's name stayed out of it if I took the deal. At the time, she was going to be a bigwig at the law firm." I wince, hating that Atlas took the deal because of me.

Though, without it he and I may have never gotten married, never met Howard, fallen in lo–

"And you," Dad's voice snaps me out of my thoughts. "You allowed that man-child to beat you? You? My daughter?" I cross my arms protectively over my torso, only to have Atlas stand closer to me, shielding me from my father's harsh words.

"You are a Judge, and you," he motions towards my mother. "Are a doctor, both of you have seen domestic abuse victims, you know it's not that cut and dry. Don't you take this out on her, she is a strong woman for coming out the other side of this." A tear rolls down my cheek at his words. This man is so fucking amazing. So protective, trusting and giving.

My dad lets out a huff of air before looking from Mom to us again. "You still should've told us. What's the point in having wealthy parents in power if you can't go to them when you need help?" I am about to make a smart ass remark, but Atlas must sense it because he grabs my hand to stop me, and he's right to do so. Now isn't the time.

"I'll look over the contract you signed when you worked at Cambridge. I am sure there is something we can do to get you out of the non-compete agreement and get you into another firm. Now let's go and eat." My dad turns to head to the dining room and–no, no this is my shot, I'm not wasting it again.

"I don't want to be a lawyer." I blurt out and my mother nearly drops the wine glass she's been holding.

"What?" My father asks slowly before letting out a small chuckle. "Bird–"

"It's Lauren or Ren. I am not a bird, I don't appreciate being called one just because I'm overweight." I say as firmly as I can through my anxiety producing shakes. "I love you both, and I don't expect your support and I don't want your money. But I am not going back into practicing law. I got a part-time job doing administrative work and I..." I look at Atlas, who is giving me the most encouraging expression I've ever seen. It gives me enough strength and courage to keep talking. "I'm going to look into taking classes on voice acting. I would like to be a book narrator, I think I would be good at it and it is what will make me happy."

Both of my parents stare at me blankly. My mother sits on the antique chair pressed against the wall and shakes her head. "A narrator? So you... read books? Oh God, not this again. Is... is that even a real job? Philip, is that a real job?" Mom looks as though she is about to begin crying, which I am not one hundred percent sure she is even capable of doing such a thing.

"Yes, it's a real job," Atlas snaps as he glares at them. "My god, you ask yourselves why she didn't come to you for help. Look at how you react when she tells you she wants to follow her own career path." He grabs my hand and gives it a squeeze. "Come on pretty girl, let's go home."

I don't fight him and I don't say goodbye as we walk out the door. I knew my parents wouldn't take my choice well, but a small part of me still hoped that I would be proven wrong.

Most of the car ride was spent with me gripping Atlas arm while silently crying. I am heartbroken over my parents, but more than anything, I'm overwhelmed. Overwhelmed with this feeling for Atlas. His determination to keep me safe, to support me and show me that I am cared for and loved...

Loved.

I stare at my lips on his right hand, his wedding ring

that he never takes off on his left ring finger. I'm laying on a custom refrigerator that he put in for me. He does love me... and I... I am so in love with him, it's terrifying.

ATLAS OPENS THE DOOR TO THE APARTMENT, LETTING ME WALK IN. I give Bruno a scratch on his soft ear before turning to face Atlas. I need to tell him. Right here, right now. Because if I don't, I might chicken out and I can't anymore. I can't go one more minute with him not knowing, not understanding how much he means to me.

Atlas gives me a mournful look as he speaks. "Ren I'm sorry if I overstepped, I just couldn't let them talk to you like –"

Just fucking say it.

"Atlas, I'm in love with you."

CHAPTER 26
ATLAS

I've died.

That's the only reasonable explanation. I've died and I am in heaven.

"Atlas?" I hear the blonde angel say my name with uncertainty and it pulls me out of my shock.

"I-I'm sorry, ummm,"

"It's okay," she states quickly and I see the wall going up around her. "I mean you don't have to say it back or anything, I just wanted to uh–"

I walk towards her and press my lips to hers. "Stop talking." I mumble as I deepen the kiss for a second before pulling back. "Ren, I love you too. God, pretty girl, you have no idea how much I love you." I kiss her again.

"Really?" She asks, pulling back, her eyes going glassy.

"Really?" I can't help the surprised laugh. "Baby, I don't think I could love you anymore if I tried. All I want is to be with you, be that person you turn to, that you rely on. I want to be the man that makes you believe that we will find each other again in another life. Because you make me feel like that. You make me feel like all I want to do is love you until our souls are put into another body, and then I want to find you and annoy the shit out of you until I get you to fall in love with me again."

She laughs as the tears spill freely down her cheeks. "And what am I going to have to do to get you to fall in love with me?"

I let out a chuckle as I run my thumb across her wet cheek. "Oh Princess, haven't you figured it out? I've always loved you, and I always will. You never have to do anything besides be you."

I watch her bottom lip quiver and I give her a small smile right before she jumps into my arms and wraps her legs around my waist. That jump may not mean much to others, but it means everything to me. She's comfortable, she trusts me to catch her, and fuck, I just want to tell her over and over again that I love her.

"Make love to me." She whispers against my lips, and I am instantly moving us to the bedroom.

I lay her down on the bed and begin removing her shoes and stockings, kissing her soft, giving thighs before moving on to the skirt. She moans as I plant a kiss on the top of her mound. I slip her panties down next and move my way back up, kissing and sucking on her inner thighs. The gasps and moans are damn near enough to send me over the edge.

"Atlas..." She breathes and I feel her grip my hair.

Spreading her thighs, I smirk as I spread her lips to see her swelling clit. I fucking am obsessed with her perfect pussy. Her tight, ribbed hole, her smell, her taste, the fact that sex with her is always messy, and her perfect fucking clit that I love to watch swell and get hard the more aroused she becomes.

I take the tip of my tongue and lick her clit before sucking the nub into my mouth.

"Shit!" She hisses as I press the flat of my tongue over her and lick before sucking again. She bucks her hips against my mouth and I growl in satisfaction before doing the motion again and again. She begins to pant and I know it's coming.

"Atlas!" She groans out as she squirts. I lap up her delicious fluids and hold it in my mouth while gripping her hips and tilting them upwards. Then I place my mouth over her hole and force my tongue and the fluids in. I lick inside her for a moment before trading my tongue for my middle and ring finger.

"That's my girl." I praise as I lick a trail back to her erect clit. God damn it, going down on her, watching her body arch and twist and shake. Her sighs and moans... it's perfection. I feel her squirt again and I know she's close, I can feel her pussy walls tightening. She begins to lift up and I splay my hand over her soft belly, pressing her back down.

Her whimpers and cries are fuel, keeping me going. It's at this point I am mildly aware I'm grinding my cock against the mattress to try and get some relief.

"Right there..." She whines. "Right... yeah... Atlas suck... Oh fuck... Atlas!" She digs her nails into my scalp and I feel her coming around my fingers and in my hand. I let her ride out her orgasm and only stop when she tells me to. I kiss my way up her stomach, lifting her sweater over her breasts. I let out a ragged breath at the sight of her large breasts tucked into the vivid blue lace bra.

"Oh my god" I bury my face into her cleavage–licking, biting, sucking.

"Mmmm... you having fun in there?" She giggles and I

pull my head up from between her breasts and give her a playful grin.

"Princess, you have no idea. Your body is absolute perfection." She snorts and I shoot her a glare. "Why do you do that?"

"Sorry," she winces as she runs her hands through my hair. "I'm trying. I'm just not used to someone accepting me."

"Accepting you? Ren, I'm not accepting you. I am attracted to you. This isn't a 'despite it all, I love her on the inside' thing. I mean yes, I love your mind and your heart, but you are fucking sexy baby. I am lucky and proud to have you, to get to touch every part of you. You have these amazing tits, soft body, these hips that I can grip a hold of and then this one spot..." I trail off as I lean down to where her outer hip meets her lower stomach, I press my lips to the spot and realize very quickly that no one has touched her there. *Perfect.*

I suck on the flesh and bite gently. Ren is nervous at first, but it quickly turns into lust and pleasure as she lets out a soft moan. After a moment, I release the spot and smirk at the dark red mark forming.

"A hickey?" She laughs lightly as I remove her shirt and bra while she makes short work of my clothes. "What are we, teenagers?"

I give her a shrug before angling her hips to meet mine and sliding my dick deep inside her wet heat.

"I mark what's mine." I shudder as I feel her squeeze her walls around my cock. I roll my head back, letting out another breath–willing myself not to come on the spot. Leaning overtop of her I stare into her pretty brown eyes as I thrust into her again, nice and slow. I watch her eyes go hazy and her pretty mouth parts into an "o".

"I love you." I whisper before kissing her softly. She tastes of the apple juice she had on the way home earlier. I run my tongue over hers, earning me a moan of approval as she bucks her hips up against me.

"I love you too." She smiles softly as our foreheads meet and we continue to stare deep into each other's eyes.

The sex is lazy, there are no rapid thrusts, erotic positions, explicit language. It's just her and I taking the time to learn the feel of each other. Every curve, every muscle, every ticklish spot–right under her left butt cheek, but not her right–and once the orgasm hits, it is long and drawn out. We finally come back down and I remove myself before laying next to her and pulling her to me. We are covered in sweat and each other; I don't care, I'm happy to lay like this forever. But my sweet Ren lasts all of two minutes before rolling over to look at me with an apologetic look.

"I'm totally down for laying in bed with you the rest of the night," she smiles softly. "But I can't do so until we've both showered and changed the sheets."

I roll my eyes before smacking her ass. "Anything for you, princess."

CHAPTER 27
LAUREN

"It doesn't have to make sense," Atlas sighs in irritation as we make our way up the steps to Fox's house. "Just know it's tradition. Thanksgiving with the shop guys involves a lot of food. And we don't want to be restricted."

I stare at Atlas' outfit–a pair of pajama pants covered in cartoon turkeys and an orange shirt that has a picture of a cooked turkey with the phrase "I came for the breasts" written on it.

"I understand that it's a pajama party. What I don't understand is why you went out and bought that set of pajamas." I laugh at his hurt expression.

"Have you no holiday spirit?"

"Some holiday," the young scratchy male voice from behind us causes me to jump. I look back to see Wade walking up the steps with Sunday. "You know over forty million turkeys are murdered every year just for this day? An American holiday, think what that could do for a starving country."

I look from the preteen to his exhausted mother.

"Wade," Sunday sighs, her southern voice coming out stronger than usual with her obvious frustration. "Son, I told you not to start that again. You already got kicked out of mamaw's dinner with the bridge club."

"Oh, what a devastating blow that was to my heart." He rolls his eyes and I see the murderous rage on Sunday's face.

"Sunday," I pat her shoulder, "There are tons of non-meat options in the house I'm sure. You know Janie is big on vegetables and what not."

"Oh," Sunday snorts and shakes her head. "This brat ain't a vegetarian. He's an asshole. He was double fisting bacon this morning. He just is mad I didn't let him stay home alone."

"Because I don't want to hang out with your old friends!" Wade groans and Atlas gasps.

"When did I become the old guy? I'm cool! That's not a cap." I smack my face and walk inside, leaving a confused, lovable idiot out front.

"Ren! That's what the kids say now!" I hear him call out but I just laugh and keep walking.

Upon entering the house, it becomes evident why Atlas picked the ridiculous pajamas — Ash and Fox were also wearing them. And then grumpy Derek sat on the couch away from everyone, watching the football game, he's not in matching pajamas.

Janie bounces over and gives me a hug before doing the same to Sunday. "Oh, and who is this?" Janie asks and holy crap, it is love at first sight. Wade's eyes would be in the shape of hearts, if that were physically possible.

Wade is almost taller than my redheaded friend, and this is giving him a major ego boost. He clears his throat and goes to say his name, but "Wade" comes out cracked because, damn puberty. Janie takes pity on the boy and gives him a hug before taking him into the kitchen where he tells her how Thanksgiving is his favorite holiday. Turning to Sunday, I cannot help but laugh at her defeated expression.

"I swear," she sighs, shaking her head. "They tell you that the hard part is when they're babies, that's a lie. When they're babies, they ain't talking. Feed me, hold me, clean me. That's it. They start getting thoughts in their heads and it's just too much. And now," she waves her hand towards the still grinning boy who is helping Janie set the table. "Now he is being a perfect gentleman. I had to pin him down to get him to put deodorant on before we came here."

I snort out a laugh as I pat the tired woman on the back. Since I found out about Wade, Sunday has been a lot more open with me and the girls. We've found out that she lives in a house across town that is owned by a woman she calls "mamaw"–the old woman also helps out and watches Wade when Sunday has to work. We also found out that about a year ago, Sunday got a divorce from a man, not Wade's father, who stole everything from her, except the dance studio, and she's had to work on rebuilding it. And, her epilepsy is getting worse, the medication isn't stopping them like they used to and after the holidays, she will be closing the studio for a while because she is having a device put in that is supposed to help lessen the seizures. It's one of the reasons I took the job to work for her, besides the pay–which isn't exactly the salary of a lawyer but I can get by–it will help Sunday out and during the downtime I can start working on taking narrating and voice acting classes.

After my parents, I realized that Atlas was right, I didn't go to them because I couldn't rely on them to really hear ***me.*** So, I am going to do what makes me happy, and if I fall, I know that I fell following my dreams.

A long whistle interrupts my thoughts, and I look up to see black eyes and flirty grin. "Happy Thanksgiving, Ash." I smile and give him a half hug.

"Happy Thanksgiving Ren, now who is this stunning creature? Have we met because I feel like you look familiar." Sunday rolls her eyes and flicks her wrist, waving Ash off.

"Not interested, Charming, try your moves on someone else." Ash, never one to be rejected, smiles and crosses his arms over his wide chest.

"Now, now... no need to be so cold. This is a day that we are to be thankful for our blessings, and I know just what I'm thankful for."

"It better not be my mom." Wade's voice nearly growls from behind Ash. Ash goes pale as he turns to look at the glaring boy. I had to admit, it was impressive, the kid shows no fear. He walks to stand in front of Sunday, arms crossed.

"Oh," Ash says and I roll my eyes. There it was, the typical look of fear that most players got when "baggage" showed its head. I got it as soon as the insulin was brought out. "I didn't realize you had a kid."

"Doesn't mean her parts are broke, you dipshit." Derek calls from the couch, not looking up from the game. I can't help but laugh, and Ash turns slightly red.

Sunday glares at the dark-eyed man. "Actually, that is exactly what it means. I'm closed for business. You'll have to find somewhere else to go, though, even if I didn't have a kid," She pauses and gives Ash a once over before huffing out a laugh. "Not a snowball's chance in hell. Call me shallow, but I have a standard, and you ain't measuring up Dash."

I watch Ash go pale as he replies quietly, "It's Ash."

"Dash, Ash... whatever. Either way, you're out of here,

so go on... get." Ash slowly turns and walks away, and I stare at Sunday in shock.

"What...the fuck?" I laugh and Sunday shrugs before motioning to Wade to go watch the television.

"He doesn't remember me." She hisses, and it's then I notice it. She's wearing a mask. Had Ash hurt her by not remembering?

"Sunday, he does have a lot of clients. Maybe if he saw your tattoo, I know Fox remembers–"

"No no," she whispers as she waves a hand. "I... I slept with him. And he is acting like he doesn't remember me." My mouth drops and I look over to Ash, who is talking to Atlas and Fox.

"Oh, I'll kill him." I growl and Sunday grabs my arm and pulls me back.

"No! If he doesn't remember me, I won't remember him either. I'm not going to let him think that the night we had was so memorable when he can't be bothered. It was a couple years ago anyway, best to keep it in the past." Sunday gives me a look as if to say to drop the subject, nodding I give her a hug as we head to the kitchen.

THE DINNER WAS SPENT LAUGHING AND JOKING WITH THE ENTIRE crew. Fox and Atlas took it upon themselves to pull out the XBOX to play some fighting game with Wade after we ate too much food. Janie, Sunday and I were in the kitchen cleaning up with a silent Derek.

"Derek," Janie patted the tall man's back and you could see him visibly stiffen, though he didn't tell her to get off.

Derek was an asshole ninety-nine percent of the time, but he rarely turned that on the women, at least not fully. In fact, he got kind of awkward with ladies a lot of the time. "Go out there with the guys, we can clean up."

"It's alright," he says as he continues rinsing the dishes. "Y'all made the food, it's the least I could do. Besides, I ain't got nothing to say to those idiots in there. I see them every day."

Janie gives me a sad look and I roll my eyes. Janie looks at Derek like a wounded puppy that needs love, whereas the rest of us look at him like a wounded wolf that we need to leave the fuck alone.

Atlas and I make eye contact, and he tilts his head, motioning for me to follow him. I excuse myself from the kitchen and follow Atlas down the hall to Fox and Janie's spare bedroom.

"Atlas, what are you–" My mouth was captured by his in the sweetest, most romantic kiss. I melt into him as I part my mouth to pull his bottom lip in.

"I love you," He whispers over and over as he moves to pepper me with hot kisses.

"I love you too, but what are you doing? We are in Fox's house!" Atlas smirks slyly as he grabs my arm and tugs me across the hall to Fox and Janie's actual bedroom.

"Trust me, I owe him this." He chuckles as he backs me up to the bed. Realization hits me and I give him a deadpan look.

"Really Hart? A revenge fuck for what he did over a year ago?"

"Princess, it was my station!" He groans as if I should be on his side. I stare at him for another second before rolling my eyes and pulling down my pajamas and kneeling on the bed.

"Make it fast, bud. If they come in here, you'll be grounded for years." I look over my shoulder. Atlas isn't listening. No, he is too busy staring at my bare ass while fisting his cock through his pajama pants.

"Atlas," I hiss, waving my ass from side to side. "I'm kind of exposed." I slip my hand between my legs, rubbing my clit to get myself wet, because there is zero chance I'll survive Atlas' large, pierced cock if I'm not properly lubricated.

"Oh, pretty girl." He growls low as he watches my hand work. He walks up and falls to his knees and grabs my hips, pulling me to his face before burying his mouth deep into my pussy. I press my face into the mattress to stifle my embarrassingly loud moans. He continues to shamelessly tongue fuck me for another minute before ramming two fingers inside and letting out a long sigh.

"Princess," He purrs as he rubs his face over my ass cheek. "You are so perfect, you are a fucking goddess that deserves to be worshipped." I gasp as I feel him bite and lick on the underside of my ass cheek.

"Then worship me Atlas." I breathe out and within seconds, Atlas is standing and I shiver as I feel him entering me, his piercing rubbing me in the exact right spot to cause my legs to shake. I start to collapse as he grips my hips.

"Nuh uh Princess, you know the rules, ass up." He groans as he does a quick swirl and I feel myself releasing around him. "Ohhhh yesss." He breathes, and he begins to pound into me over and over. I keep my face buried, unable to stop the screams or the fluid coming out of me. Fuck, I will owe Janie new sheets after this.

My body starts shaking and I gasp as he grips my ass cheeks, and begins to spread and roll my cheeks apart and together. Oh god, I am going to come, every thrust he drives into me causes me to cry out in need.

"You fucking perfect goddess." He pants as his thrusts become jerky. "I. Worship. You." He growls as I scream into the blanket, my body exploding around his exploding cock.

We stay still for several moments before he removes his softening dick. I look over my shoulder and watch as he heads to the bathroom that joins the bedroom and comes back with a damp towel. I go to clean myself, but he smacks my ass before kneeling.

"A goddess doesn't do this. It's my job." He proceeds to clean and kiss every part of me before helping me get dressed and remove the sheets.

We open the door and I nearly scream upon seeing Fox's scowling face. Atlas gives him a smug smirk. And they are both silent for a moment before Fox scoffs and rolls his eyes. "Fine," he mutters as we head back to the living room. "We are even."

CHAPTER 28
ATLAS

I'm going to barf, or pass out... maybe both.

"Will you stop!" Janie hisses as she puts the finishing touches on the fence posts.

"What if she says no?" I groan and Fox snorts.

"Then I guess you just stay married–Ow!" He cries as Janie pinches his forearm.

"Honestly," she blows a fallen curl out of her face. "If she says no, I'll accept the proposal. Not like anyone around here is asking me. Let alone re-asking." She shoots a glare at Fox, who has conveniently become very focused on the sunflower bouquets, making sure they are completely straight. Truth is, I'm not the only one that picked out an engagement ring last week, but apparently he is making her wait and continue to hound him and berate him so that when he does ask her on Christmas Morning, she can look like an asshole. Their relationship is the weirdest, most enviable one.

"Okay," Janie clasps her hands together as she looks around at the pasture. "I think it's done." Small twinkle lights line the split rail fence with a bouquet of flowers tied to each post, leading to a dimly lit, flowy canopy where I would be standing like the nervous idiot I am, waiting for her to either accept my proposal, or crush my soul.

I wave Fox and Janie off as I stand under the canopy, listening to the crickets and the cows while going over my speech in my head.

I cuss again as I look at my watch. She is forty-five minutes late, it's no longer "romantic dusk". It's full fucking night and I'm annoyed. Grabbing my phone out of my pocket, I go to call her and it's then I see the crescent moon icon on the top corner of my phone.

Do Not Disturb

I had turned it on after Janie and Fox left, so I wouldn't be interrupted by anyone during my proposal. I am jogging to my vehicle as I see the fifteen text messages from Ren, along with the glucose monitoring alerts that had been silenced. I'm a fucking idiot. I try to remain calm as I look at the texts, my dyslexia making it harder to decipher. Saying fuck it, I use my app to read the messages to me and back out of the farm.

Princess: Hey I'm finishing up reading at the nursing home. I'm not feeling too hot, can we just hang out at home?

Princess: Leaving now, I know my alarm is going off, I'll drink some juice.

Princess: Atlas?? Why didn't you answer me?

Princess: You're worrying me, I'm calling Fox.

Princess: Atlas, I really feel sick... where are you?

I hit the touchscreen and pull up Ren's name, hitting the phone icon. It rings, and rings, and rings.

"Hi! You've reached Lauren Hart, please leave a message and I'll return your call as soon as possible! Thanks."

I wait for the beep before speaking. "Ren? Baby, fuck, I am so sorry, I had my phone on silent. Jesus Christ, please be okay. I am headed home now. Please, please. PLEASE be there. Call me as soon as you get this. I love you....Baby, I love you so much."

I hang up even though I don't want to. I've never felt so far away and helpless. What if she was low on the ground alone? What if she wrecked? What if she's in the elevator and the creep downstairs–No...I can't think about any of this.

I press my gas pedal to the floor and speed down the road, praying that she's just napping.

I DON'T EVEN PARK MY TAHOE IN THE GARAGE, I LEAVE IT RUNNING out front as I race through the doors and to the elevator. I would take the stairs, but if she's in the elevator...

I get in and breathe a sigh of relief when it's empty. I hit her floor and pace as the elevator takes its sweet fucking time reaching my destination. That's it, we are moving. A house, something with no fucking elevators that I have to watch crawl up to our floor when I need to be there ***now.*** The doors don't even open fully as I squeeze myself out. I try the door, it's locked. I unlock it and I feel my knees go weak and buckle under me.

Ren is laying on the couch in my hoodie, snoring away with Bruno curled up by her butt. I completely collapse to my knees when I reach her. Her nose is red and sounds stuffy. I touch her head with my hand, she's a little warm.

A cold. She just has a cold. Looking around, I find her phone tucked into the couch cushions. I feel like crying. She's okay.

"Atlas?" Her scratchy, sleepy voice may as well be angels singing in my ears. I look at her reddened eyes and smile softly.

"Hi baby," I whisper and kiss her head. She shoves me back.

"I'm sick, don't touch me." She goes to cover her face as she sits up but stops when she looks me over. I'm in dark wash jeans, a white button-down shirt with the sleeves rolled up and a deep blue vest. "Wow," she breathes and winces. Her throat must be bothering her. I stand and go to the kitchen, returning a second later with a cold bottle of water.

"Why are you so dressed up?" She asks after taking a long drink. "I thought we were going to pet cows."

I rub the back of my head. "Yeah, well, I thought maybe a nice dinner beforehand or something." I mutter, feeling the heat rise to my cheeks. I would have to text Fox and Janie and make sure they didn't say anything.

"Let me go change and we can watch a movie, okay?" She smiles softly and I grab my cell out of my pocket, needing to also see if the front desk had towed my car. There is a small thud as something else comes out of my pocket with the phone. My eyes widen as I watch Ren grab the small box off the floor for me.

"Here–wait... what is this?"

Shit! This isn't right. I look at her and my shoulders slump over.

"I'm sorry Princess," I say lowly as I grab the box and kneel in front of the couch again. "I had the whole night planned, lights, flowers, music, I even memorized a speech... okay partially memorized. I wanted everything to be perfect for you. I wanted you to have the super special grand gesture engagement that you wanted with the ring you deserve."

Ren stares at me quietly for a moment, her eyes calculating.

"You were going to propose again?" She asks, surreptitiously. I nod, slowly "Because I deserve a grand gesture?" I nod again, staring into the brown depths of her eyes

"Yeah, you do," I breathe out. Knowing that I would do anything for this woman. ***Anything.***

"And what? You marrying me to make sure I had what I needed to stay alive wasn't a grand gesture?" I furrow my brow and look at her.

"What? No! That wedding wasn't what you deserved!"

"Yeah, I thought that too." She whispers softly. "I thought for a long time that I deserved the men that used me. That, my size, my illness, meant I should be grateful anyone would pity me enough to go out. But then, you came along. Not just the friendly flirting, but you came and helped me with Andrew, and then without question you protected my name, and when you found out I was losing my health insurance, you selflessly protected me again." She stops and coughs lightly before taking a drink and continuing. "When I stood in that chapel, in a dress that you got me because the ones they had there were too small, I didn't feel like I deserved any of it. But not because it wasn't enough."

She pauses and I can see her emotions pooling in her eyes, "Atlas. Baby, you are a grand gesture! You've given me all that you could without a second thought and I'll be damned if you try to take my proposal and wedding from me. It may not have been what others would call romantic, But I'm telling you now, our love story, exactly the way it's been, is the greatest love story I've ever heard, and I would never want to rewrite any of it."

I crash my lips into hers, even though she temporarily protests about her cold. Fuck that cold, I'll gladly get sick. I grip a fistful of her blonde hair as I pull her as close as I can, I need to feel every part of her against me. I need to know that this is real, that she is real and I'm not going to wake up from some amazing dream.

Ren pulls back and I see her eyes go soft and wide. "Y-You're crying!" She gasps as she wipes the tears off my cheeks.

Pulling her to me, I inhale her scent so deeply it touches my soul. "Lauren," I whisper her name into her neck. "Thank you."

"For what?" She asks, pulling me into her tighter.

"For giving me what I didn't know I deserved too."

EPILOGUE

ATLAS

TEN MONTHS LATER

"I'm not kidding!" Ash groans over the speakers of my car bluetooth as I continue the drive.

"I am sure you believe you saw it." I humor him as I make the turn off the busy road to a smaller, quiet one.

"At, it was a hot chick... running... with a fucking chicken. In the middle of the night, on the side of the road."

I have been listening to this story since he called me at four this morning to tell me what he claims to have witnessed.

"Ash, I'm telling you, lay off the scotch." Ash snorts at my comment and mutters something about me not being fun anymore.

"How's country life treating you?" Ash asks just as I turn into the gravel drive of the dark green bungalow, nestled tightly into a large mass of trees.

"It's not country life, I live ten minutes from the city."

I hear him groan. "Might as well be another state."

"Anyway," I sigh as I park my vehicle. "It's amazing. Ren

loves it, as does Bruno. Plus, her sound booth is getting delivered tomorrow, so I know she's excited about that."

"Well, I hate that I'm alone in this game now, but I'm glad you got your girl, man. Ren is a catch."

Don't I know it.

We say our goodbyes and I walk into the house that Ren and I got together about four months ago because Ren couldn't properly record in her apartment that had thin walls and noisy new neighbors.

"Hey handsome." Ren beams from the couch where she is planning out her next reading session with the senior citizens. I thought maybe she would stop once I was off probation, but after two months free, both she and I still make weekly visits to hang out with the seniors. They adore Ren and I have weekly gin games with some of the men. It's not the same without Howard there, but I feel like we have built some kind of community now at the center. Betty and the center's director have told us that our weekly visits are the highlight to some of the seniors, especially the ones who have been unfortunately forgotten by their families. They've adopted Ren and I as their kids more or less since she and I are not on speaking terms with our families. Well, most of our family. I am hopeful for my sister, Millie. She came to me a month ago and asked for real help getting clean, which I did. Ren and I got her into a very nice rehabilitation center and she's three weeks into her ninety day stay and they say she's an absolute delight to have there. I know things between her and I will never be the typical brother and sister relationship, but I am hopeful that we can mend some of the broken pieces and become a family.

"Hey princess," I kiss her temple as I sit on the couch next to her and pull her to my chest.

"Ew, why are you so sweaty?" She tries to squirm away, but I hold her firmly to me.

"I went to the gym, I gotta keep myself looking good for you!" Which is becoming more difficult as the weeks and months go on. Turns out when you are happy, in love and married to the hottest woman in the world–you start getting a little lax in your vigorous training. And then throw into the mix that your girl does amazing things in the kitchen and her best friend owns a bakery... let's just say it was a humbling day about a month ago when my ass had to go to Derek to ask him to help whip me back into shape. Which he did, brutally.

"I love you soft just as much." She says as she pokes my side. "But, I don't love you sweaty, so go shower. We are supposed to be at the shop in an hour, and I believe Sunday is going to meet us there. Supposedly, she's nervous she might be in some legal trouble and wants to talk to me in person. Your job is to distract Wade." I raise a brow as I stand to head towards the shower.

"Oh yeah? What did she do?"

Ren lets out a laugh. "Get this, she stole her ex's chicken."

SUNDAY DIDN'T SHOW UP TO THE SHOP, WHICH IS FINE BY ME because having Ren all to myself to do this tattoo makes everything better. I smirk at her as she holds still while I continue to finish the piece in ***my*** spot.

"I can't believe I'm doing this." She lets out a soft laugh

as I wipe the excess ink away to look and see if there are any spots I need to go over.

"I have your lips on my hand." I deadpan as I grab my bottle of green soap and rinse off her tattoo.

"I know, and you are nuts!" She laughs as I help her sit up.

I give a half shrug. "Valid. Now go look in the mirror, tell me if you like it. And be honest. It's my first tattoo on you."

I watch her go to the full-length mirror and the grin on her face is so mischievous it makes my dick twitch. She stares at the tattoo on her soft hip of my bite mark and I watch her teeth sink into her bottom lip.

She whips around and looks at me. "I love it and I love you. This is awesome, my first bad girl tattoo!"

I laugh lightly as I snake an arm around her and slide a finger into the front of her panties.

"You know, if you really want to be a bad girl," I purr in her ear. "There is a certain station that could use defiling. And then another that needs to be cleansed."

She raises a mischievous brow at me before reaching out and licking my lips. "Well then, sounds like we had better get busy."

THE END

Acknowledgments

Cover - Kate Farlow - Y'all That Graphic
Editor & Fake PA - Raeleen Nelson - Book Witch Author Services
Narrators - Paige Reisenfeld & Christian Leatherman

All of my Beta & ARC Readers

ABOUT THE AUTHOR

Crowned the Queen of Banter, DJ Krimmer is known through the community for her witty, smart mouthed characters. In real life she will often say her slogan is:

"Purposely Awkward, Accidentally Funny."

And it's a slogan she takes very seriously.

When DJ isn't making inappropriate jokes or hiding from the worst imposter syndrome known to writer-kind, she's weaving contemporary romance stories filled to the brim with imperfect alpha-holes and witty females whose love conquers every hurdle thrown their way. In her books, representations of the imperfect sides of life are not hidden in the shadows, they're front and center, a reminder that everyone deserves a happy ending.

Also by DJ Krimmer

Closing the Distance

Chasing Noelle

Must Love Cat - Sapphic Novella

Remnants - Dark Sapphic Novella

A Thousand Little Memories - Sapphic

Fox - Hel's Ink Book One

Ash - Hel's Ink Book Three

Derek - Hel's Ink Book Four

Stevie - Hel's Ink Book Five

Janie - Hel's Ink Novella Five & a Half

Phoenix - Hel's Ink Book Six

Stray - Rowe Brother's Ranch Book One

Wayward - Rowe Brother's Ranch Book Two - Sapphic

Drift - Rowe Brother's Ranch Book Three

Home - Rowe Brother's Ranch Book Four

Always Waiting - Always Series Book One

Always Wondering - Always Series Book Two

Always Wanting - Always Series Book Three

Always Wishing - Always Series Book Four

Printed in the USA
CPSIA information can be obtained
at www.ICGtesting.com
LVHW022259270924
792345LV00015B/274

9 798868 964817